An Amish Mystery

Suspendered
Sentence

D0035834

Laura
Bradford

National Bestselling Author
of *Shunned and Dangerous*

BERKLEY
PRIME
CRIME

$7.99 U.S.
$9.99 CAN

S › EAN

ISBN 978-0-425-27302-9

9 780425 273029

5 0 7 9 9

continued . . .

"The Amish customs and traditions are fascinating and blend nicely into the mystery, while the author's ability to provide an authentic sense of community makes this story engaging."   —*RT Book Reviews*

"Engaging characters fill this well-plotted mystery. The Amish community of Heavenly is realistically depicted and English (as the Amish call non-Amish) characters are woven into the community in believable ways."
        —*The Mystery Reader* (four stars)

Hearse and Buggy

"A really great, well-written mystery. The characters all had depth and dimension, and were easy to relate to . . . The plot itself was excellent . . . A delightful book, and I cannot wait to visit Heavenly again!"   —*Fresh Fiction*

"Undoubtedly one of the best cozy mysteries I've read this year. It is meaty, with an intriguing background, and it provides an education as to the Amish culture. And, Bradford's characters are some of the best developed, most interesting ones I've come across in a cozy mystery. With *Hearse and Buggy*, Bradford has taken the Amish mystery and successfully made it her own."
        —*Lesa's Book Critiques*

"An engaging amateur sleuth that interweaves Amish society with an enjoyable whodunit. Claire is a terrific protagonist whose wonderful investigation enables readers to obtain insight into the Amish culture . . . [A] delightful Amish cozy."   —*Genre Go Round Reviews*

Suspendered
Sentence

LAURA BRADFORD

BERKLEY PRIME CRIME, NEW YORK

THE BERKLEY PUBLISHING GROUP
Published by the Penguin Group
Penguin Group (USA) LLC
375 Hudson Street, New York, New York 10014

USA • Canada • UK • Ireland • Australia • New Zealand • India • South Africa • China

penguin.com

A Penguin Random House Company

SUSPENDERED SENTENCE

A Berkley Prime Crime Book / published by arrangement with the author

Berkley Prime Crime Books are published by The Berkley Publishing Group.
BERKLEY® PRIME CRIME and the PRIME CRIME logo are trademarks of
Penguin Group (USA) LLC.

For information, address: The Berkley Publishing Group,
a division of Penguin Group (USA) LLC,
375 Hudson Street, New York, New York 10014.

ISBN: 978-0-425-27302-9

PUBLISHING HISTORY
Berkley Prime Crime mass-market edition / March 2015

PRINTED IN THE UNITED STATES OF AMERICA

10 9 8 7 6 5 4 3 2 1

Cover illustration by Mary Ann Lasher.
Cover design by Sarah Oberrender.
Interior text design by Laura K. Corless.

For my family, with all my love.
You really do make my world so much brighter.

Acknowledgments

Regardless of the book I'm writing, I invariably come across a question that sends me in search of answers. Sometimes, in respect to the Amish Mysteries, those questions mean a research trip to Lancaster County (I love my research trips). Sometimes, those questions send me rifling through my pile of books and newspaper clippings (thank you, Kevan Deardorff). And sometimes, those questions lead me to my cell phone and the really smart folks who inhabit my contact list.

J. D. Rhoades was one of those "smart folks" this go-round as I played with the plot for *Suspendered Sentence*. His willingness to answer my law-related questions (sometimes several rounds of questions) proved invaluable. Thank you, Dusty!

Equally important to the writing of each book, is the support I get from my readers. Your letters (via my website), posts on my social media pages, and willingness to come say hi when I'm doing an event always provide just the right boost at just the right time. Thank you!

Chapter 1

Claire Weatherly didn't need to trade glances with her aunt to know what the woman was thinking. It was as palpable as the flames that danced in the hearth and the contentment she felt as she watched them.

Life was good. Great, even. And the man seated beside her on the floral couch was, without a doubt, a contributing factor in that assessment. The only question that remained was whether he was there as the friend she repeatedly tried to convince herself he was, or the something more Diane's eyes were desperate to convey via their usual arched brow or deliberate blink.

Oh, how she wanted to lose herself in the kind of certainty reserved for the unhurt, but fear held her back. Instead, she turned yet another page of the paperback mystery novel she'd stopped absorbing the moment Jakob

Fisher showed up at the door of her aunt's inn, and mentally pleaded with herself to enjoy the moment.

"I think you were about fifteen when I opened the inn, weren't you, Jakob?"

Claire lifted her head just in time to catch the detective's faint nod. "I will never forget your smile the day you came out to my father's farm to buy some pumpkins for your front porch. It was different than any I'd ever seen on an adult."

"Different?" Claire echoed across her book. "How so?"

He trained his hazel eyes on her, eliciting a slight but audible intake of air from her lips in the process. "I don't know. I guess the adults in my world at that time were more subdued. They smiled, sure, but not like your aunt did that day."

"As I remember it, I wasn't the only one smiling that day," Diane teased before rising to her feet to add a log to the fire. "In fact, you were so smitten by that young girl walking along the road, I'm surprised you noticed anything else."

Jakob's momentary hint of confusion was quickly chased from his face by an expression more befitting a painful memory, piquing Claire's curiosity in the process. "Do tell. Please."

Hesitation gave way to an answer peppered by starts and stops. "That would have been Elizabeth Troyer."

"That was Benjamin's Elizabeth, right?" The second the words were out, she cringed. "Wait. You don't have to answer—"

He shrugged. "Yes. Benjamin's Elizabeth. But she was not Benjamin's at that time."

She noted the lingering bitterness in the man's voice at the mere mention of Benjamin Miller and held it against everything she'd learned about the pair since moving to Heavenly, Pennsylvania, thirteen months earlier. The two men had grown up together, their proximity in age and common interest in all things outdoors helping to forge a friendship within the confines of their small Amish community. When they hadn't been helping their elders on their respective farms or sitting side by side in their district's one-room schoolhouse, the boys had often met at the creek to catch frogs, skip stones, and swim. It was a friendship that had soured, though, as they approached their teenage years, thanks to a jealousy Jakob's own father had stoked in his son. Jakob's departure from the Amish fold before his twentieth birthday simply served to sever the tie completely.

Diane returned to her upholstered lounge chair on the other side of the oval hooked rug and sank into its depths, a worried expression creasing her brow. "I didn't mean to bring up a sore subject, Jakob. I'm sorry."

"No apologies needed. Elizabeth's heart did not belong to me. I accepted that fact seventeen years ago."

"Is that why you *really* left the Amish?" Claire whispered.

He shifted his body ever so slightly, grazing his shoulder against hers as he did. "No. I left because I wanted to help solve John Zook's murder—as a *policeman*."

It was a decision that had cost Jakob everything, not the least of which was any hope of a relationship with his childhood family or anyone else from his former Amish life.

"When Elizabeth first told me of her feelings for Benjamin, I was angry. I saw it as yet another way I didn't measure up. But, years later, when I had time and distance to reflect, I knew it was more than that. Elizabeth had changed during Rumspringa. At first, it was a change that brought us closer. But then, like everyone else, she could not accept what I wanted to be."

"I don't understand."

"I was fascinated by the police long before Zook was murdered. The uniforms that made my family and friends wary, excited me. I wanted to know what they did and where they went. During Rumspringa, while my Amish friends were wearing English clothes and listening to English music, I was spending my time talking to police officers and watching what they did. When Rumspringa was over, my fascination with law enforcement had only grown. Which is why, looking back, I should have *known* baptism was not right for me. But I resisted. Had I not, I could be a part of my sister's and brother's lives now."

It was a part of the Amish culture she would never understand. The notion that a man like Jakob could be excommunicated from his family for choosing to serve the public simply didn't sit well. But it was not hers to judge, as Diane always said. Had Jakob made his decision to leave prior to baptism, everything would have been different.

"And Elizabeth?" Claire prodded. "She was bothered by your fascination?"

"When her own Rumspringa was over, she was very quiet. I remember her crying a lot. She would never really say why, but she'd let me hold her sometimes when she was really upset. Oftentimes I would ask her if she was sure she wanted to be Amish. Each time I asked, she insisted she was.

"I was skeptical until the moment I told her I was thinking about becoming a police officer. She got so upset at the mention of me becoming a cop that I knew, at that moment, that she was confident in her decision to be baptized."

Diane reclaimed her copy of the *Heavenly Times* from its spot atop the end table and smoothed it across her lap. "Did you happen to know that young Amish girl who left during Rumspringa and never came back?"

"Sadie Lehman?" Jakob clarified. "Sure, I knew her. She was Elizabeth's closest friend. They were like two peas in a pod, as my mother used to say. They played together, dreamed together, went on Rumspringa together. Having Sadie take off like that in the middle of it all was hard on Elizabeth. She thought they were friends, she thought they would be baptized together."

Diane clucked softly under her breath. "Hence the tears that you dried when Elizabeth's Rumspringa was over . . ."

"Hence the tears I dried," Jakob confirmed. "But it was Benjamin, not me, who was finally able to convince Elizabeth that Sadie's decision was God's will."

There was something about Jakob's tone that made Claire want to reach out and smooth away any and all lingering hurt from his features, but she resisted. There was simply too much uncertainty where his feelings for her were concerned.

"And then, only a few years later, it was *Benjamin* who had to accept God's will." Diane shook her head slowly, the downward turn in the room's atmosphere beginning to weigh on the sixty-three-year-old's shoulders.

Jakob stiffened ever so slightly beside Claire. "What happened to Elizabeth, exactly? All I've ever been told is she passed away shortly after she and Ben got married."

"Oh, Jakob, it was such a sad, sad tragedy," Diane murmured. "It was early December, if I remember correctly. She was walking out near those thick woods next to Bishop Hershberger's farm and—"

"Wait. That's hunting season."

"Yes, it was."

Jakob raked his fingers through his dark blond hair, groaning as he did. "Awww no . . ."

Claire looked from Diane to Jakob and back again. "What? What am I missing?"

Pitching forward on the sofa, Jakob dropped his head into his hands. "She was killed by a stray bullet, wasn't she?"

Her gasp wasn't loud enough to drown out Diane's affirmation and Jakob's subsequent, louder groan. "I . . . I had no idea," she stammered. "I . . . I just assumed she'd been sick or something." A glance to her right confirmed she wasn't the only one who'd made a similar assumption.

"In some ways, I think an illness would have been easier for Benjamin. It would have given him time to prepare. But a simple case of being in the wrong place at the wrong time? There's no way to prepare for something like that . . ." Diane's words whispered off only to return on the heels of a weighted sigh. "They'd been married less than three weeks. *Three weeks.*"

She searched for something to say—for Jakob, for Benjamin, for the woman who'd clearly meant so much to both men—yet she was speechless.

"I always knew it would take someone mighty special to make that poor man even consider the notion of getting married again. It's just a shame that—"

Desperate to keep her aunt from finishing, Claire cleared her throat, then trained her attention on their guest. "Hey . . . you okay?"

Jakob's hesitation gave way to a reassuring pat on her hand. "Yeah. I'm okay. I'm just stunned. Stunned and saddened for Elizabeth . . . and Ben." Then, squaring his shoulders, he plucked a familiar red-and-white-checked bag from the pocket of his coat and handed it to Claire. "I stopped by Shoo Fly Bake Shoppe after work today and thought maybe you'd like one of Ruth's famous chocolate chip cookies . . ."

The rustle of newspaper on the other side of the rug did little to disguise her aunt's cluck of approval, but it didn't matter. Diane was right. It was a sweet gesture. By a sweet man.

"I'd love one, Jakob, thank you—"

"I'm still not sure what I think of this." Diane adjusted her reading glasses atop her nose and then tapped the paper with the back side of her hand. "But I know Ryan O'Neil must be absolutely beside himself."

Reluctantly, Claire broke eye contact with Jakob to address her aunt. "Who is Ryan O'Neil?"

Jakob's non-cookie-holding hand shot into the air. "Wait. I know this. He was the mayor of Heavenly during the last few years I lived here as a teenager."

"That's right. And he held that office for another three terms before losing to Don Smith about seven or eight years ago. Folks around here thought Ryan would run again the first chance he got, but his pride was wounded and he never did."

Claire took a bite of Ruth's cookie, savoring the instant burst of chocolate. "Mmmm, okay, so what's going on now?"

"His son, Mike, is throwing his hat in the ring for the next mayoral race."

"Yeah, some of the guys in my department were talking about that this morning. They seem to be divided on how he'd be as mayor. The ones who grew up around here seem to find the notion funny; the ones who didn't, think he'll do a decent job."

"That's because the ones who grew up around here remember the Michael of old and it's not a very flattering image. Especially in conjunction with someone who wants to hold a position of power in our town." Diane took one last look at the article, then peered up at Claire's sofa mate. "Do you remember Mike from back then, Jakob?"

"Vaguely. I know from my time hovering around the police department during my Rumspringa that he set something on fire once. But nothing happened to him on account of being the mayor's son . . . And I know he was part of Elizabeth's Rumspringa crew a few years later, thanks to Miriam Hochstetler."

Claire stopped chewing. "How could he have been a part of Elizabeth's Rumspringa? He's English."

"And that's exactly why he was part of her crew . . . because he *wasn't* Amish," Jakob said.

"Oftentimes, it's through those English counterparts that Amish teens come in contact with things they might not have otherwise," Diane added by way of explanation. "Cigarettes, alcohol, mischief, et cetera."

"Which brings us back to the limited memories I have of the mayor's—"

The wail of a siren as it raced past the inn brought Jakob's sentence to an end and him to his feet. "That's the fire department."

Diane pushed the paper from her lap and stood, her stride and her destination matching that of both Jakob and Claire. When they reached the bay window that overlooked the Amish countryside, they dispensed with the traditional pull string and, instead, parted the curtain with their hands to reveal a bright orange glow in the distance.

Claire felt the gasp as it escaped her throat, knew it had been echoed by her aunt, but all she could truly focus on was the sound of Jakob's voice as he barked into the phone now clutched to his ear.

"Detective Fisher. What's going on? Copy that address, please . . . Okay, got it. I'm on my way."

He snapped the phone closed inside his hand, returned it to his pocket, and then gathered Claire's hands inside his own. "Stoltzfus's barn is on fire and they're worried about the house going next. I've got to get out there and help. But I want to thank you"—his gaze left hers just

9

long enough to offer a quick yet deliberate nod in Diane's direction—"for tonight. For the conversation, the warmth, and the sense of normalcy. I can't think of the last time I felt so at home anywhere."

And then he was gone, his strong, confident footfalls disappearing as he made his way through the front door and into the night, the rising pillar of flames in the distance guiding his path.

Chapter 2

Claire stood at the lone window overlooking the alley-way between her store and Shoo Fly Bake Shoppe and watched as Ruth Miller carried one box after the other through her side entrance.

The boxes, in varying shapes and sizes, were a normal part of the workday for each and every shopkeeper along the cobblestoned thoroughfare that connected the English and Amish sides of Heavenly. But unlike the other shop-keepers, the Amish bakery owner didn't carry her own boxes. Ever.

It wasn't that she wasn't capable—because she was. And it wasn't that the twenty-two-year-old beauty was some sort of kapp-wearing diva—because nothing could be further from the truth. But she *was* Eli Miller's twin sister. That, coupled with being Benjamin Miller's unmarried little sister, was all the explanation needed.

Every morning, while the gas-powered lampposts still burned bright up and down Lighted Way, Benjamin delivered the bakery's supply of fresh milk in his horse-drawn wagon. Once the shop opened, Eli showed up at various points throughout the day to attend to any deliveries and carry out the trash that had accumulated between visits. They came quietly, performed their tasks quietly, and left quietly, the only indication they were around coming via the whinny of their respective horses in the now-empty alley.

Something was wrong.

It had to be.

Squaring her shoulders amid the lull in customers, Claire wound her way around the counter and into the back room, the hinges of the screen door announcing her presence in the alley as surely as any verbal greeting ever could.

Ruth looked up from the dwindling stack of boxes at her feet and smiled shyly. "Good morning, Claire."

She took a moment to study her neighbor and the many features that made the young woman more suited to a high-end fashion runway in Paris or Milan than a small Amish bakery in Lancaster County, Pennsylvania. Only with Ruth, her beauty didn't hinge on one particular feature and an artist's ability to highlight a few others. No, the youngest Miller's beauty was a complete package—one that included large, ocean blue eyes, high cheekbones, and long golden blonde hair parted severely down the middle and pinned into place beneath a plain white kapp. And that was just the exterior.

The true beauty that was Ruth Miller transcended the

obvious and resided in an inner genuineness that was recognized by everyone. Except, perhaps, by Ruth herself.

"Is everything okay?" Claire finally asked by way of a response that had taken far too long in coming.

Ruth's brows furrowed ever so slightly. "Everything is fine. God has made it so."

She crossed the alley and gestured at the two remaining parcels on Ruth's top step. "I guess I'm just used to seeing Eli carrying your deliveries inside . . ."

"I have been telling them for years I can do such things myself, but they do not listen. Even now, when Eli is married, he still spends too much time worrying about things I can and want to do by myself."

"He loves you. Benjamin does, too. They just like to make sure you're okay, is all."

Ruth glanced over her shoulder and through the screen door, the lull of customers in Claire's shop holding true inside the bakery as well. "I know they do. And I am grateful." Slowly the young Amish woman lowered herself to the top step and invited Claire to do the same. "But it is okay for me to look after them, too."

Claire claimed the cold concrete step just below Ruth and raised her face to the late winter sun just starting to peek itself over the top of her store. "Of course it is. That's what loving someone is all about."

"Eli did not return to Esther until dawn. It was even later when Benjamin's wagon went past the house. It was a long night of much worry and hard work."

And then she knew. Ruth was referring to the fire that had cut her unexpected evening with Jakob short—a fire that had burned for hours before night had finally reclaimed its hold on the view from Claire's bedroom window. "Did it spread to the house?" she asked.

Ruth shook her head.

"Was anyone hurt?"

Ruth's shapely shoulders rose and fell beneath her simple, plain blue dress. "No people. But a few horses perished."

Claire turned her body just enough to afford a clear view of her friend. "I was told the barn belonged to the Stoltzfus family?"

"Yah. Jeremiah and Miriam Stoltzfus." Ruth fiddled with the front of her apron for a moment and then continued, "I did not speak to Benjamin long this morning, but he said the barn is gone. There is nothing left."

"I know how important a barn and horses are to an Amish farmer. To start over must be difficult."

Ruth waved aside Claire's worry. "The Stoltzfus farm will have a new barn by week's end."

"By week's end?" she echoed. "But how?"

A hint of surprise raised Ruth's perfectly arched brows. "The men will come together to raise a new one. They will work all day long and the women will make sure they are fed."

"And they can raise an entire barn in less than five days?"

"With many able hands they can raise it in two."

She was less than a hundred yards from Sleep Heavenly when she heard the car approaching, the quiet whir of the engine and the slow rotation of the tires making her step onto the strip of gravel shoulder separating the grass from the pavement.

A familiar black sedan rolled up alongside her and stopped. Seconds later, the window lowered to reveal Jakob's smiling face and knee-weakening dimples. "Isn't it a little chilly to be walking home?"

She felt the flutter in her chest and the way it manifested itself in a matching smile she couldn't contain even if she'd wanted to. "According to the calendar, the official start of spring is only three weeks away."

"Mother Nature doesn't follow a calendar in these parts."

She laughed while simultaneously pulling the flaps of her jacket a little closer. "Exactly. And that's why I'm getting a jump on things now. You know, the whole early-bird thing . . ."

"You're a nut, do you know that?"

"I do. But when you've spent most of your adult life thus far sidestepping people and taxis in order to walk five blocks, I guess I find walking around here almost therapeutic. Besides, you can't beat the fresh air or the uninterrupted quiet time."

He winced dramatically. "Ouch."

She felt the color drain from her face as her last three words looped their way from her mouth to her ears. "Wait. No. I didn't mean that the way that it sounded. It's just that there's no song on the radio to cloud my thoughts or—"

"Hey, I was just kidding. No offense taken, I promise." His gaze left hers long enough to note her royal blue sweater and partially zipped coat. The appreciation on his face as he returned his focus to hers warmed her cheeks

15

instantly. "Any chance I could entice you into getting in the car with me? There's something I'd love to show you if you're game. Unless"—he leaned forward against the steering wheel to gesture toward her aunt's inn—"you need to get home to help Diane with dinner?"

There was no mistaking the hope in his eyes or the renewed flutter in her chest as she contemplated the answer she was all too eager to give. "We're in the middle of a trio of rare guest-free nights at the moment. While not necessarily good for Aunt Diane's bottom line, it does provide a rare opportunity for her to get out. Tonight, she's meeting friends for dinner in Breeze Point. So, in answer to your question, yes, you can entice me into your car . . . provided it has a heater."

"You're on."

She opened the door and slid into the passenger seat, the blast of warm air from the dashboard vents a welcome reprieve from an evening that had gotten cold, fast. "Oh. Wow. It's nice in here."

"I'll pretend you're referring to my company rather than my heater," he teased before a rare shyness took over. "Thanks for saying yes. I've been wanting to take you to see this since they started showing up a few hours ago."

"Since who started showing up?"

He swiveled in his seat just enough to gain an unobstructed view of the road, then did a U-turn that took them back toward Lighted Way. "Did you have much of a chance to look out your window at the shop today?"

Settling her head against the back of the seat, she took a moment to look out at the scenery as blacktop gave way to cobblestones and the quaint shopping district she'd left on foot less than ten minutes earlier. "Now that Esther isn't working at the shop any longer and I've yet to hire a replacement, I don't have much time to do anything except take care of customers, stock shelves, and keep the books straight. Although, today, I did get to spend a few minutes in the alley talking with Ruth."

"You need to hire some help. Working seven days a week isn't good for anyone."

She swung her focus back to Jakob. "You sound like my aunt right now."

"There could be worse things. Diane Weatherly is a wise woman as you well know." The *thump-thump* of cobblestones beneath the tires gave way to the distinctive ping of fine gravel as they left the shopping district and headed out into the Amish countryside. "Anyway, if you'd been able to look outside, you'd have seen far more Amish buggies than normal moving along Lighted Way this afternoon. Dozens and dozens of them, actually."

"Did someone die?" she asked quickly.

"Nope."

"Did someone get married?" Though, even as the question left her mouth she knew it was a silly one. Wedding season among the Amish took place in late fall. And even in the rare instance when one took place in late winter, they were held only on Tuesdays and Thursdays—never Wednesdays.

"They came because of last night's fire."

"But the fire was put out last night, wasn't it?"

A hint of a smile tugged at the corners of his lips as he nodded. "It was."

"Then I don't understand . . ."

"You will in about two minutes."

He returned his full attention to the road in front of them and she followed suit in time to notice the parade of empty buggies now lining both sides of the quiet Amish road as dusk settled around them. "What's going on?"

They rounded the next corner in a near-crawl and then came to a complete stop on the far side of the driveway belonging to Daniel Lapp and his wife, Sarah. "Come on, it's just past that tree line over there."

She followed the path made by his outstretched finger but saw nothing out of the ordinary except the continued line of buggies and an usually bright light in the distance. "I've never seen a light like that on this side of town," she mused.

"It's propane powered and it's a necessity tonight." Unlatching his door, he stepped onto the road and met her on the passenger side of the car, his hand finding hers in the growing darkness. "Come on. This is a sight not many people outside of Lancaster County ever get to see, and they should."

She quickened her pace at the slight tug to her hand and, together, they made their way along the winter brown grass that bordered the gravel road. A curious horse or two turned their head to watch as they passed, but, for the most part, it was just the two of them and whatever mission Jakob had in mind.

"Can I have a clue?"

"Nah." He dropped back a step, put his hand to the small of her back, and guided her around an outcropping of trees. "You're smart. I think you'll figure out why I brought you here in about five seconds."

"I'm not too sure what I think of this cryptic side of you . . ." She stopped speaking midprotest as they reached the next clearing. Jakob was right. She didn't need an outstretched finger or verbal directions to know which way to look. The sheer volume of men working to clear burned and mangled debris from the spot where Jeremiah Stoltzfus's barn had stood twenty-four hours earlier took care of that all on their own.

"By the day after tomorrow, there will be a brand-new barn in that exact spot."

She heard Jakob's voice, even processed his words, but the nonstop motion less than twenty yards away claimed the bulk of her attention and made her jaw go slack. "There are so many of them . . ."

And there were. Hundreds of hatted Amish men in black pants and suspenders worked together to move charred lumber and cover the site with fresh dirt. Teenagers carted fresh lumber from wagons and lined it up along the ground at a safe distance. Still younger boys sorted tools and passed out shovels for those who turned over the earth in hopes of accelerating the cooling process for anything still smoldering.

"The apostle Paul said that to fulfill the law of Christ, brethren must bear one another's burdens," Jakob explained. "The Amish believe that it is God's will for them to assist each other through financial ruin, disaster, fire, sickness, and even old age.

"When there's a fire like this one, the Amish come

from all over to help. They bring bales of hay, tools, food, and anything they think the family might need. Once the fire is cool and the debris is removed, they start raising a new barn." He leaned against the nearest tree and raked a hand through his hair. "The womenfolk come, too. See?"

Shifting her gaze toward the farmhouse, she noted the gaggle of women in their aproned dresses and kapps wearing a path between the front porch and a slew of tables. "Ruth said they would feed the men who came to help, but I didn't realize she meant *that* many men."

"A happenstance like a fire has a way of turning into a social occasion."

She nodded and then looked back at the men and boys who showed no sign of slowing down. "Ruth said they can build a new barn in its entirety in just a few days, but I never imagined she meant *now*. It hasn't even been twenty-four hours yet," she whispered.

"The Amish don't wait. When help is needed, they come."

"It's hard not to imagine what the world could be like if everyone responded to another person's suffering like the Amish do," she commented, engrossed.

"I couldn't agree more." Jakob pushed off the trunk of the tree and came to stand beside Claire, his upper arm gently brushing against her shoulder as he did. "So . . . Are you glad you got in my car instead of just going home to an empty inn?"

"How could I not be? This is absolutely amazing." She allowed herself a moment to really look at Jakob, to see the awe in his face and know it was surely mirrored on her own. For not the first time since they met, she couldn't help but wonder if he regretted his decision to leave his Amish upbringing behind. But, as was always the case, she kept the question to herself. "I almost want to stand here and watch until the whole process is done."

"They will be calling it quits for the night soon, which is a good thing for that young man right over there." He pointed her attention toward the object of his and laughed. "I think someone needs to tell him they don't need any more dirt."

Sure enough, a young Amish boy Claire judged to be about thirteen was painstakingly digging and transferring dirt into a waiting wheelbarrow. The dirt, she now knew, would then be used to sprinkle in and around the footprint of the former barn. This particular boy, unlike his many counterparts, seemed oblivious to the fact that the goal had been met.

"He'll figure it out when he looks up and realizes everyone else has moved on to dinner," Jakob teased before reaching for her hand once again. "How about I buy you dinner since I interrupted your evening with—"

"Dat! Dat!"

The fear-filled cry echoed across the open field and brought their attention back to the boy and the shovel now hovering above a hole he'd no doubt be tasked with refilling once his father got a close-up look at his handiwork. "Dat! Please! Come quick! I found bones!"

Chapter 3

For the first time since Esther got married, the sight of the twenty-year-old standing in the doorway of Heavenly Treasures didn't bring Claire joy.

Oh, it wasn't that she was unhappy her former employee had stopped by—because nothing could be further from the truth. In fact, not a single day went by that Claire didn't wish things could be different, that a married Amish woman could work outside the home right up until the moment she became a mother. But seeing her best friend standing there with swollen and red-rimmed eyes changed everything.

"Esther? Oh my gosh, sweetie . . . what's wrong? Are you hurt?"

Undeterred by the emphatic shake of her own head, a fresh round of tears began the slow descent down Esther's face. "I . . . I . . . I am not hurt."

Claire grabbed hold of the young woman's shoulder and guided her over to the counter and the stool that sat vacant on the other side. "Is it Eli? Did the two of you have a fight?"

Esther's soft gasp was quickly followed by a hiccup. "No! Things with Eli are wonderful. He is a good man and a good husband."

Claire's shoulders sagged with relief only to tense up once again as her thoughts traveled in a different direction. "Is something wrong with your mother? Your father? One of your siblings?"

Esther settled onto the stool and wiped her eyes with the back of her hand, sniffing as she did. "No. All are well."

"Then what's wrong, Esther? What has you so upset?"

"I saw her mother today. I saw the sadness in her face. It is a different one now. Because she no longer has hope."

She tried to follow Esther's words, tried to fill in the gaps with people they both knew, but she came up short. She had absolutely no idea what her friend was talking about and she said so.

A second round of sniffing and tear-wiping was finally followed by some clarification. "Waneta. Waneta Lehman."

"I'm sorry, Esther, I don't know who that is. Did something happen to her?"

"N-not Waneta. H-h-her daughter . . . Sadie."

Maybe it was a by-product of the relief she felt at the realization that Esther and her loved ones were okay. Maybe it was the tossing and turning she'd done during the night as she worried about Jakob and what he'd found at the site of the barn raising. But whatever the case, she could feel her patience running a bit thin. She took a deep breath, let it release slowly, deliberately. "You lost me, Esther. I don't know who either of these women is."

"Sadie is Waneta's daughter. Or was when she was still alive." Esther leaned her upper body against the edge of the counter and took a deep breath of her own before continuing her narrative in more of a straight line. "Sadie disappeared in the middle of her Rumspringa when I was a baby. Everyone said she went to the city to live the life of an Englisher.

"I remember, as a little girl, seeing Waneta in church. Her eyes did not smile with her mouth. I remember asking Mamm why she looked so sad and Mamm said it was because Sadie did not say good-bye before she left."

Claire started to speak but stopped as Esther continued. "I touched Waneta's hand after church a few years ago. I said that maybe Sadie would come back one day. That she would come back to say hello and give Waneta a hug. She squeezed my hand and said we would hope for that day together. And, until this morning, that hope has kept her eyes from being so sad."

Once again, the tears began to fall, the force and velocity of their encore preventing the young woman from uttering another word.

"You said this girl's name was Sadie, right? Is this the one who was friends with Benjamin's late wife?"

"Y-yes."

"And they went on Rumspringa together, didn't they?"

"Y-yes. Only Elizabeth c-c-came home for a few years before she died. S-Sadie did not."

Claire squatted down beside Esther's stool as the meaning behind her friend's statement hit its mark. "Wait. Did news come that Sadie died somehow?"

"Not news," Esther wailed. "Bones!"

Jerking back as her thoughts instantly rewound eighteen hours, Claire said, "Are you talking about the bones they found on the Stoltzfus farm last night?"

Esther pulled her gaze from her lap and fixed it, instead, on Claire. "You know about the bones?"

"I was with Jakob last night. We were standing on the edge of the Stoltzfus property, watching the men clear away the last remnants of the barn fire, when a young boy started yelling about finding bones. Jakob ran to him right away and you know how fast your uncle is. By the time I reached him and the hole, he was telling me to step back . . . telling everyone to step back."

"Eli stayed into the night with some of the other men. He says the bones are Sadie's." Esther's hands shook as she brought them to her face. "All these years Waneta walked over the place where her daughter was buried and she did not know. She did not know!"

Claire searched for something, anything to say as Esther's tears morphed into racking sobs that literally shook the young woman's body. "Shhhh . . . Esther. You need to take a deep breath. It's not good to get this upset. Besides, I don't know how you can be so sure those bones are Sadie's. The police can't even be certain of that without testing DNA or whatever it is they do when the only thing they have is bones. And surely, even with that, verification would take weeks, maybe even months."

"I do not know what is worse, Claire. The loss of

Waneta's hope . . . or knowing that I am the one who gave it to her in the first place."

"Maybe Eli misunderstood," Claire hypothesized. "Maybe the bones aren't human at all."

"No, they're human, alright."

Startled, Claire sprang upward, grazing her arm against the edge of the front counter as she did. "Oh. Jakob. I didn't hear you come in."

"You just didn't hear the bells." He crossed the showroom floor and stopped beside Claire, his gaze leaving hers just long enough to note his niece's presence. "Hey. I wanted to stop by really quick to apologize for the way last night ended. I hated having to shove my keys into your hand like that and tell you to drive yourself home. I just knew it was going to be a long night and I didn't want to keep you out there in the cold any longer than absolutely necessary."

"No. I understand. Truly." Mindful of Esther's gaze richoceting between them, Claire took a deep breath and released it slowly through her nose. "I dropped off the keys and your car with the dispatcher as I drove through town last night."

"I know. I got 'em." He ran his finger along the top of the counter and sighed. "But I didn't give you the car so you could walk home in the dark from the station."

"I didn't. I called Aunt Diane and she was back from her dinner in Breeze Point. So she picked me up."

"Good. I don't want to have to worry about you, too." He peeked over the edge of the counter and addressed his niece. "Esther, I heard what you said when I came in. You have nothing to blame yourself for in all of this. Nothing."

Claire silently waited to see whether Esther would

acknowledge her uncle despite the ban of communication his postbaptism departure demanded. But, as was often the case with the twenty-year-old, her actions were guided by her heart more than the Ordnung and its unwritten rules for behavior among the Amish.

"Sadie was buried on her parents' land," Esther said between sniffles. "I do not understand how they could not know."

"That's what I'm going to try to find out, Esther. You have my word on that."

Claire held up her hand. "Wait. I thought the barn that burned was on the Stoltzfus property."

"It was. But this time last year, that particular parcel of property belonged to the Lehmans. They sold it to Stoltzfus at the same time Daniel Lapp sold them acreage on the other side."

"So if those bones really belong to this Sadie Lehman, she's been buried on her own property this whole time?" She heard the disbelief in her voice but could do little to stop it. Like Esther, the notion that a woman could spend years looking forward to the return of a child whose remains were within yards all along was truly heartbreaking.

"It sure looks that way."

"Is there a specific reason why you think these bones are Sadie's?" She stopped, tilted her ear toward the back room, and lifted her index finger into the air. "Actually, can you hold your answer for just a second? I've been waiting for a delivery from that Amish soap maker you put me in touch with, Esther, and I think it may have finally arrived."

With a quick nod at Esther and then Jakob, Claire made her away toward the back room, the promise of new inventory quickening her steps. But as she approached the door that led to the alleyway, she realized her error. For there, standing just on the other side of the screen, was Benjamin Miller.

Like his younger sister, Ruth, Ben's eyes were as blue as the ocean on a sunny day. His cheekbones were high as well, but on his masculine face they appeared almost chiseled. His light brown straw hat contrasted nicely with the darker shade of hair barely visible around its base.

He raised a callused hand in greeting, then let it slowly slip down his clean-shaven face. "Good morning, Claire. It is good to see you."

Oh, how she wanted to believe him, to know beyond a shadow of a doubt that he harbored no hard feelings where his ill-fated marriage proposal was concerned, but she couldn't. Not entirely, anyway.

Sure, she'd seen him countless times since that day in the woods behind the shop. And yes, he'd been a driving force in her continued presence as a shopkeeper on Lighted Way. But despite all of that, the quiet yet powerful camaraderie they once shared was different now. It was a bit more awkward and a little less special.

Still she'd made the right decision. The last thing she wanted was for Ben to suffer the kind of gut-wrenching hurt Jakob experienced every day as an excommunicated Amish man.

Finding her smile, she pushed open the door and motioned him inside. "It's good to see you, too. How are you?"

"I am well. Thank you. Is Esther ready to leave? I am to drive her home to Eli."

She lowered her voice to avoid any chance of being overheard, but peeked around the corner and into the storeroom to be certain her friend was otherwise engaged. "I'm worried about her. She's taking the discovery of those bones on the Stoltzfus property extremely hard."

"If Eli is correct that Sadie Lehman has been found, it is a shock, of course, but it is God's will. I will speak with Esther in the buggy."

"Before you go, why don't you come into the store with me for a minute? Jakob is here and I was just asking him why he seems so certain the bones are Sadie's." She led the way back into the showroom, stopping every few feet to straighten a stack of bibs, a display of homemade candles, and a collection of wooden spoons hand-painted by Esther's mother, Martha. "While there was no soap delivery to be had, I did find Benjamin. He's ready to bring you home now, Esther."

Esther looked up from her lap and wiped at the remaining wetness on her cheeks. "I am sorry, Benjamin. I did not mean to keep you waiting."

Jakob stepped forward and extended his hand. "Ben."

Claire held her breath for a beat, releasing it slowly as Ben's momentary hesitation gave way to an answered nod. "Jakob. Eli spoke of what happened last night. He said you were still at Stoltzfus's farm when he left to milk the cows."

Jakob shrugged. "Even after all these years, we still have to take care to preserve any evidence we might find."

"For prosecution purposes?" she asked quickly.

Jakob pitched his upper body forward and planted his elbows on the counter, the exhaustion from his sleepless night clearly beginning to weigh on his body. "Prosecution *and* initial identification. And it's what we found in terms of the latter that makes me virtually certain we found Sadie Lehman."

"I don't understand."

"There was jewelry mixed in with the bones."

Esther's head dropped forward into her hands, prompting Claire to leave Jakob's side and move closer to her friend. Then, with one hand on Esther's back, she gave voice to the protest that seemed so simple. "Doesn't that say, right there, it can't be Sadie? The Amish don't wear jewelry."

"They do if they're on Rumspringa."

Rumspringa.

The time when Amish teenagers experiment with English life in order to make an informed decision as to whether baptism is right for them . . .

Slowly, methodically, she moved her hand in a circular motion at the base of Esther's neck, the young woman's breathing coming in fits and starts. "But it's been almost twenty years since she disappeared, right? How could anyone possibly remember what jewelry she was wearing?"

"Because one of the pieces was a silver necklace with her name dangling from the chain."

She swallowed hard. "And the other?"

"Was the right side of a friendship bracelet."

Esther lifted her head just enough to peer over the top of her fingers. "W-what is a f-friendship bracelet?"

"It's got a pendant that looks as if it's been broken in half. English girls and their friends often give or get them as gifts. One friend's bracelet has the right half of the pendant and the other friend has the left half. At least that's the way the chief explained it to me this morning."

Seeing the confusion in Esther's eyes, Claire stepped over to the register and the canister of pens tucked neatly to its side. "Here," she said as she plucked a blue pen from the mix and brought its tip to the first piece of scrap paper she could find, "I'll show you what he's talking about."

Carefully, she drew a small circle with a jagged cut through the middle. On one half she wrote *best* and on the other she wrote *friends*. When she was done, she showed it to Jakob for confirmation she was on the right track.

"Yeah, that's it. Only the one we found was heart shaped and had the word *forever* written in cursive across its half."

"Oh. Okay. I can do that." She flipped the paper over and drew a heart with the same jagged line through the middle. On the left side she wrote *friends* and on the right side she wrote *forever*. "Now, keeping in mind I'm not the most skilled artist in the world, this gives you a pretty good idea of what your uncle is talking about."

She handed the paper to Esther and watched as the young woman studied it closely, every detail, every line scrutinized as the novel concept it was. "I would have liked a bracelet like this when I was on Rumspringa, too." Squaring her shoulders beneath her burgundy-colored dress, Esther scooted off the stool, stood, and handed the drawing back to Claire. "Thank you for helping me to understand what Jakob found. Maybe, one day, I will have a girl and she can have a bracelet like this on her Rumspringa."

The sadness in Esther's voice was as impossible to miss as its very source. Esther was a sensitive soul living in a stoic community. What her family and friends saw as God's will still tugged at the young Amish woman's heart.

It was one of many ways in which Esther favored her now-English uncle.

"Everything will be okay, Esther," Jakob said, stepping forward. "If this is Sadie, as I believe it is, I *will* find out who did this to her and why."

Without thinking, Esther reached out for her uncle's hand only to jerk it back as she became aware of Benjamin's presence and the Amish infraction she was mere inches from committing in front of her brand-new brother-in-law. "I am sorry," she whispered. "I should not have done that."

Claire glanced at Jakob, the hurt in his eyes raw. There was so much about the Amish she admired—their simple way of life, the way they helped one another through tragedy and strife, and their big beautiful families. But the one thing she would never understand was the way they could forgive a stranger for such atrocious things as murder and rape, yet they couldn't forgive one of their own for a far more noble infraction.

It made no sense.

"Jakob. Could you please see Esther out to the buggy? I must check to see if Claire needs another chest for the shop."

She opened her mouth to weigh in on the notion of

another homemade blanket chest for the shop, but closed it as reality dawned. Blinking against the sudden moisture in her eyes, she turned a shaky smile in Benjamin's direction as Jakob and Esther disappeared into the alleyway. "Thank you for that, Ben. I'm not sure who needed the time together more . . . Esther or Jakob."

Benjamin pointed. "May I?"

Confused, she followed his finger to her hand and the picture still clutched inside. "I'm sorry, I guess I was so intent on helping Esther visualize what Jakob was saying, I forgot to show you, too."

He took the picture from her hand and stared down at it, his brow furrowed. "This is what Jakob found?"

Claire rocked forward on the tips of her toes for a closer look, then flipped the paper over in Benjamin's hands. "No, that was my first attempt. You know, before Jakob told me it was heart shaped and I had to draw it all over again, like this. See?"

It was quick, fleeting, but something about Benjamin's breath made her glance upward in time to see his complexion blanch.

"Benjamin? Are you okay?"

Crushing the drawing inside his hand, he stepped backward, his expression unreadable. "I must go. It is time to get Esther home to Eli."

Chapter 4

Somehow, despite the many times Claire had viewed it from the rock atop the hill, Benjamin's small, simple farmhouse looked very different while she stood at the base of the porch steps, trying to decide whether or not to knock.

Suddenly, the tangible tug it had held on all those star-filled nights felt a lot more like a push now, and she knew why.

Yes, she and Ben were friends.

Yes, friends checked on each other when they were worried.

Yes, she'd been worried about Ben since he'd abruptly left her shop earlier that day.

But there was also that other yes—the one that reminded her he was Amish and that he'd been willing to walk away from his family and his community to be with her.

"Oh. Claire. I did not know you were here." Ruth stepped onto her brother's front porch and quietly pulled the door closed. "I am glad. My brother will not talk to me about whatever is troubling him. Perhaps he will tell you, his friend."

She fiddled with the zipper pull on her jacket then released it along with a heavy sigh. "I don't want to intrude if he just wants to be alone."

Ruth looked left and then right, her gaze sweeping across the patch of gravel roadway that separated her brother's home from the one she still lived in with her parents. "Benjamin may be smart and strong, but he does not always know what is best for himself. So please, go inside. See if he will talk to you."

Reaching behind her statuesque frame, Ruth pushed Benjamin's door open and stepped aside. "Go. Please."

"I can't just walk in without knocking, Ruth," she whispered in protest. "He's not expecting me."

Ruth's blue eyes left Claire's face long enough to roll ever so slightly. Then, with the faintest hint of a smile, she poked her head into the open doorway. "Benjamin? Claire has come for a visit. She would like me to tell you that she is coming inside to see you."

Then, with a gentle shove, Ruth pushed Claire through the door and into the utter silence that was Benjamin's home. Before Claire could argue, before she could resist, the door was closed and there was no turning back.

"I am in the kitchen, Claire."

She closed her eyes and began a mental count, willing her mind not to read anything into Benjamin's monotone voice except the same end-of-day exhaustion she felt throbbing behind her own temples. This was Benjamin. Benjamin Miller. The same man who'd stepped forward with his wood-crafting ability in order to help keep her in Heavenly—something that transpired *after* she'd turned down his attempt at a marriage proposal. They were friends, and he was Amish. He didn't hold ill feelings.

When she reached ten, she opened her eyes and noted her surroundings. The large front room that served as the entryway into the home was sparsely furnished and reminded Claire of a similar room in Esther's parents' home. Although not an expert on the Amish by any means, Claire had learned enough from Esther to know the room's primary function was to accommodate roughly a hundred people for church service two or three times a year. The empty space allowed for the necessary benches to be brought in and utilized during the service and then converted into tables for the lunch and dinner that always followed.

Step-by-step, she crossed the room, picking out a few things as she went—a simple lamp atop a wheeled cabinet, a German songbook, a Bible, and a single pair of boots placed neatly beside the door.

It was hard not to wonder about Elizabeth and her three-week-long stint as Benjamin's wife. But she also knew such details wouldn't be visible inside the home. Even if the woman had still been alive, there would be no photographs framed on walls, no knickknacks dotting the mantel. The Amish didn't take or pose for pictures and they didn't put their stamp on a room with a certain wall-color choice or a particular prized treasure. If it had function, it was used; if it didn't, it wasn't.

She peeked around the open doorway into the kitchen,

the sight of Benjamin sitting alone at the large wooden table as dusk slowly claimed any natural light from the room, bringing an unexpected hitch to her breath. So many times Ruth had made reference to her brother's solitary existence—his lonely nights, his quiet meals, his empty home—but somehow the widower's reality hadn't truly sunk in.

Not until that exact moment, anyway.

Suddenly, the sight of the man with the shy smile who'd listened to her babble on about stars and wishes, helped save her shop from financial ruin, and had been willing to leave the only world he'd ever known in order to be with her, was almost more than she could comprehend without bursting into tears.

She took a deep breath, held it a beat, and then let it release slowly through pursed lips. No. Tonight was not about her. It was about Ben . . .

"What are you doing in here all by yourself?" she finally said before crossing to the table and taking a seat on the opposing bench. "It's starting to get dark and your propane lamp is in the other room."

"I prefer candlelight. It is enough to read by."

"Psst . . . you'd need a book in order to read."

The smile she'd hoped to entice didn't come; instead Ben simply laid his left hand over his right fist and propped the pair against his mouth.

She cast about for something to say, something to bring the Benjamin she knew out of this uncharacteristic shell. "I would imagine you're getting close to planting some of your crops. I bet that'll make your days long again."

"It will."

Her gaze fell on a basket on the counter beside the stove and she switched topics once again. "Looks like Ruth brought you some dessert, yes?"

"She brought dinner."

"Wow. I can only imagine how good her cooking must be if her baking makes my mouth water from across the alley at work."

Shrugging, Benjamin let his hands fall to the table. "She said it is chicken. You are welcome to have it if you would like."

"No, I wasn't hinting for dinner, Ben."

"I did not think that you were. But it is a shame to see good food go to waste."

"Then eat it," she said, not unkindly.

"Tonight, I am not hungry."

She looked around the room, at the simple propane-powered appliances, the spotless surfaces, and the overall empty feel of the space, any hunger pangs she may have felt upon news of the basket's contents faded. It was as if the loneliness that emanated from Ben and his surroundings made the prospect of a meal almost painful. The thought that he lived that way night after night made it even worse.

No, tonight would be different. She would see to that . . .

Rising to her feet, she stepped around the bench and walked over to the counter that housed the picnic basket, a quick peek inside confirming Benjamin's guess and adding homemade rolls, potatoes, and green beans to the mix. "Ruth made this for you and, judging by what I see, there's plenty for me, too."

"She does not seem to remember I am one person."

"Well, tonight, you're not." She opened the first cabinet she came to but found only glasses and pitchers. The second cabinet held the plates she needed but in a quantity that was downright agonizing. Benjamin had obviously imagined he'd have a life like his own father's, with a wife and a half-dozen kids. Instead, thanks to a poorly timed walk, seven of the eight plates went unused.

Night after night after night.

Shaking the mood-altering thought from her head, she set the plates on the counter and filled them with food from Ruth's basket. Then, armed with a pair of napkins and two glasses of cold milk at the ready, she brought everything to the table.

For a moment, she wasn't sure if Benjamin was going to stay and eat or get up and leave, the hollowness of his eyes making it difficult to know what, if anything, he was thinking. But when he reached across the table for her hands and bowed his head in prayer, she knew she'd won at least part of the battle.

She, of course, did most of the talking as they ate, his answers to her questions coming in mostly nods and shakes, but that was okay. It was progress, even if only a little.

"Ruth is a great cook. This chicken is delicious."

He forked a helping of beans into his mouth and nodded.

"I used to like to cook a lot back when I was living in New York City. But, after a while, when I was the only one eating it ninety percent of the time, I lost interest. Diane is trying to help me reclaim that."

"Is it working?" he asked quietly.

She tried not to show too much surprise at the sound of his voice and his sudden desire to engage in conversation, but it was hard. "I—uh . . . yes, it is. The people who stay at the inn are always so appreciative of the food we make. Knowing someone is not only eating it but also enjoying it, too, helps a lot."

He nodded slowly and with understanding.

"I imagine you know exactly what I'm talking about after going from your childhood home with your parents and siblings to sharing meals with Elizabeth and . . ." The rest of her sentence disappeared as a spasm of pain ripped across Benjamin's face.

"Ben, I'm sorry. I didn't mention your wife to cause you pain."

He wiped his mouth on the napkin Claire had placed beside his plate and then pushed back from the table, stopping short of actually standing.

"Ben . . . please. Talk to me. I saw the way you reacted to that drawing I did this morning. I saw the way your skin paled. What's going on? Maybe I can help somehow."

Seconds turned to minutes as the last of the day's light disappeared from the room's only window, bathing them in total darkness save for the lone candle Ben lit without a word. But just as she gave up any hope of him talking, he stood and motioned for Claire to follow him into a tiny sitting room off the back of the house. There, he lit another candle, palmed something small and silver from atop a plain end table into his fist, and then turned, flipping his hand over and slowly opening it in front of Claire.

She leaned forward and waited for her eyes to adjust to the dim light. When they did, she inhaled sharply.

"Ben?" she half whispered, half gasped. "Where did you get that?"

"It was Elizabeth's."

She tried to process his words, to make them fit with the familiar bracelet and charm in his hand, but it was hard to do amid the sudden roar in her ears. "But I don't understand . . . I . . ."

"She and Sadie were good friends. They must have bought bracelets together. On Rumspringa."

"Where did you find this?"

"It was in her chest. At the foot of my bed."

"So you knew about it before today?"

He nodded but said nothing.

"And that's why you reacted the way you did when you saw my drawing? Because you recognized it as being the half that went with Sadie's bracelet?"

Again, he nodded. Only this time, he followed the barely perceptible motion with background. "Elizabeth was a good woman. She was a fine wife for the short time we had together. But there was a sadness I did not understand. I often wondered if she wished she had made a different choice for her life. One day, just after we were married, I found her crying and I asked if she wished she had gone with her old friend Sadie."

"What did she say?"

"She did not answer. She just bowed her head and cried more." Benjamin looked down at the bracelet as if it were toxic. "I did not know what to think. I did not know if I was right. I did not want to start a life with someone who did not want that life, too. But then we went to the Lehmans' home about three weeks later to receive our wedding gift."

"Receive your wedding gift?" she echoed.

"Yah. We do not receive gifts at our wedding. They are presented to us in the weeks that follow, as we visit the friends who celebrated our day with us."

It was her turn to nod. "Okay, I think I understand."

"Sadie's mamm and dat were so happy for us. So happy for Elizabeth. Waneta—that is Sadie's mamm— said she was excited to see the children we would have, that it would be like watching Sadie's children grow."

"How did Elizabeth react?"

"She did not speak on the buggy ride home that night. And that is when I knew her sadness was not because she wanted to run off with Sadie, it was because she missed her." He rocked back on his feet and stared up at the flickering shadow on the ceiling. "The next day I bought her a notebook and pen. I told her to write to Sadie as if she was still in Heavenly. I told her to talk about our wedding and our new home and our plans for the farm."

"And?"

"She did as I said. Sometimes I would see her sitting on the front porch, writing. At lunch, while I ate, she would sit and write at the table. And at night, when I read, she would write in that chair." He lowered his chin and pointed at the wooden chair behind Claire.

"Did it help with the sadness?"

"I am not sure. I lost her three days later."

She felt the lump of emotion working its way up her throat and did her best to try to swallow it back down.

What she wouldn't give to turn back the hands of time and make things different for Ben . . .

"Did you ever read what she had written in those three days leading up to her death?"

A long, low sigh filled the air between them. "No. I put her book in the chest after she was buried. I did not see it again until I took out the bracelet this afternoon."

"And you still didn't read it?"

"I did not."

She looked from Ben to the bracelet and back again, the hurt and anguish on her friend's face making it difficult to breathe, let alone speak. But still, she tried, her hand finding his in the dark and squeezing them gently. "Maybe it's time you did."

Chapter 5

Sitting there, looking out over the moonlit fields that comprised the Amish side of Heavenly, Claire marveled at the absolute serenity. So much of her existence in New York City had been about hurrying and waiting.

First, she'd hurry through her day in anticipation of an evening with her then husband, Peter, only to wait at the table, alone, as their meals grew cold. Next, she'd hurry through the week in the hope the weekend would be different. But it never was. Instead, she spent her Saturdays and Sundays waiting for him to return from whatever golfing or dining engagement he had with yet another important client.

Five years of her life had slipped through her fingers playing that hurry-and-wait game.

Now, though, things were different—as different as New York City was from Heavenly, Pennsylvania, in fact.

Here, there was no more hurrying unless she happened to linger over coffee and breakfast with her aunt's guests a little too long. And as for waiting, that was gone, too, unless she counted silly stuff—like the wait for brownies to be done baking or customers to arrive.

"Claire, dear? Don't you think you should come inside now? It's awfully cold out here to be sitting on that porch swing."

She turned her head toward the hushed voice, the woman's features difficult to make out in the narrow swath of light streaming onto the porch from the partially opened front door. "I'll be in soon, Aunt Diane."

"Is everything okay? You seemed mighty quiet when you got home this evening."

"I'm fine. Just a little tired is all."

"Which is why it makes more sense for you to come inside and get some sleep, rather than continue to sit out here by yourself in the cold . . ."

She heard the sigh as it slipped past her lips and hoped her aunt didn't take it as rude. She loved Diane more than words could ever describe, but sometimes she needed a little space to ponder, even if she wasn't sure what, exactly, she was pondering. "I'll be in soon. I promise. I'm just enjoying the last guest-free night for a little while longer."

"Okay. I'm heading up to bed now, so just make sure to lock up, will you?"

"You've got it. Good night, Aunt Diane."

"Good night, Claire. Sleep well."

She lowered the side of her cheek back onto her out-stretched arm and focused again on the dark fields in the distance, the swing moving ever so slightly with the push of her right foot. Forty-eight hours earlier, the same land-scape had been bathed in a fiery glow. Twenty-four hours earlier, it had been peppered with a pulsating mixture of red and white emergency lights atop police cruisers. And now, it was dark again, with all the Amish likely fast asleep.

All except, perhaps, Waneta Lehman and her husband, Zebediah . . .

For years, Sadie's parents had surely lain in bed won-dering about their daughter's whereabouts.

But tonight, they wondered no more.

She traced the tip of her finger along the top edge of the swing and tried to imagine what it would be like to get such awful news. To realize that all your years of hope had been for naught . . .

The familiar *clip-clop* of an approaching horse broke through her reverie and forced her thoughts back to the porch. Rotating her body to the right, she brought her left foot down to the floor and leaned forward, the darkness that enveloped the inn's driveway making it difficult to see much of anything.

When the sound stopped, she stood and made her way over to the porch railing. "Hello? Who's there?" she called.

"It is me. Benjamin." And then he was there, standing at the foot of the steps, peering up at her with a troubled expression. "Can we talk?"

She took a step back and waved him onto the porch. "Of course. Please. Come up. Sit with me."

Retracing her steps back to the swing, she lowered herself onto the evenly spaced wooden slats and patted the vacant spot to her left. "If you hurry, you can take advantage of any leftover heat from my leg."

The soft light peeking around the parlor curtain was enough to illuminate the pained expression in the Amish man's face as he shook his head and remained standing. "I will not keep you. It is late and you must sleep."

"Aunt Diane said pretty much the same thing not more than ten minutes ago. But I'm not tired."

"Why?" he asked.

It was such a simple question yet she knew it merited anything but a simple answer. Still, she tried. At least in regard to the part that involved him, anyway . . . "I guess I've been worried about you. About the pain that will invariably be stirred up again when you finally read Elizabeth's journal for the first time."

"I have read it."

She drew back, surprised. "Already?"

He gave a slight nod. "I took care of my chores after you left. I even stopped by Mamm and Dat's house to thank Ruth for our dinner. When I was done, I went upstairs to bed. But when I walked into my room, all I could see was Elizabeth's chest."

"So you took out her journal and read it?" she prompted.

Again he nodded, his gaze slipping past hers and settling somewhere in the distance. "I did."

"And?"

"I am confused."

Something about the raw uncertainty in his normally confident voice caught her by surprise. "Oh? How so?"

He reached into the part of his waistband she couldn't see around his coat and pulled out a simple black spiral-bound notebook. "I would like you to read Elizabeth's words. Maybe you can understand what I cannot."

Surprised, she reached for the book only to drop her hand back to her lap, empty. "I don't know, Benjamin. I'm not sure I should read something so private. I never even knew your wife."

"Please. I would not ask if I did not need your help."

She looked from the book to her friend and back again, her heart thumping slowly but deliberately inside her chest. "If you're sure . . ."

"I am sure." He deposited the book onto Claire's lap and then gestured toward the inn. "You will need light to read her words."

"Do you want to come inside? Or would you rather I turn on the porch light?"

Ben stepped toward the porch railing and exhaled into his fist. "I would like to be here if that is okay?"

"Then I'll be right back." She laid the book beside her on the swing and then rose to her feet, the necessary light switch no more than three feet away. "Ready? It'll be bright."

At his nod, she flipped the switch and returned to the book, the absence of a title or any outward markings exactly what she'd expect from a married Amish woman. Slowly, she opened the cover and stared down at the uneven writing, the hastily scrawled sentences filling the first page from top to bottom.

"Are you absolutely sure you want me to read this?" she whispered, glancing up.

"Yah."

She held the page into the light now streaming down from the exterior wall of the house and began to read, the words of Benjamin's deceased wife filling the air between them.

For too long I have kept this secret for fear of what would happen to me. I did not want to live in a small room. I did not want to drink only water and eat only bread. I did not want to hurt Mamm and Dat. I did not want to cry each night.

> *I did not tell, yet I still cry each night.*
> *Not because I am afraid.*
> *Because I am sad.*
> *Because I did not do the right thing.*
> *Your mamm is so happy for me and Benjamin. She smiles like I am good. Like I am kind. But I am not good. I am not kind.*
> *I am a very bad person.*
> *You know that more than anyone.*
> *I am sorry, Sadie.*

Claire reread the last sentence and looked up at Benjamin when she reached the end. "I . . . I don't understand."

"Go on," he said, pointing at the book. "There is more."

Turning the page, she did as she was told, Elizabeth's penmanship becoming more and more difficult to read.

Benjamin asked me if I had made a mistake in marrying him. At first, I did not understand his question. I am happy to be his wife.

> *But I do not smile as a wife should, he says.*

I have tears I should not have, he says.

I want to tell him why I do not smile. I want to tell him why I cry at times. But if I do, he will not look at me with love anymore. He will look at me as if I am bad.

Something roiled in the pit of her stomach. Ever since the very first moment she'd learned of Elizabeth's existence as both Benjamin's late wife and Jakob's once romantic interest, she'd had an image in her mind. That woman had been beautiful, sweet, and good at everything she did.

Yet now, in a matter of two pages, her image was changing. Rapidly.

Elizabeth may still have been beautiful.

Elizabeth may have been good at everything she did.

But now, the sweet factor was definitely in question . . .

"There is more, Claire. Much, much more."

This time, she turned the page without stopping to look up at Benjamin, the wooden quality of his tone telling her more than any glance ever could. She felt a sudden chill race down her spine and shivered in response, but if Benjamin noticed, he said nothing.

I have tried to forget, just like Leroy and Miriam and Michael.

But I cannot.

I see your skin and it is like a new snowfall.

I see your eyes. They are wide and looking at me.

Sadie, you were my friend.
But I was not a friend to you in the end.

She sucked in a breath and flipped to the next page.

I cannot do it anymore.
I cannot stay silent.
What we did was not right.
It was not God's will.
It was ours.
Sadie's mamm and dat may not know.
My mamm and dat may not know.
Benjamin may not know.
But I know.
God knows.
I cannot forget like they can.

Suddenly, the bits and pieces of a tortured mind were starting to assemble into a workable picture far different from anything Claire could have ever imagined.

Glancing upward, she saw the troubled look on Benjamin's face and knew it reflected her own. "Benjamin, I—"

"Do not stop. Please."

Her hands trembling, Claire dropped her focus back to the book and turned the page again, any positive effects from the quick fortifying breath she took disappearing in mere seconds . . .

I am not the only one who cannot forget.
Miriam cannot forget.

But she tries.

Leroy cannot forget.

I do not need his words to know this.

It is in his eyes when we talk.

It is in his head when he looks into the valley.

It is in the lines beside his eyes when I talk of that night.

I do not know about Michael but Leroy is sure he cannot forget, either.

How could he?

How could any of us?

I do not want to live in a small room. I do not want to drink only bread and water. I do not want to hurt my mamm and dat. I do not want to hurt Benjamin.

But it is time for God's will to be done.

The chill from earlier returned, only this time, instead of a quick skitter down her spine, it spread outward to every nook and cranny of her body and remained.

There was a part of her that wanted to read on, to see if the picture now fully formed in her head was, in fact, correct. But there was also a part of her—the part that cared deeply for Benjamin and Jakob—that wanted to shut the book and marvel at Elizabeth's obvious gift for compelling fiction even in first-draft form.

Which part would win out, though, was decided by the man standing against the rail.

"I have always wondered what Elizabeth's last thoughts were before she died. Now, because of that book, I must wonder no more."

She ricocheted her focus between the book and Benjamin, the date in the upper right-hand corner of the page winning out in the end. "This is the day Elizabeth died?"

"Yah."

"Aunt Diane says Elizabeth was walking by the woods when she was killed. That she was struck by a stray bullet from a hunting rifle . . ."

"Yah."

Closing her eyes, she put herself on the same road that wound its way through Heavenly's Amish country, the stretch of woods her aunt had mentioned, the same stretch of woods she'd passed with Jakob twenty-four hours earlier . . .

On the way to the Stoltzfus farm . . .

The same farm that had once been owned by Sadie's parents . . .

Elizabeth's journal thudded to the ground as Claire rose to her feet and started toward the house and her cell phone, the final piece of the puzzle slipping into place with startling ease. "Oh dear Lord, she was trying to tell them! She was on her way to tell the Lehmans what happened to Sadie, when that bullet hit her!"

At the door, she turned to see Benjamin's head hung low, his shoulders hunched forward. "Ben?"

When he didn't respond, she swallowed. Hard.

There was no doubt whatsoever that Elizabeth had known Sadie was dead. The woman's journal entries made that virtually crystal clear. But just as that picture had come into focus for Claire, the one Ben had always had of his late wife had surely blurred into the unrecognizable.

"Ben," she whispered just loud enough for him to hear. "Ben, I'm so sorry."

After what seemed like an eternity, her friend finally looked up, the various stages of pain she'd seen in his eyes throughout the day slowly disappearing behind a heartbreaking resolve.

"We must show Jakob, yah?"

Chapter 6

At any other time and under any other circumstance, Claire might have been vaguely amused at the way Jakob's fingers tapped along with the ticking of his office clock. But when she took into account the almost two-to-one ratio of her heartbeat to that duet, suddenly the music it created in her ears wasn't terribly appealing.

She swallowed and nudged her chin toward the now-closed notebook atop his desk. "Are you upset to learn Elizabeth may have been privy to details of Sadie's death?"

A long hesitation gave way to a single nod of the detective's head.

"What else is bothering you?"

Jakob turned his troubled eyes in her direction. "Else?"

For not the first time since handing him the deceased Amish woman's journal, she wished she could slip it back into her purse and simply bypass the white, clapboard-sided building completely. Especially now, without Esther as backup, the opening and closing of Heavenly Treasures fell on Claire. The last thing she needed to do was fill her morning with other people's problems.

Then again, Benjamin and Jakob weren't *other* people. Benjamin was her friend and Jakob was possibly something more. Or could be if she stepped out of her own way like Diane was always encouraging her to do.

"I . . . I don't know. I guess I'm picking something else up from you right now." The second the words were out, she wished she could recall them. Really, who was she to think she knew Jakob well enough to translate his thoughts?

Shifting uncomfortably in her seat, she cast about for something to say that would serve as both an apology and a reset button. She settled on the straightforward approach. "Look, I'm sorry. Can we just chalk it up to a short night of sleep and the fact that my brain is still a little groggy? I tend to have a rather overactive imagination and sometimes . . ."

The corners of his mouth lifted ever so slightly as she continued to babble. "Whoa. Slow down a minute, would you? I'm not upset that you're picking up more. Quite the contrary, actually."

"Quite the contrary?" she echoed before indulging in a second, slower swallow.

"Yeah. I guess I find your ability to see inside my head rather encouraging."

She didn't need a mirror to know her cheeks were turning red. She could feel the increasing warmth of her skin just as surely as the unmistakable flip-flop in her stomach. "So . . . I'm right, then?" she said quickly, the question as much an attempt to take control of the conversation as it was a fact-finding mission. "There *is* something else bugging you about Elizabeth's journal?"

All hint of a smile disappeared as Jakob's focus shifted back to the notebook she'd handed him roughly twenty minutes earlier, the entries she'd read and reread throughout her sleepless night now responsible for a third set of troubled eyes.

"Do you remember the other night? At your aunt's? When I was talking about Elizabeth?"

"I do. You were talking about the way Elizabeth changed during Rumspringa. How having Sadie leave was hard on her because they'd been such good friends."

"That was my speculation three nights ago, yes." He fingered the cover of the plain notebook before pushing it to the center of his desk, punctuating his action with a weighted sigh. "Though now we know differently, don't we?"

"Meaning?"

"If nothing else, we know Sadie didn't just *take off*."

"Okay . . ."

"And now, *that*"—he pinned the book with a sharp glance—"has me questioning a lot more than all those tears I wiped from Elizabeth's face back then."

She leaned forward, the urge to smooth the worry from Jakob's brow strong. Instead, she merely rested her hand atop his and squeezed. "I'm sure she was hurting, Jakob. You can feel it in every sentence she wrote. I'm sure the tears were real. Especially if she knew her friend was gone forever."

Flipping his hand over, he linked his fingers with hers momentarily before releasing them to stand and wander over to the window that overlooked the fields behind the station. "Oh, I don't doubt her tears were real. I'm just starting to question the driving force behind them."

She waited a minute to see what else he'd say, but there was nothing. The tension emanating from his body, though, spoke volumes.

"I'm not sure what you're saying, Jakob."

"When Elizabeth's Rumspringa was over and she said she wanted to be baptized, I doubted her conviction because of her tears."

Claire, too, stood and made her way around the desk, perching against the side closest to the window. "Yes. That night at Diane's you told us you had asked her if she was sure she was making the right choice."

Slowly, he turned away from the late-winter fields, his eyes tired but focused solely on Claire's face. "I guess I didn't understand why leaving Rumspringa behind was so upsetting to her if it was what she really wanted."

"Makes sense, based on what you knew at the time."

He shrugged in agreement. "But then, when she got so upset about my never-ending fascination with the police, I figured she had truly embraced everything about the Amish ways—including their wariness toward men in uniform."

"And now?"

He cupped his left hand over his mouth and exhaled against his palm.

"And now?" she repeated.

Letting his hand drop, he tipped his head toward the ceiling, a second, uninhibited burst of air echoing around the room. "*And now* I'm wondering if there was an entirely different reason for her reaction."

"To what? Being baptized?"

"No. To my endless talk about being a cop."

"What other reason could there be?"

Slowly, he lowered his chin until their gazes locked, the raw pain in his eyes catching her by surprise. "If I became a cop, maybe I'd figure out the truth."

"You mean about Sadie's death?"

He looked past her to the notebook still sitting on the middle of his desk, the wooden tone of his answer befitting the difficult thoughts he finally unleashed. "I'm thinking more along the lines of *Elizabeth's involvement* in Sadie's death."

Claire sunk onto the stool behind the cash register and rested her head on the countertop. Somehow, despite her best efforts to the contrary, she'd managed to have decent sales during the first half of the day thanks to the tour bus of senior citizens that had parked itself at the end of Lighted Way as she was opening the shop.

Within ten minutes of debarkation, Heavenly Treasures, and every other shop on the quaint street, was reaping the rewards of having so many seasoned shoppers intent on bringing a slice of Amish country home with them. One of Martha's quilts had sold, as had three of Esther's hand-sewn shawls. A hand-carved footstool and coatrack of Eli's had gone as well.

She'd tried to be cheerful to each and every customer who had wandered in, some asking specific questions about her inventory, others asking more general questions about the Amish. But, no matter how hard she'd tried to focus, her thoughts hadn't been able to stick on anything except Elizabeth's journal entries and Jakob's bone-chilling suspicion.

Oh, how she'd wanted to laugh at the detective's theory until he saw its absurdity, too. But she hadn't and she couldn't. Because as much as she hated to admit it to herself, the contents of the notebook proved Ben's late wife had known of Sadie's true fate. And, as Jakob went on to outline for Claire in his office that morning, only the guilty tended to keep quiet.

She closed her eyes, tried to stop her thoughts from revisiting the moment Ben verbalized Jakob's need to see Elizabeth's journal, but to no avail. The memory was as clear as if they were standing on the porch and she was still looking into his troubled face.

"Claire?"

Hadn't Ben been through enough already? Did he really need to entertain the possibility his late wife had played a part in someone's death?

"Claire?"

Her name, in conjunction with a cough, brought her attention to the back of the store and the twenty-two-year-old staring at her from beneath the rim of a straw hat. For a split second, she thought it was Benjamin, the ocean blue eyes a near-perfect match. But as quickly as the impression came it was gone, thanks to the mop of blond hair peeking out around the edges of the hat, and the three-month-long beard taking shape along his jawline.

"Oh, Eli, I didn't hear you come in." She stepped down off the stool and made her way around the counter, the sight of her friend's new husband bringing a much-needed lift to her step. "How are you? How is Esther?"

"Esther is well, thank you. But she would worry if she saw what I saw just now."

She tilted her head and peered up at Eli, the visual similarities between the young man and his older brother multiplying with each passing day. "What did you see?"

"A deep frown where there is usually a smile."

Before she could make sense of his words, he continued, his brows arching upward as he did. "Is something the matter, Claire? Something I can help fix?"

Her confusion gave way to understanding and she tried her best to brush his observations off with a laugh. The fact that it was forced was not lost on Eli.

"It seems there are many frowns these days. The kind of frowns men with tools and boards cannot fix."

She allowed the pent-up sigh past her lips then motioned for him to follow her back to the counter and the pair of waiting stools. "I wish all problems in life could be solved as quickly and efficiently as the Amish tend to a burned barn. I've never seen anything like that in my life. It was truly awe-inspiring."

Eli took the stool his wife frequented during her days as Claire's employee. "Galatians 6:10 advises, 'As we have therefore opportunity, let us do good unto all men, especially unto them who are of the household of faith.'"

"It's a beautiful thing to see, Eli." Claire leaned her back against the edge of the counter and pointed toward his chin. "You wear your beard well."

She watched as his callused hand rose to touch the new growth, a peaceful smile lifting his cheeks in the process. "It is good to be married to Esther."

"I knew it would be." A familiar lump formed in her throat and she worked to clear it away. "I miss her being here with me."

"That is not the only reason for your frown, yah?"

She considered arguing, but knew it was fruitless. Eli was a sharp man but, more than that, he was fiercely loyal to those he cared about. Claire's link to Esther put her squarely in that camp. "I guess I'm just worried about a lot of people right now."

"Jakob?"

Glancing up, she met Eli's eyes and realized the question was more rhetorical than anything else.

"Yes."

"I have seen him at Stoltzfus's farm. Sometimes he has paper and pen, sometimes he just walks around the hole where the body was found."

"It's his job to figure out what happened to Sadie Lehman," she said, her voice quiet yet steady.

"And he will do it well."

She couldn't help but marvel at the genuine conviction in Eli's tone despite the ban that made so many of his Amish brethren turn away from the very mention of Jakob Fisher. The sentiment itself didn't really surprise her, not coming from Eli, anyway. Eli seemed to be able to look at Jakob in a way few Amish could. As a result,

Claire was certain Esther was free to speak of her uncle inside her home without worry of being shunned by her husband.

"I will tell him you said so," she whispered.

Eli nodded once, his gaze never leaving Claire's face. "I often think of you and Jakob at the wedding. I could not speak with him, but I did look his way. He is happy with you."

She felt the instant warming of her cheeks and gave the only response she could. "And I am happy with him. Jakob is a good man."

"Yah."

A comfortable silence fell across the room as she mentally revisited the day Esther and Eli got married. So much of the day had been a blur as she tried to focus on the joy she felt for her friends rather than the sadness in her heart at losing Esther from Heavenly Treasures' day-to-day operations. But the one part that remained crystal clear was standing next to Jakob as Eli and his niece became husband and wife. Nothing—not the countless backs that had been turned in his direction or the fact he couldn't speak to his family members—could have wiped the joy from Jakob's face the moment Esther had smiled at him in her plain white wedding dress.

"Now that is much better. Esther would be pleased."

She pulled her thoughts back to the present and the man seated on the opposite stool. "What's much better?"

"You are smiling again."

Indeed, she was.

"It is because of Jakob, no?"

"You're as bad as Diane, do you know that?" she joked

before granting the nod she knew Eli sought. "Yes, Jakob was part of my smile just then. But so, too, was Esther . . . and you."

"Then it is set."

She drew back, confused. "I'm sorry, Eli, you lost me. What's set?"

"You will come to dinner tonight."

"Dinner?" she echoed.

"Yah. That is why I am here. To ask you to dinner tonight."

"I—"

"Esther said I am to tell you she is making chocolate cake for dessert. She said that will convince you to come."

It felt good to laugh, to leave her worries about Jakob and Ben behind if even for just a little while. "I accept." Leaning forward she winked up at Eli, her smile still huge. "But between you and me, I didn't need the cake to convince me."

Chapter 7

If she'd had any hint of doubt that Eli was a hard worker, it disappeared the moment his and Esther's farmhouse came into view around the bend. Suddenly, the dilapidated building that had housed the late Harley Zook as recently as five months earlier looked like a true home.

Gone were the shutters that hung from the window by a precarious nail or two—replaced, instead, by brand-new freshly painted versions.

Gone was the spray-painted graffiti from the foundation of the home, the murderous threat to the previous owner covered over by the same fresh coat of white paint that gave the rest of the house a much-needed lift.

Gone, too, were the rotting boards of a once-expansive front porch—in their place sturdy two-by-fours and a simple, yet tastefully painted railing that gave the outdoor space a brand-new lease on life.

Sliding the gearshift into park, Claire stared up at the house, flabbergasted. Sure, she'd known Eli was working to restore the house, but to make such night-and-day progress during the winter months was simply mind-boggling, at best.

"Claire! Claire!"

Esther's voice seeped through the closed car and propelled Claire from her seat, the utter shock she'd felt only moments earlier a distant blip compared to the excitement now coursing through her body at the promise of some real time with her best friend.

"Hi, Esther," she called out as she pushed the car door shut and fairly ran toward the front porch. When she reached the top step, she pulled the Amish girl in for a hug and held her close, the much-missed aromas of soap and hearth pricking her eyes with unshed tears. "It is so good to see you again, Esther."

"It is good to see you again, too, Claire. I am sorry I was so sad when I saw you last."

She released her friend from her embrace and stepped back to afford a closer look. "I'll take time with you any way I can get it. But, I have to admit, I much prefer seeing you with this smile."

"I am happy."

Claire gestured toward the house, her earlier surprise rearing its head again. "This place looks amazing. I . . . I can't believe the work you've done in just a few short months. It looks like a different house."

"Eli has worked hard. He wants everything to be nice for me and for the baby."

Her jaw slacked as she processed her friend's words. "You mean you're pregnant?"

"Yah."

"Oh, Esther . . . I didn't know."

"I asked Eli not to tell. I wanted to do it. But I was too upset about Sadie the other day to tell you. So I waited until now."

She hugged her friend a second time then stepped back to place a gentle hand on the tiniest hint of a mound Claire had failed to notice beneath the black aproned dress. "When are you due?"

"Harvesttime. Mamm says it will be a busy time for Eli."

Looking again at the house and then Esther, she offered what she hoped was a reassuring smile. "If anyone can handle it, it's Eli."

"That is what I told Mamm."

She gathered Esther's hands inside her own and gave them a gentle squeeze. "Can I tell Jakob?"

A smile made its way from Esther's mouth to her eyes in quick fashion, stealing Claire's breath in the process. "I was hoping you would say that. Yes . . . please. Tell him."

"He's going to be so happy."

"I am glad." Then, turning toward the door, Esther looked back at Claire. "Please. Come. Eli and I have been working to get things ready inside, too."

She shadowed her friend through the door and into the large front room that was the norm in so many Amish homes. The floors in the wide-open space gleamed. "We are to host church next weekend."

"Isn't that a lot in your condition?" she asked, curious. "I mean, you can have as many as a hundred people here that day, right?"

"Mamm will help with the cooking and I will be fine."

"You are a marvel, Esther King—I mean, Miller." She shook her head, embarrassed. "I'm sorry, Esther. I guess I'm just not used to your married name yet."

Esther waved aside her apology. "I have made that mistake many times since the wedding. Eli does not get mad. He says it will get easier to say, and he is right. I am saying Miller with more ease now." Then, hooking her thumb over her shoulder, she made a face more reminiscent of the Esther Claire remembered from the shop. "This is not my favorite room. Come. Let me show you the kitchen. It is where I spend much of my days cooking, or painting."

She followed Esther into the heart of the home. There, the wood-planked floor and soft green walls enveloped her in an instant feeling of warmth that had little to do with the delightful smells wafting from the simple stove on the opposite side of the room. "Oh, Esther, it's lovely."

A hint of red rose up in Esther's otherwise pale face at the praise and she brushed it off with the required humility, drawing Claire's attention to specifics, instead. "Eli said we were to have a big kitchen table. For our growing family and for when people come to share supper."

"It's perfect." And it was. Like the large dining room table at Sleep Heavenly, Esther's lent itself to good food and conversation. She pointed at the sparkling appliances around the room and looked back at Esther. "Those all run on gas?"

Esther nodded and then directed Claire's attention to a hand-carved shelf on the wall above the sewing machine. "Those are the bowls you gave us for our wedding. Eli said they looked nice on his shelf."

She blinked away a new set of tears, the presence of her gift in such a prominent spot touching her deeply. "Eli is right."

"Claire? Are you okay? You seem sad."

"I'm not sad, Esther. I'm happy you and Eli have each other and this beautiful home."

"As you will have with Jakob one day." Esther ducked her head then peered back up at Claire with a sweet smile. "Mamm says I should not say such things to you. That I should wait for my uncle to decide, but I am sure. Mamm is, too."

She staggered to the table and dropped onto the bench closest to the entryway, her friend's words more than she could process at that moment. "Esther, it's too soon. We're really still trying to figure out what's going on between us, if anything."

"Oh, there is something going on. It is plain as day every time I see my uncle look at you." Esther crossed to the oven and opened it, her nose lifting into the air in perfect time with Claire's. "We shall eat soon."

Claire listened for Eli's footsteps on the floor above but heard nothing. "Where is Eli? He will be joining us, won't he?"

"Of course. But he must check the cows first." Esther

closed the oven door and then began adding butter to something in a large pot. "It is good that he is busy in the barn. It quiets his worry about Ben."

She sat up tall, her curiosity aroused. "Eli is worried about Ben? Why?"

Esther covered the pot, stepped to the left, and grabbed the threesome of dishes stacked on the counter. "Ben has been quiet since Sadie's body was found. He keeps to himself in the field and does not say much when Eli stops by their dat's farm. He says it is as if Elizabeth has passed all over again."

Claire stood and took the plates and utensils from Esther's hands. "Please, let me set the table. You tend to the meal." Then, as she moved around the table, setting each place, she brought the conversation back to Ben, curious as to what Esther might know. "I would imagine it would be hard, at times, for Ben to be around Elizabeth's friends and family just in the course of a regular day, let alone in the wake of one of their deaths."

"That does make sense. I know I cannot stop thinking of Waneta and how she must be feeling now that she knows she will never see Sadie again. There is comfort in knowing it was God's will, but it is still sad."

"It is." She set a cup beside each plate and then reclaimed her spot at the end of the wooden bench as Esther put bread in a basket and carried it to the table. There was so much she wanted to know about Elizabeth's friends—people who'd been on Rumspringa when Esther had been just an infant, yet very likely remained in the same district today. "Do you know a Miriam? A Miriam Hoster-something?"

Esther shook her head at Claire, laughing as she did. "You mean Hochstetler?"

Claire rewound her thoughts to the night of the fire and did her best to recall the name her aunt had mentioned. "Yes, I think that's right. It *sounds* right."

"I don't really remember her as Miriam Hochstetler at all. I was a baby when she was still with her mamm and dat. But I know her well as Miriam Stoltzfus."

She felt her mouth gape and worked to recover it quickly. *"Stoltzfus?"*

"Yah. She is married to Jeremiah."

"Stoltzfus?" she repeated. "As in the owner of the barn that burned to the ground the other night?"

"Yah. But the new barn has been raised."

Wrapping her left hand around the edge of the table, she stared, unseeingly, at the basket of bread and the accompanying slab of butter, Esther's response barely registering before the next rhetorical question made its way past her lips. "And Stoltzfus is also the owner of the land where Sadie's body was found?"

"The current owner, yes. But the land was first owned by Sadie's dat. He sold it to Jeremiah when it became too much for him to farm." Esther returned to the oven and, this time, transferred the roasted chicken to the now-empty counter. "I spoke of this the other day, at the shop."

But I hadn't read Elizabeth's journal then . . .

She shook off the troubling thought and did her best to lighten her tone. "That's right, you did. So what is she like? This Miriam?"

Esther poked at the chicken a few times before deeming it done. "Miriam is quiet. I believe that is because

71

she has five boys. Mamm said it happened before that, after her Rumspringa."

"She wasn't quiet as a young girl?"

"I only know what Mamm said."

Intrigued, Claire made a mental note to speak with Jakob's sister, Martha, before moving on to the next name she remembered from Elizabeth's journal. "How about a Leroy?"

With careful hands, Esther carved the roast, each slice making its way onto a waiting plate. "Leroy is married to Bishop Hershberger's oldest daughter. They, too, have five children, but Eva is to have her sixth soon."

The front door swung open, admitting Eli into the house, his purposeful footsteps prompting Esther to cut faster. He made short work of the front room and joined them in the kitchen. "Are you speaking of Beiler?"

Esther turned and smiled at her husband, the love she had for the man intensifying her normal glow. "Yah."

"I would imagine it must have been hard to court the bishop's daughter," Claire mused. "Do you know if it was?"

Eli shrugged and took his place at the end of the table, smiling up at his wife as she placed the plate of meat in front of his spot and then returned to the stove for the covered pot. "I cannot say. But there would be no room for angry outbursts like I once had."

Esther returned to the table again, the now-uncovered pot revealing homemade mashed potatoes. "You were not ready to marry then, Eli."

"I was, I just did not stop to think how my anger could hurt you. But I have learned from my mistakes."

"How about Michael?" Claire asked as she accepted the potatoes from Esther and spooned a small helping onto her plate. "Do you happen to know someone with the first name of Michael?"

"I know of no Michael," Eli replied before bowing his head in time with his wife. "It is time to pray."

Chapter 8

There was something therapeutic about waiting for dough to rise and then punching it back down to its original size. It had a way of relieving stress while simultaneously making you feel as if you were accomplishing something—two things she was in dire need of that morning as she kept one eye on Diane's recipe card and the other on the clock above the sink.

"The table is all set. The guests will be down in about thirty minutes," Diane said as she breezed into the kitchen from the dining room. "How are those donuts coming along?"

"I'm getting ready to roll and cut the dough now. Then, they need about twenty minutes to rise one more time before I drop them into the deep fryer." She pointed at the white mixing bowl to her right, the spoon she'd used for mixing still inside. "The maple glaze is all ready to go the second they come out of the fryer."

"Perfect. I was telling the Finnegans about Amish donuts when they checked in yesterday and I thought it would be a nice surprise to serve some with breakfast this morning." Diane opened the refrigerator and pulled out a dozen eggs and a carton of milk in preparation for the scrambled eggs on the morning menu. "We missed you last night. Did you have fun?"

She couldn't help but smile at the hopeful tone Diane didn't even try to hide. "I did. Very much. But I wasn't with Jakob . . . in case you were wondering."

Diane crossed to the stove and the waiting skillet. "I wasn't."

Securing a knife from the utility drawer beneath the center island's countertop, Claire began a silent count to ten, her aunt's anticipated next question coming before she even got to three. "So who were you with?"

If it were any other adult, she may have found the inquiry nosy, but, considering it was Diane, she simply laughed. "You really are very transparent, you know that?"

Diane's hand stopped just short of cracking an egg against the side of the skillet. "Transparent? Me?"

Claire cut the dough into slices and set them back on the floured board to rise one last time. "Don't think I haven't seen how dog-eared that bridal magazine is in the parlor. Because I have . . ."

"I don't know what you're talking about, dear."

"Oh . . . okay. I suppose Wendy Finnegan has been looking at it and reminiscing about her marriage to Todd, right?"

"Maybe."

When she had a dozen slices lined up on the board, she covered it with a dishcloth and noted the time on the clock. "Diane, we're just trying to figure out what this is right now. See if we're meant to date or remain friends."

Diane cracked a few more eggs and then adjusted the temperature on the burner. "That's the problem with young people today. They spend too much time thinking and analyzing. Just live. Date. See what happens."

She bit back the urge to say Peter's name, the mere memory of her ex-husband and their failed marriage a springboard for a bad day. Instead, she changed the subject and hoped it would stick. "I had dinner with Esther and Eli last night."

Diane bit. "Oh? How are they?"

"They're—" She stopped, inhaled, and searched for something to say that would finish her statement without divulging news of the couple's impending new addition. Jakob needed to be the next to know.

"They're enjoying the house and, Diane, you should see what they've done with the place. Harley would be pleased, I'm sure."

"Was Benjamin there?"

The question brought her up short as did the wooden tone in which it was posed. "No. He wasn't. Not that that would have been a bad thing. We're friends, Diane. Nothing more."

Diane glanced over her shoulder at Claire, the worry in her eyes impossible to miss. "I want to believe that, Claire, I really do. But I know that he stopped by Thursday evening and that he spent time with you on the porch."

She grabbed hold of the bowl and began to stir the glaze mixture, her thoughts quickly traveling back to the porch and the reason for Ben's visit as she did. "He came because he was upset. He wanted to know if he was reading into her words."

"Her words?" Diane parroted just before she added a pinch of salt and a dash of pepper to the bubbling mixture in the skillet.

"The last few weeks of Elizabeth's life, she kept a journal. It was Ben's idea. He'd hoped it would be a way for her to work through whatever was bothering her."

"Go on . . ."

"He thought she was second-guessing their marriage. She insisted she wasn't. But she wouldn't tell him what was wrong. He figured it had something to do with Sadie, so he gave Elizabeth the notebook. When she died, he put it in her hope chest and didn't read it until the other day, when he went into the chest after Jakob mentioned a bracelet found alongside Sadie's remains."

Pushing aside the glaze bowl once again, Claire lifted the dishcloth from the board and inspected the puffy dough. "I think these are just about ready for the deep fryer."

Diane pointed a spatula at Claire. "Don't stop. Keep talking."

She slipped off the cushioned stool and carried the floured board and dough slices over to the deep fryer and the waiting fat. "Unfortunately, it looks as if Elizabeth knew Sadie was dead."

The gasp from the other side of the kitchen wasn't much different from the one she herself had made when she got to the page in Elizabeth's journal that brought that fact home. "Trust me, I know. I feel so bad for Ben right now. This has to be eating him up inside."

A glance in the direction of the stove showed that Diane was wrapped up in the tale Claire was weaving. "Diane . . . the eggs?"

Diane shook her head and turned back to the skillet, her attention still riveted on their conversation. "What did she write?"

One by one, she dropped the dough slices into the fryer and hovered above them at the ready. "She talked about knowing and not telling anyone. She talked about a few of her Rumspringa friends and how they seem to have forgotten . . . but she couldn't."

"Forgotten Sadie?"

"Forgotten her death, we believe." When the slices were a golden color, she plucked them from the fryer and placed them on a rack. "Last night, at Esther's, I was able to figure out who two of the people Elizabeth mentioned are. But there was one I couldn't figure out."

"Who is that?" Diane retrieved a large serving bowl from the cabinet to the left of the sink and set it beside the stove in preparation for the eggs. "Maybe I can help."

Returning to the island, Claire retrieved the bowl of maple glaze and gave it another quick stir. When it was the right consistency, she carried it back to the waiting donuts and began the process of dipping each one. "She mentioned Miriam—"

"Miriam Hochstetler, now Stoltzfus."

Claire nodded. "And Leroy Beiler."

"Eva Hershberger's husband."

"And a Michael . . ."

"O'Neil," Diane supplied without so much as a hint of hesitation.

She looked up from the second to last donut and studied her aunt. "Why does that name sound familiar?"

"Because we were talking about him the other night. When Jakob was here. He's running for mayor of Heavenly."

"You mean the one that's the son of the former mayor?"

"*Ryan* O'Neil," Diane said with a quick but firm nod. "Yes, he's the one. He—"

"Wait. Didn't Jakob say something that night about this Mike guy being part of Elizabeth's Rumspringa crew on account of Miriam Hochstetler?"

Diane nodded again then scooped the eggs into the bowl. "Yes, because he was."

"How did the son of an English mayor get involved with an Amish teenage girl?"

Yanking a nearby drawer open, Diane fished out a dishcloth and draped it over the bowl to keep the eggs warm. When she was done, she retrieved a basket from the corner hutch and brought it over to Claire for the freshly glazed donuts. "Michael was a bit of a trouble-maker. Some folks in town chalked it up to his being the mayor's son and knowing he could get away with things—which he did, often. Some folks chalked it up to a desperate plea to get his father's attention—which was always on other things. But, regardless of the reason, he was drawn to trouble and *creating* trouble. Befriending a sweet Amish girl and her friends and then leading them astray was just another way to accomplish that goal."

"And this guy actually has a chance to be mayor?" She set the basket back on the island and grabbed a pot holder from a nearby drawer. "Does he even have a shot?"

"A very good one, from what I can see." Diane lifted the bowl of eggs with one hand and the basket of donuts with the other and headed for the kitchen door. Claire followed behind with the piping-hot casserole dish. "Mike's father was ousted from his mayoral seat eight years ago by Don Smith. Don is running again, but he's getting tired. Couple that with the fact that Mike is willing to address road problems and other little bothersome issues we've had in this town in a way that won't affect people's wallets, and, well, that speaks to people."

Diane set the bowls on the serving table and waited for Claire to do the same with the casserole. Footsteps on the stairs let them know they were right on time. "But can he handle the job?"

"I think he can. He's grown into a fine young man in spite of being pushed around by his father. He's engaged now, I believe, and wanting to raise his own family here one day. His troublemaking days are over." Diane smoothed her hands down the sides of her waist-tied apron and smiled at the first pair of guests who entered the dining room from the front hallway. "Good morning, Wendy. Good morning, Tom. How did you sleep?"

What the Finnegans said in response, Claire didn't hear, her thoughts ricocheting in different directions even as she, too, managed a greeting for the next two couples. Once everyone was settled at the table with full plates and mugs, she returned to the kitchen with Diane, her eyes automatically shifting to the clock.

"Has Jakob seen Elizabeth's journal?" Diane leaned against the refrigerator for a well-earned, albeit quick break.

Claire grabbed a bottle of disinfectant and moved around the room, wiping and cleaning counters as she walked. "He has."

"I can't imagine Benjamin is too happy about that."

"It was his idea." She stopped beside the fryer, double-checked everything was turned off, and then continued on, stopping every few feet to spray and wipe. "Though, now that I say that, I realize I owe him an update."

"What did Jakob say?"

She finished the final counter and moved on to the oven doors, her cloth sliding across the handle with a practiced hand. "He's worried about the extent to which Elizabeth may have been involved in Sadie's death. If she knew and didn't say anything, it makes it look an awful lot like she had something to hide."

"Oh dear. I can't imagine that sweet young thing being involved in someone's death. It just doesn't fit."

Claire finished with the handle and turned around, an unexpected anger rising up inside her chest. "That sweet young thing knew a woman's child was dead and buried and said nothing."

"Claire!"

"I'm sorry, Diane, I know you thought highly of Elizabeth, as did Ben and Jakob." She crossed to the sink and set the cleaner and cloth beside the faucet. "That said, I can't keep from thinking about Sadie's mother, Waneta. Esther said the woman was certain she'd see her daughter again. Elizabeth *let* her believe that."

"Didn't you say that Elizabeth was likely on her way to tell the truth when she died?" Diane reminded.

"I did."

"That should count for something."

Did it?

"But what about Waneta? And all the false hope she had?"

"It's a tragedy, dear. But she *will* see her daughter again one day." Diane closed the gap between them and pressed a gentle hand to Claire's back. "Jakob will find the truth. You know that."

"But what happens if that truth hurts Benjamin? What then?" She hadn't realized the question was on the tip of her tongue until it was too late to call it back. Instead, she rushed to explain it before there was even a chance for misinterpretation. "I mean, isn't it bad enough he had to lose his wife in such a tragic accident? Does he really need to remember her as being dishonest at best? And a potential *murderer* at worst?"

Diane pulled her hand away and covered her gasp. "A *murderer*?"

"She knew, didn't she?"

"Yes, I suppose, but . . ." Diane's words trailed off only to reappear in starts and stops. "Didn't you say others knew, too?"

She turned to face her aunt as the woman's meaning took root. "Elizabeth mentioned Miriam Hochstetler, Leroy Beiler, and this Michael O'Neil and wondered if they thought about Sadie, too."

"Then perhaps the guilt lies elsewhere."

Claire reached behind her back, untied her apron

strings, and then looped them around the hook beside the refrigerator. "You're right, Aunt Diane. If nothing else, Elizabeth's journal makes it very clear she wasn't the only one in on the secret. And at least it *bothered* her."

Diane peeked out the window at the Amish fields in the distance, the morning sun bathing the brown earth in golden rays. "The truth has a way of making itself known. Sometimes it takes longer than we'd hope, but eventually it comes out . . . as it did when the Stoltzfus barn burned to the ground. If it hadn't burned, that body may have gone undetected for another eighteen or nineteen years."

"Makes you almost wonder *why now?* Doesn't it? Why now—when Elizabeth has been dead for so many years? Why now—*after* the Lehmans no longer own the property where their daughter has been buried all this time? Why now—when Michael O'Neil has finally decided to run for mayor?"

"Because timing is ultimately up to God, not us." Slowly, Diane returned her focus to the room and Claire, her finger shooting upward to the wall clock and the approaching ten o'clock hour. "Getting to your shop in time to open, though, is up to you. I've got the rest of this under control so, please, go. The last thing we need in Heavenly is a busload of disappointed tourists."

Chapter 9

She didn't need the rumble of her stomach to know she'd worked through lunch. The near-constant hum of the cash register and virtually empty pile of shopping bags beside it told the story of her day all on its own.

Something about the ten-degree bump in the forecast, and the promise of spring it ushered in, had done a better job of bringing foot traffic to Lighted Way than any newspaper advertisement ever could. All day long the string of bells over her front door jangled away as the curious arrived and the satisfied departed. And all day long she'd answered questions, restocked shelves that seemed to empty as quickly as she filled them, and added more and more money to her bottom line.

It was, in three words, a perfect day.

Save, of course, the simple fact that a busy day made her miss Esther in very different ways than a quiet day did. When customer traffic was light, she longed for the camaraderie she'd shared with her Amish friend. When it was high, as it was that day, she mourned the extra set of capable hands that allowed her to answer questions and replenish inventory all at the same time.

Still, missing lunch and running ragged were very good problems to have when the reason behind both meant customers. Without their buying the beautiful items her Amish friends made, she wouldn't have her shop. And without her shop, she wouldn't be able to live in Heavenly.

Taking advantage of her first lull in customers all day, Claire closed her eyes against the image of a reality that had almost come true. Yet, because of talented craftsmen like Eli and Ben and their belief in her and her shop, she'd been able to keep Heavenly Treasures open.

"Ruth thinks you have not eaten today and that I must bring you food."

She peered at Ben through freshly parted lashes and laughed. "Well, aren't you and that basket a sight for sore eyes."

"So it is true? You have not eaten?"

Slumping onto the closest stool, she allowed herself the first big sigh of the day. "People were waiting outside the door when I opened this morning and they didn't stop coming until about two minutes ago."

"That is a good problem to have." He set the basket on the counter and pointed at the red-and-white-checked covering. "Ruth said there is a sandwich inside. Cookies, too."

Her stomach rumbled long and loud, eliciting a smile

on Ben's otherwise tired face in response. "Perhaps you should eat now before you cannot hear the next customer."

"Very funny." She pushed aside the covering, reached for the sandwich, and made short work of its matching red-and-white-checked parchment paper covering. "I imagine your sister's place has been nonstop all day, too."

Ben's ocean blue eyes briefly disappeared beneath the rim of his straw hat as he nodded. "She is out of Shoo Fly Pie and apple pie, too. I believe she has her lemon meringue and a dozen or so more of those cookies"—he gestured again, toward the basket—"left. But that is it. It was a good day for her bakery, too."

She looked from Ben to the remaining half of her sandwich and back again. "Would you like half?"

"It is not food that I need."

Something about the way he spoke made her look up again and really focus on her friend. There, in his eyes, she saw more than just fatigue.

She set her half-eaten lunch back on the parchment paper and patted the vacant stool to her right. "Will you sit?"

"No."

"I wish you would. Since Esther stopped working I never have anyone to talk to during lunch."

"Claire."

An unusual rasp to the man's normally steady voice brought her up short. This time, when her stomach rumbled, it wasn't from hunger. "Is Esther okay? Did something happen with the baby?"

"Esther is fine."

Relieved, she reached for her sandwich and took another bite. "Then what's wrong? Why do you look so—so—" She stopped, lowered her sandwich back to the paper, and silently chastised herself as she rose to her feet. "Ben, I'm sorry. I should have gotten back to you after I spoke to Jakob yesterday morning. But when I finally left the station, I came straight back here. Then, after I closed, I went to Eli and Esther's for dinner. I had hoped you might stop by so we could have a private word, but you didn't."

"What did Jakob say? Does he think as we do? That Elizabeth knew of Sadie's death before her accident?"

She considered how much to say, how much the widower really needed to know at that point. Did she tell him his childhood friend must now consider his late wife a suspect in Sadie's death? Was that something he needed to know?

Unsure, she opted to confine her answer to the question at hand. "He does. But, like you, that is not a thought he enjoys."

"I do not know how she could keep such a secret. Waneta and Zebediah are good people—God-fearing people. They would have been sad to learn of Sadie's death but they would not have been angry at Elizabeth."

She studied Ben closely for any indication his thoughts had traveled in the same direction as Jakob's, but saw nothing. No, he hadn't put two and two together. If he had, they certainly weren't adding to four.

He continued, his hands clenching and unclenching

at his sides in a rare show of emotion. "I wish only that I could know why Elizabeth did not tell. But it is too late to know such things."

"Maybe it's not."

Ben pinned her with a stare. "My wife died many years ago, Claire."

"But the others she mentioned in that notebook are very much alive." She hoisted herself back onto her stool and snuck a quick peek at the remaining sandwich half. "Maybe one of them can shed light on why Elizabeth didn't speak up. Or, better yet, why *none* of them spoke up when it happened . . . or came forward with an explanation when the body was found three days ago."

Confusion gave way to surprise as the meaning behind her words appeared to sink into his head. "I . . . I had not thought of that. But it is true. There are others who would know. Three others, if I remember correctly."

"Miriam Stoltzfus—then, Hochstetler—Leroy Beiler, and Michael O'Neil."

"I do not know a Michael O'Neil."

She paused to take another bite of her sandwich. "He is English. He is running for mayor of Heavenly."

"Perhaps they will talk to me. Tell me why Elizabeth kept such a secret."

"No!"

He drew back at the fierceness of her response and she rushed to explain. "You have to let Jakob take care of this, Ben. It's his job and he's very good at what he does. He'll find out all of those answers in due time. I promise you that."

"I cannot ask Miriam? I cannot ask Leroy? I cannot ask this Englisher?"

"Not directly, no."

"I do not understand."

"There are subtle ways to find information, Ben. Like in casual conversation with Miriam. Esther said she is a wonderful seamstress. Perhaps she would have items to sell here in my store . . ."

A pop of understanding fired across Ben's face just before he reached for the remaining piece of sandwich. "I am to go to Stoltzfus's farm this afternoon to bring supplies to Jeremiah. If you are not busy, you could come. Speak with Miriam about the store."

Her stomach rumbled as Ben nearly swallowed his half sandwich whole. Licking her lips, she reached into the basket and retrieved a still-warm chocolate chip cookie. "Now that sounds like a great idea."

The buggy pitched to the right and then the left as Ben guided his horse around the corner and up the dirt driveway belonging to Jeremiah and Miriam Stoltzfus. To Claire's naked eye, the land on either side of them appeared brown and somewhat barren, but she knew better. Because just below the surface, waiting for the first hint of spring, were rows and rows of what would soon be rye and barley.

Straightening on the narrow wooden slab, she shifted her gaze to the brand-new barn that had been nothing more than a goal three days earlier. "Wow. It still amazes me that something so large could be built so quickly," she mumbled, as much to herself as the man seated beside her.

"When many hands work together, much can be accomplished."

"I can see that," she said. "Jakob brought me here Wednesday night to see the volume of people who had come to raise the new barn. He said they would raise it quickly, but I guess I didn't get it until now."

Ben's hands tightened ever so slightly on the reins as they rounded a slight bend in the dirt lane, the buggy lurching to the left and the right as he navigated them through a series of ruts. "The barn was to be where the old one had been, but it was raised a bit to the right at Jakob's request."

"*Jakob's* request?" she echoed, only to have her question answered by the path of Ben's outstretched finger. There, not more than ten yards from the new Stoltzfus barn, was a ten-by-ten stretch of land cordoned off by yellow crime scene tape. "Ahhh. That makes sense. That way the family could still get their new barn without having to wait until the scene is released."

"I do not know why there is still tape. They have found Sadie's body."

"Because, in the event they need to revisit the site, it won't be compromised any further than it already is."

The horse stopped beside a long water trough and Ben dropped the reins. "How do you know such things?" he asked quietly. "Is police work something all English know?"

She gathered her purse from the board beneath her feet and hoisted it onto her lap in preparation for their exit from the buggy. "Those with an aunt who must be in front of the television every Tuesday night at nine o'clock to watch *Investigators* sure do."

He returned her smile with a slight one of his own and then jumped down from his seat. She followed suit and met him in front of the horse just as Jeremiah Stoltzfus emerged from the new barn.

"Good evening, Benjamin." The man's bushy eyebrows arched upward as he took in Claire with a quick nod. "Ma'am."

"Stoltzfus, this is Claire Weatherly. She owns one of the shops on Lighted Way."

Again, Jeremiah nodded, his dark eyes narrowing in on her black trousers and simple white sweater. "Mizz Weatherly."

"Please, call me Claire." She extended her hand and watched as it disappeared inside the man's large, callused one. "My store is next to Shoo Fly Bake Shoppe and Ben happened to mention that he'd be coming out here this evening to bring you some supplies. I asked if I could come along . . . to talk to your wife."

Hooking his thumbs inside his suspenders, he jutted his chin in the direction of the simple white farmhouse just beyond Benjamin's buggy. "Miriam is in the house. Preparing supper. Just go on in."

"Thank you." Then, excusing herself from the pair, she sidestepped as many ruts as possible and headed toward the sparsely furnished front porch. At the open door, she stopped and cleared her throat. "Hello? Miriam?"

The sound of running footsteps was her response, followed by the sight of two disheveled-looking boys in black pants, suspenders, and pale green shirts. "Mamm says you should come in," the older boy said. He tapped his younger sibling on the head and rocked back on his bare feet. "He is Daniel. I am David."

Claire stepped into the front room and held out her hand to each boy, the warm sticky feel of their skin a perfect accompaniment to the sweet smile they each wore. "My name is Claire. It's very nice to meet you."

A woman in her midthirties with a simple maroon dress and black aproned front poked her head around an interior wall and shooed the boys away with a few last-minute chores before dinner. When they were gone, she addressed Claire. "Sometimes I do not know what to make of their energy. It is boundless."

Claire laughed. "I imagine yours must be as well, then." She followed the center hall to the kitchen and stopped inside the doorway. "I told your husband I was hoping to speak with you and he told me to come up to the house. I hope that's okay."

"Of course. I am Miriam Stoltzfus, Jeremiah's wife."

"And I'm Claire Weatherly. I—" The introduction died on her lips as a burst of pastel hues registered in the corner of her eye. Turning, she clapped her hands together. "Oh, Miriam, that quilt is absolutely beautiful."

"It is not done quite yet. But soon."

"Do you sell your quilts?" she asked.

"If someone wants to buy my quilts, I sell."

She watched as Miriam returned to her dinner preparations, the Amish woman's simple black lace-up boots making nary a sound against the wooden floor. No more than a few years older than Claire herself, Miriam's face was lined, her eyes void of anything resembling a sparkle. How much of that was indicative of a hard life and how much of that came from harboring an awful secret, though, Claire could only guess. For now, anyway.

"I happen to know a quilt like that would go very fast in my store."

Miriam pulled a stack of dishes from a corner cabinet and carried them to the table. "You have a store?"

"Yes, I own a specialty gift shop in town, called Heavenly Treasures. Esther King—I mean, Esther *Miller* and I worked there together until she and Eli married." She stopped and smiled. "In fact, now that I think about it, I think I remember seeing you at their wedding in December. I was the only English person there. Well, actually, I was one of two. Jakob Fisher, Esther's uncle, was there with me, too."

"The police detective," Miriam whispered.

"That's right. I imagine you've seen him out here a lot since your friend Sadie's body was found on your property the other—"

A strange garbled sound emerged from Miriam's throat just before the stack of plates clattered onto the table. "Yes, Daniel, I will be right there." Keeping her eyes cast downward, the woman made her way around the table and in the opposite direction of Claire. "I am sorry, Ms. Weatherly, but my boy needs me. I must go. Good evening."

Startled by the abrupt dismissal, she grabbed for the only delay she could find. "When would be a good time to talk about selling your quilts in my shop? I really think they would sell quickly and at a very good price."

Miriam moved toward the stairs and the call for help Claire was certain had not come. "I do not know. I must first talk to Jeremiah."

"Can I check back with you in a few days?"

The woman paused, her back to Claire. "That would be fine."

Chapter 10

Claire rolled onto her side and plucked her phone from the nightstand, its vibrating alarm welcoming her to a new day. Yet even as she fumbled for the button in exactly the same way she did every morning, she knew something was different.

She looked down at her wrinkled trousers and long-sleeved blouse and then around the room, taking care to shield her eyes from the brighter-than-normal morning light that poked around the edges of her window shades. A quick glance at the digital clock beside her bed reassured her she hadn't overslept.

Slipping out of her bed and into her slippers, she pulled her door open a crack and listened. But, try as she could, she couldn't make out any of the sounds she'd come to equate with morning since moving in with Diane.

There were no creaky floorboards as her aunt made her way down the stairs and into the kitchen . . .

There was no soft humming as the woman moved from room to room on the first floor, opening drapes, fluffing pillows, and preparing coffee for the guests' breakfast that would commence in just under an hour . . .

And there was no greeting of the paperboy at the front door . . .

Instead, there was only deafening silence, punctuated every so often by a rhythmic scraping that sounded as if it was coming from the front porch, or, perhaps, the stone walkway that linked the inn to the parking area. Pushing the door shut once again, Claire turned, crossed to the window, and pulled back the shade, sucking in a breath at the unexpected winter wonderland below.

A thick blanket of muting snow covered the porch roof, the yard, the driveway, the guests' cars, the tree-mounted birdhouses, the main road, and the Amish fields in the distance. Rays of morning sun reflected off the glistening snow-covered limbs outside her window and accounted for the added brightness in her room. And as she stood there, watching, a quick blast of snow from somewhere underneath her window, followed by the now-familiar rhythmic scraping sound, filled in the final piece of the puzzle.

Pulling her hand from the shade, she reached into the closet, retrieved the parka she'd pushed to the back when spring had begun to announce its premature arrival two weeks earlier, and slipped it on. A quick trade of her slippers for some boots had her out the door and down the stairs in record time.

Only this time, instead of heading to the kitchen as

she would every other morning, she zipped her coat all the way to the top and stepped out onto the porch, shaking her head at a smiling Diane as she did.

"Did you know it was supposed to snow like this?" she asked in greeting.

"I did when I closed the drapes in the parlor around nine thirty. It was falling fast and furious." Diane propped her shovel against the porch rail and tightened the wrist straps on her waterproof gloves. "When I came up to bed, I poked my head in your room to tell you but you were fast asleep in your clothes and I didn't have the heart to wake you. So I simply covered you with your afghan and tiptoed my way back out of your room."

"I guess I was more tired than I realized after we got everything cleaned up after dinner. I'd intended to put on something more comfortable and then come back down and spend time with you in the parlor, but I guess I fell asleep." She met her aunt beside the railing and leaned forward enough to see the main road. "It doesn't look like a plow has come through yet."

"Oh, it's come through. It's just snowed again since then." Diane pointed to the top of her car in the small parking area beneath the snow-covered weeping willow tree. "Near as I can tell, we've gotten a good ten inches, maybe a foot. Either way, I think it's safe to say you've been given a much-needed and well-deserved day off from the shop."

She looked from Diane, to the car, to the road, and back again. "You mean I shouldn't open the shop?"

"You shouldn't open the shop."

"But why?" she asked.

"Because any tour buses scheduled to come into Heavenly today have canceled on account of the weather, and the locals aren't going to venture out of their homes to buy much of anything besides cat litter for their sidewalks and provisions for their refrigerators. Heavenly Treasures doesn't sell those items so you might as well stay closed and take a little time for yourself. You've earned it, dear."

Rocking back on the heels of her boots, she couldn't help but squeal just a little. Diane was right. She needed a day off. "It's been so long since I've had a day away from the shop, I'm not even sure what to do."

Diane went back to shoveling, her tone light and playful. "Well, if you hadn't fallen asleep by eight last night, I'd say sleep. But, since you did, maybe you should just read the hours away."

"Read the hours away," she echoed in a whisper. "That sounds wonderful . . ." She reached out, hijacked the shovel, and shooed her aunt toward the door. "First, though, you need to go inside and make sure the egg and ham casserole you have planned for the guests is on target. I'll get the rest of the porch, the steps, and the walkway cleared. When I'm done, I'll join you inside for whatever breakfast prep still needs to be done."

Diane folded her arms across her down-covered chest and shook her head. "Shoveling and helping me with breakfast isn't taking the day off, dear."

"I'll take the day off *after* I shovel and help you. Now, go on inside before my reading time is marred by cranky guests."

"You don't know how to slow down, do you?" Diane said, shaking her head in mock frustration.

"Gee, I wonder where I learned *that* . . ." She brought the edge of the shovel to the porch floor and began to push, her breath marked by a plume of smoke in the chilly air. "I'll be in soon. This won't take long."

She'd just settled onto her favorite couch in the parlor when she heard the quick knock at the door. Part of her wanted nothing more than to ignore the sound and wait for someone else to answer. But, considering the fact her aunt was in the basement doing laundry and the guests were playing a rousing game of cards in the dining room, the task fell to Claire.

Marking her page with a bookmark, she dropped her stocking-clad feet onto the floor and stood, a second and slightly louder knock guiding her to the front hallway. When she reached the door, she took a deep breath, turned the knob, and mustered the closest thing she could find to enthusiasm—an emotion that turned genuine the second she caught sight of the man standing on the other side. "Jakob! Hi! Isn't this a nice surprise . . ."

A smile raced across his face like wildfire, calling his dimples into service as it reached the finish line. "Looks like someone got that day off she's been needing for quite some time now."

She leaned against the doorframe and allowed herself a moment to take in the hint of blond hair visible around the edges of the royal blue knit hat, the strong, capable arms that filled out the sleeves of his navy blue parka, and the amber-flecked hazel eyes that gazed back at her with unmistakable fondness. "To listen to you and Diane,

I must have been acting like a real shrew, with the way you both were so determined I have a day off."

"The word *shrew* doesn't belong on the same planet as you, Claire," he said matter-of-factly. "Your aunt and I just know that working seven days a week, every week, for coming up on three months now, isn't healthy for anyone, *including* you."

"The two of you worry too much. I've got this." She pushed off the frame and waved the detective inside. "Come on in. I've got a nice fire going in the fireplace, and the parlor feels really cozy right now."

He remained exactly where he stood, his smile giving way to a mischievous grin. "I'll take you up on the fire soon. For now, though, I was kind of hoping you'd put on your coat and gloves and come on outside with me for a little while."

"In the snow?"

"Yup."

"But why? It's cold out there."

"True. But I'm pretty certain this"—his hands disappeared from her sight only to reappear holding an old-fashioned wooden sled—"would mark up your aunt's floor if we tried to ride it down the stairs."

"You want to go sled riding?" she gasped.

"With you, yes." He nudged his chin in the direction of the coat closet and flashed another of his dimple-laden smiles. "So come on, put on some warm socks and boots and come play. This snow will be gone by midweek."

There was no disputing the surge of excitement she felt at the image of spending a few hours outside with Jakob. The fact that he came up with the idea made it even better. "Give me five minutes and I'll be right out."

* * *

She climbed onto the wooden sled and nestled her back into Jakob's chest, the long snow-covered hill in front of them making her giggle in anticipation.

"You ready?" He tucked his arms around her waist and his legs around hers and inched the sled forward. "We're gonna go quick."

"Let's go!"

With a quick lurch of their bodies, they sped down the hill, the winter air lapping at their cheeks. The more she squealed with delight, the more he laughed and the more he leaned forward, increasing their speed until they toppled off into a heap at the bottom.

"That was so so *so* much fun," she said between breaths. "I can't remember the last time I was on a sled."

He sat up and extended his hand in order to help her do the same. "Me, neither. But I can say, with absolute certainty, that it's been entirely too long."

She squeezed his hand but remained sprawled out in the snow, its wet chill beginning to seep through her jeans to her skin. "I think it's been even longer since I made a snow angel." Stretching her arms and legs wide, she began to scissor them back and forth, the answering spray of snow chilling her even more.

"You should see your face right now," he murmured. "You're glowing."

"What I want to see is my angel." Bringing her legs and arms to a stop, she sat up and reached for Jakob's hand. When she was safely on her feet, she turned to examine her handi-work. "Hmmm . . . Not too shabby, if I do say so myself."

Her breath hitched in surprise as he draped an arm over her shoulder and pulled her against his side, his warm breath atop her head paling against the feel of his lips on her hair. "Thank you for coming out with me today. I needed this time with you."

Snaking her arm around his lower back, she matched his squeeze with one of her own, the happiness she felt at that moment nearly overwhelming. "Thank you for asking. I can't think of the last time I felt this—this alive."

He turned to face her, his gloved hands rising to her wet and cold cheeks. "I know you've been hurt in the past, Claire. I know it's going to take you a while to trust your heart again. But when you do, I'll be here . . . waiting. And praying."

"Praying?" she parroted. "For what?"

"That when you *are* finally ready to trust your heart, you'll trust it with me."

She blinked back the tears that threatened to turn into mini icicles against her skin, and buried her face in his chest, the answering feel of his strong embrace warming her from the outside in. "I'm getting there, Jakob. Faster than you realize."

For several minutes, they simply stood there, wrapped in each other's arms, surrounded by the beauty of the day. When they were ready, they stepped apart.

"Well, should we give it another whirl?" he asked as he retrieved the sled from the ground and tucked it under his left arm. "Maybe see if we can go even faster this time?"

"Absolutely."

Chapter 11

She placed the serving tray on the coffee table and handed the first of two mugs to the wide-eyed man seated on the sofa beside her.

"Too much whipped cream?" she asked quietly before retrieving the second mug and pulling it close. "Aunt Diane is always scolding me for how much I put on her hot chocolate, too. But it's a habit, I guess."

"No, no, it's not that. It's the whole thing—the whipped cream, the peppermint stick, the chocolate chips on top." Jakob cocked his head and smiled. "I guess I'm used to making it for myself. Only when I do it, I rip open the powder, dump it in the mug, and add water. That's it. This feels . . . I don't know . . . sweet, I guess. Like you."

Not quite sure how to respond, she took a sip instead, the steaming-hot liquid a perfect tonic for the chill that had come to roost the moment they walked into the inn and removed their soaking-wet outer layers. "I wish I'd had my camera out there. I'd have loved to get a picture of you next to your snowman."

"I was thinking the same thing when you struck that pose next to yours." He captured a line of runaway cream on the side of his mug with his finger and inserted it into his mouth. "But I don't think that's an image I'll be forgetting anytime soon, so I'm good."

She took another, longer sip and then bent her legs at the knees and pulled her calves up onto the couch. "I love this room in the evening. It's almost magical."

He grinned as he took in the room, too. "I feel it, too. Thanks for inviting me back here after our snow day. Sorry if I made you late for dinner with the guests."

"You didn't. Diane gave me the night off. If we get hungry later, I'm pretty sure I can rustle up some really good leftovers from whatever was on the menu."

"I'll keep that in mind." He raised his mug to her and then took his first long sip. "For now, though, this is enough."

She looked down at her own drink and then back up at him. "I talked to Miriam yesterday after work. Or, rather, I tried to talk to Miriam after work."

"Stoltzfus?"

"Yes. Ben was heading out there to bring a few more supplies to Jeremiah and I tagged along." Tightening her hands around her mug, she revisited the previous day in her thoughts, Ben's anguish hard to forget. "I feel sorry for him. He's really struggling with this new information about Elizabeth."

At Jakob's silence, she shivered and held her mug

closer. "I imagine you're struggling with many of the same things on account of how you felt about her, too." She hated the pensive quality to her words but it was too late to correct.

"My feelings for Elizabeth were a long time ago. A lifetime, actually. Back then I was a different person. My world was confined to a few streets inside Heavenly. Elizabeth was someone I grew up with, someone who went from a little girl to a young woman at about the same time I was changing, too. I was drawn to her quiet nature. At times, I have to wonder if one of the reasons I was drawn to her was because Benjamin was, too, and I was determined to have someone see me before him."

Her heart ached for the pain in Jakob's voice and the reference to the yardstick his own father had used to measure the two boys—a tool that consistently had Jakob coming up short. She cast about for something to say but he continued before she settled on the right words.

"It's not that way with you. I felt something the first moment I laid eyes on you in the lobby of the police department. You were so beautiful, standing there with that bag of goodies you brought by to welcome me to town. Or *back* to town, as Diane surely told you at the time." He leaned forward, set his mug on the tray, and sat back, his gaze mingling with hers. "But since then, I've often wondered if you have feelings for Ben. Feelings that are preventing you from really seeing me the way I wish you would."

Nibbling her lower lip, she took a moment to compose her thoughts and words. When she was ready, she addressed the elephant that had frequented their space for far too long. "If I said I wasn't drawn to Ben those first few months I owned the shop, I'd be lying. But I've come to realize that what drew me to him was his gentle nature. From a distance, he seems so stoic, so rigid, but he's not. There's a depth of thought and feeling there that spoke to my curiosity. And, in doing so, he became my friend. But we're from two different worlds and it's meant to be that way. I like the window Ben and Eli and Esther give me into their world, but I love my world for me—the world I have here in Heavenly with Diane, and the shop, and . . . *you*."

Pulling her left hand from atop her right on the mug, she reached out, gently touched the side of the detective's cheek, and smiled. "I see you, Jakob. I really do. And trust me, I like what I see."

He captured her hand with his and moved it to his lips. "You have no idea how glad I am to hear that."

"Probably as glad as I am to finally say it out loud to someone other than my pillow."

"Your pillow?" he said from behind her hand before lowering it to his lap and holding it tight. "And? What did it say?"

"To stop being a chicken and admit my feelings." She closed her eyes briefly, enjoying the feel of his thumb as it caressed the back side of her hand. "I guess I feel more vulnerable saying it out loud. Like I'm putting my heart out there to be broken even worse than before."

"Even worse?"

She met his questioning gaze head-on. "With my ex-husband, I think I was trying so hard to be what *he* wanted me to be that I was able to protect the real me on some level. But with you, it's all me—the me that likes taking walks and riding on sleds and building snowmen. I'm showing you who I really am and it scares me, a little."

"It shouldn't. Because I adore everything about you." He cleared his throat, released his hold on her hand, and reached for his mug. "Even the excessive whipped cream."

It felt good to laugh, to relieve some of the intensity in the room with a little lighthearted fun. "That's good, considering there's a lot more where that came from."

He swirled the remaining liquid around in his mug and then took a long sip. When he was done, he swung his focus toward the fire crackling in the hearth. "Miriam say anything of interest?"

"No. We spoke for a moment or two and when the conversation turned to the discovery of Sadie's body, she ended it by pretending her son called for her."

"Pretending?"

"Uh-huh." She plucked the peppermint stick from her drink and sucked off the last of the whipped cream, her thoughts traveling back to Miriam's kitchen. "She just wanted me out of her house."

"I remember when Miriam went on Rumspringa. I'd see her sneaking out of her window sometimes at night. Headed to the covered bridge on Route 50, no doubt."

"Why would she go there?"

"That's where the local English kids congregated to drink and smoke when I was growing up. And, from time to time, they were joined by a few Amish kids on Rumspringa."

107

"And Miriam was one of them?"

He nodded. "I never could understand why Elizabeth and Sadie followed her around the way they did."

She considered everything she was hearing and posed the first question that came to mind. "Do you think they drank and smoked, too?"

"I imagine they tried it, if nothing else. It's one of the things I often blamed Elizabeth's mood swings on when she made the decision to pursue baptism. That she regretted some of the experimentation she may have done. Now, I know it was something more."

"You'll figure it out, Jakob. I know you will."

He studied her closely. "If she murdered Sadie, it's going to shake Ben to the core. You know that, don't you?"

"I do."

"I don't look forward to doing that, I really don't."

She rested her hand atop his and squeezed it gently. "I know you don't. And neither do I. Ben is my friend."

He looked up at the ceiling and released a frustrated breath. "I'm quite sure Miriam isn't going to be all too excited about talking to me, either."

"Any chance Leroy Beiler will be any easier to talk to?"

"I guess it depends on what he's known all these years and what he's kept secret from members of his own community—including his father-in-law, Bishop Hershberger."

She thought back to her conversation with her aunt the previous morning about the third and final person mentioned in Elizabeth's journal. "I can only imagine how unexcited—"

Teeing his hands in the air, he lowered his gaze back

to hers. "You know what? Another workday will come soon enough for both of us. How about we shelve this conversation until then and just enjoy the rest of the evening talking about happy stuff."

She heard her stomach rumble and let it guide her words. "Happy stuff? You mean like cookies to go with a refill of our drinks?"

"Yeah. Sure. That works." He placed his mug onto the tray and laughed. "Unless you've got something even happier to share."

"Wait!" She dropped her legs to the ground and clapped her hands. "I've got the happiest news ever, actually."

His left eyebrow arched. "You already shared that."

She drew back, confused. "I did?"

"Yeah, earlier . . . when you told me you have feelings for me, too. It doesn't get much happier than that."

Pleased, she smiled and allowed herself a moment to catch her breath. When she was ready, she continued, the excitement and awe she felt over Esther's news infusing its way into her voice. "How about finding out you're going to have a great-niece or -nephew in about six months?"

He bolted upright on the couch. "A great-niece or— wait! Are you telling me that Esther is pregnant?"

Taking his hands in hers, she held them tightly, grateful for the courage she'd finally mustered to admit her feelings to the kindest, sweetest man she'd ever met. "Yes, that's exactly what I'm telling you."

"When did you find out?"

"Friday night. When I had dinner with her and Eli in their home."

"How is she? Is she feeling okay? Is Eli excited?"

She rose to her feet and pulled him to a stand, too. Then, placing her hands alongside his face, she let her feelings for him shine through in her smile. "She is feeling good so far and she and Eli are very, very excited."

"Aww, Claire, this is great news. *Wonderful* news. Thank you for telling me."

"How could I not?" she asked as she leaned forward and planted a kiss on his chin. "Especially when Esther specifically asked me to share the good news with you."

Chapter 12

Claire stepped off the curb and studied the front window display with what she hoped was an objective eye. All morning long she'd agonized over the right combination of items to both lure customers into her shop and herald spring's impending arrival despite the pile of plowed snow that lined both sides of Lighted Way.

Martha's latest hand-painted milk can instantly drew one's eye to the right with its focal scene of hillside wildflowers basking in the sun. Beside it, but slightly elevated thanks to the inch-high riser she'd placed under the cover, was the hand-stitched gardening tool bag Esther's younger sister, Hannah, had made. Closer to the center of the window sat Eli's newest high chair, each spindle leg hand-carved with careful precision. To the left of that were the Amish dolls Claire was hard-pressed to keep on the shelf—their presence in every seasonal window display a must. They were, of course, still faceless, but the latest cropping of hand-sewn dolls boasted lighter-colored dresses beneath the traditional black aprons. Pastel-colored hair ribbons and baby bibs strategically placed above and below the dolls would make it impossible for grandmotherly types to pass Heavenly Treasures without going inside to shop.

"It looks perfect, Claire."

She smiled at the familiar voice and turned to greet her friend with a quick embrace. "Esther! What a nice surprise!" Then, pointing to the basket in the young woman's arm, she stepped back. "Do you have new items for me?"

"Yah."

Claire took one last look at the window and then guided her friend onto the sidewalk and into the shop. "I hosted the Lighted Way business owners' meeting here this morning and there's still some coffee and juice left if you'd like something to drink."

"I am not thirsty."

"I have donuts, too. Maybe even a sliver of cinnamon breakfast cake if you'd like? Ruth brought the donuts so you know those are good. And I got up at five this morning to make the breakfast cake."

Esther crossed the shop to the counter and swapped her basket for Claire's clipboard of daily tasks. "Did you do some of these things yesterday?"

"I didn't come in yesterday. Diane said Lighted Way would be deserted with the snow, and from what Howard and Al said at the meeting this morning, she was right."

Looking down at the clipboard once again, Esther

shook her head slowly. "It is just eleven o'clock. You have already had the meeting, set up your new window display, and taken down last week's sale prices?"

"I'm getting ready to set up this week's sales now."

"Have there been no customers today?"

"We've had customers. Some even made purchases," she said before curiosity over her friend's questions won out. "Why?"

"It is too much for you to work here alone." Esther unwrapped her black shawl, folded it neatly in fourths, and then held it to her lap as she claimed one of the two cushioned stools behind the register. "I have worked here. I know."

Claire grabbed a dry-erase marker from the cup of pens and consulted her sale list for the coming week, her thoughts ricocheting between the stack of signs she needed to make and Esther. "Esther, you and I both know there were plenty of times when you opened or closed by yourself. And when you were doing the one, I was doing the other. We managed those shifts alone just fine . . . although they were never as much fun as the ones we worked together."

"But we did not take care of customers and make window displays alone. When we had such jobs as these"—Esther ran her finger down the side of Claire's task list—"we worked together. Now, you do all of this alone."

Glancing up from the stack of blank signs, she made a face at her friend. "That's because you had to go and marry the dashing Eli Miller . . ."

A hint of crimson rose up in Esther's cheeks just

before disappearing behind a shy hand. "That does not mean you must work alone each day. You cannot open and close each day by yourself. It is a long day."

"Ruth does it," Claire reminded her, not unkindly.

"Ruth has Eli and Benjamin to look after her. And she does not open on Sunday . . . or on some Tuesdays and Thursdays during wedding season."

She noted the dollar reduction on crocheted baby bibs onto the sign and then waved it back and forth to dry. "Ruth practically has a line waiting outside her door the second she opens each day. I don't. I can't afford to close."

"But things have been better since Eli and Benjamin started making bigger items, yah? I think you can afford to hire a new person. Someone who can help with the customers and stock shelves when it is quiet."

It was a sentiment she'd heard many times in the three months since Esther left to get married. Howard Glick of Glick's Tools 'n More had said it. Al Gussman, her landlord and fellow shopkeeper, had said it. Drew Styles, owner of Glorious Books, had said it. Her aunt had said it. And even Jakob had hinted at her hiring a little help in order to cut down her hours at the shop.

On some level, she knew they were all right. Dream job or not, working seven days a week was difficult, even exhausting at times. The lightness she'd felt during her unexpected snow day was proof of that.

Yet, every time she considered the notion of hiring someone, she came back to one indisputable fact: if she couldn't have Esther, she really didn't want anyone.

She gave the same reply she gave everyone else. "I'm getting along just fine."

"Why do you not want to hire a new person, Claire?"

Dropping her marker onto the counter, she gave Esther her undivided attention, the emotion in her voice more apparent than she wanted. "The customers loved you, Esther. They loved asking questions about the Amish and having a real Amish person to answer them. And when they learned that many of the items in the store were made by you and your mother, they got even more excited. I can't replace you, Esther. Not as an employee and certainly not as a friend."

"As your friend, I am just down the road. But there are others who could do the things I did here."

"Like who?" she challenged.

"Like Annie Hershberger. She is Amish. The customers could ask her questions."

"Annie *Hershberger*? Is she any relation to *Bishop* Hershberger?"

Esther nodded. "Yah. Annie is the bishop's youngest child."

"How old is she? Do you know?" she asked, her curiosity aroused.

"She is on Rumspringa, so maybe sixteen?"

"Sixteen," Claire repeated, slowly. "Is she a good kid?"

"She is Amish."

"Do kids on Rumspringa work?"

"Most, yah."

She came around the counter and sank onto the stool beside Esther, the image of being able to come in late on some days, or head home at lunchtime on others, more intriguing than she wanted to admit. Instead, she shrugged a second time.

"I could stop by and speak with Annie on my way home if you'd like," Esther offered.

"Give me another month. If I feel overwhelmed as traffic picks up in April, I may ask you to send her my way at that time."

The jingle of bells over the front door brought an end to further discussion and Claire to her feet. "Good day, welcome to Heavenly—oh, Jakob, hi!" She dropped her hands to her sides, smoothed the lines from her formfitting khaki pants, and stepped out from behind the counter. "I had a really great time yesterday. Thank you."

"Thank *you*. I've been able to think of little else all morning." He raised her smile with her favorite dimples then followed her eyes over to the counter and the young Amish woman seated quietly behind it. "Esther . . . hello."

Esther bowed her head shyly in greeting then stepped down off the stool as he approached.

"Claire told me the wonderful news last night, sweetie. I couldn't be happier for you and Eli."

Esther slowly lifted her chin until she was looking at her English uncle. Then, without uttering a word, the young woman reached out, took hold of Jakob's hand, and brought it to rest on the tiny mound barely visible beneath her aproned dress. "Mamm thinks it will be a boy," she whispered.

Startled, Jakob looked from Esther, to her hand on his, and back again, the emotion that misted his eyes finding its way into his voice. "Either way, you and Eli will make wonderful parents."

"Thank you," Esther whispered in the direction of her

feet before unfolding her shawl in preparation for the retreat Claire knew must come.

And come it did.

But when Claire looked back at Jakob to gauge his reaction, she saw only euphoria.

"I'm sorry she had to leave like that, Jakob."

If he heard her, he didn't react. Instead, he simply raked a hand through his hair and leaned his back against the paneled upright in the center of the store. "Did you see that, Claire? She let me touch the baby."

Blinking back the tears she was desperate to keep hidden, she offered the most convincing smile she could. But even as she stood there, silently cursing a set of beliefs that made Jakob a veritable pariah within his own family, she couldn't help but acknowledge the aura of pure joy that radiated out from the detective.

Jakob had accepted his fate in regard to his family seventeen years earlier when he left the Amish, postbaptism, to become a police officer. It was a decision he still stood by despite its unbelievable cost. But for just a moment, when Esther had guided his hand to her unborn child, his place in the family had been acknowledged, remembered.

"She loves you, Jakob. So does Martha," she whispered around the rising lump in her throat. "You are their blood, their family. Even the Ordnung can't change that."

He opened his mouth to answer but closed it as the door-mounted bells announced Esther's reentry. "I forgot my basket."

"Oh, that's right. We got so busy talking you never showed me what you brought." She met Esther in the center of the store and then followed her back to the counter. "What goodies do we have for the shop this week?"

Esther pulled the basket close and began removing items from its depths. "I made a few springtime aprons, a few dishcloths, and a baby blanket."

"Don't you think you should keep the blanket for your own baby?" she asked as she unfolded the blanket and held the soft fabric to her cheek. "Ohhh, this is so nice."

"I will make a blanket for my baby as it gets closer. For now, this will make money Eli and I need."

Claire nodded and reached for the red leather book she used to keep track of her inventory. She jotted each new item into the section assigned to Esther and Eli and then handed the empty basket to Esther. "I'm sure all of these things will go quickly once the spring tourists start coming around in a few weeks. Howard and Al said it gets busy fast once April rolls around."

"I'm working on a quilt, too. I hope to have that to you by week's end."

"That would be great. If Miriam Stoltzfus comes through with a quilt or two, the way I'm hoping she will, maybe I'll have enough to display one of them in the front window."

Esther slid her arm beneath the basket handle, retraced her steps back to the door, and then turned to look at Claire and Jakob before she stepped outside into the cold. "I don't believe you will be getting any quilts from Miriam for a while. She left town in a hired car yesterday after church. Jeremiah said something about her wanting to look after a sick relative in upstate New York."

"*Who*?" Jakob barked.

"Jeremiah did not seem to know." Esther lifted her hand in something resembling a parting wave and then stepped outside, the jingle of the door barely noticeable against the sudden roar in Claire's ears.

"How could Miriam's husband not know where, exactly, his wife was going?" She heard the question as it left her mouth but knew it paled in comparison to the second and more important one she posed on its heels. "Do you think Miriam ran to avoid being questioned?"

Jakob pushed off the upright and strode straight toward the door, his brief but tender moment with Esther shoved to the side by the reality of Sadie Lehman's unexplained death. "I don't know, but that won't be the case for long."

Chapter 13

There was something about crossing off the very last item on her daily to-do list that never ceased to lose its thrill for Claire. It was like a mini pat on the back for a job well done.

But at that moment, looking down at the now-completed list, she felt little more than total exhaustion. From the moment she'd stepped out of her room that morning, she'd been running on overdrive—baking, playing host to her fellow Lighted Way shopkeepers, stocking shelves, pricing inventory, arranging displays, and serving her customers. There'd been no time to really sit and think, no time to process the news of Miriam's sudden departure from Heavenly or to even have so much as a cracker from the lunch she'd hastily packed before heading out to the shop at the crack of dawn.

Lunch.

She looked up at the clock on the shop's back wall and noted the time: three thirty. No wonder she was starving . . .

Tucking the clipboard under her arm, she headed toward the back hallway and the tiny office beyond. Barely big enough to accommodate the beat-up metal desk left behind by the building's previous tenant, the room was rarely used for anything other than a coat closet now that Esther was gone. Without the extra pair of hands her friend's presence had provided, Claire had little to no time to balance the shop's books during normal business hours. Instead, that cumbersome task was now done in her room at the inn, after the guests had been fed and the kitchen cleaned.

She reached into the windowless room and flipped on the fluorescent overhead light for as long as it took to deposit the clipboard onto her desk and to retrieve her paper lunch sack from her oversized purse.

"Finally," she mumbled as she turned the light off and made her way back to the front room, the cushioned stool calling to her tired body every bit as loudly as the trio of chocolate chip cookies in her lunch sack were calling to her stomach. Flopping down onto the stool, she reached into the bag and pulled out its contents one item at a time.

Ham sandwich.

Grapes.

Crackers.

Cookies.

She arranged her late lunch on the counter in front of her and resisted the impulse to start with dessert. As tempting as a sugar boost was at the moment, she needed a more sustaining kind of energy if she was going to make it through the remaining ninety minutes that stood between her and closing.

She scooted closer and reached for the sandwich only to drop it back to the counter as the all-too-familiar jingle announced the arrival of another customer. Stifling the groan that threatened to earn her and her shop an online thrashing for unfriendliness, she stood and smiled. "Good afternoon. Welcome to Heavenly Treasures."

A young Amish girl paused just inside the entryway and glanced around, her wide-set brown eyes missing nothing, including the buffet of uneaten food in front of Claire. "Are you Claire?"

"I am." She rounded the counter and met the teenager on the other side. "Can I help you?"

The girl said nothing as she continued to survey her surroundings with an air of grudging approval. "Is it always like this in here?"

She followed the teenager's gaze to the display of baby items she'd spent a chunk of her day fiddling with and gave a half-nod, half-shrug combination. "I tend to base the front window display on the season, but this particular rack leans more toward a special sale or a peek at a new category of items. Are you looking for something in—"

"I mean, is it always quiet like it is now?"

"Quiet?" she echoed in confusion.

"Yah. No customers to talk to, no bags to carry . . ."

"I—"

"Because if all I have to do is sit behind a counter and eat, I will take the job." The girl reached up, pulled her kapp off her head, and crumpled it into a ball in her hand.

"It's like Kendra said, having a little cash in my pocket might not be such a bad idea."

Startled, she allowed herself a moment to really study the teenager, to catalogue the usual giveaways that someone was Old Order Amish, as opposed to a slightly more relaxed sect.

No jewelry—check.

No buttons—check.

Plain clothes—check.

No makeup . . .

The girl leaned backward as Claire leaned forward, rolling her eyes as she did. "Yes, I took off my kapp . . . yes, I'm wearing eyeliner. I'm on Rumspringa."

Claire straightened. "Do I know you?"

"I'm Annie. Annie Hershberger."

"*Hershberger*? As in *Bishop* Hershberger?"

This time, Annie's eye roll was followed by a snort of irritation. "I know, I know. What a disappointment I must be for my father, yah?"

"I didn't say that," she protested weakly.

Annie waved her off. "It doesn't matter. You have no idea what it's like to grow up an Amish kid. And you have no idea what it's like to have an Amish bishop as your dat."

Claire walked backward until she reached the paneled upright and leaned against it heavily, the day's lack of food starting to take its toll. But at that moment, if given the choice between food and the conversation taking shape in her store, she'd pick the conversation a hundred times over. "Does he have higher expectations for you than other Amish parents do?"

"Nah, not really." Annie wandered over to the counter and stared down at Claire's lunch. "But people act funny around me because he's my dat."

"Help yourself to a cookie if you'd like." She smacked a hand over her stomach but not before its growl earned an odd look from Annie. "They're really good."

"I would enjoy a grape, if that's okay."

"Sure. No problem." She pushed off the upright and joined Annie at the counter. "So how do people act funny around you? You know, because of your father?"

Annie popped one grape and then another into her mouth before moving on to the pile of crackers. "Some girls do not speak to me because they are afraid. I think some speak to me because they want to be good."

"I don't understand."

"When someone is shunned for doing wrong, it is my father who decides. I think some think to be nice to me is to . . ." Annie cast about for the right words, only to shake her head in frustration when she came up short. "I do not know how to say it."

"Do you mean that you think your friends try to curry favor with your father by being nice to you?"

Annie nodded, fast and furious. "Yah."

"Can kids your age be shunned?"

"No, but their mamm and dat can."

She contemplated the teenager's words and compared them to everything she knew about the Amish at that point. On one hand, the girl's gripe sounded plausible, if not more English-like. On the other hand, it was hard not to chalk the whole thing up to Annie's status as a teenager—a time when everything lends itself to being angst-worthy, especially on the family front.

"I'm sorry to hear—"

Annie moved on to the cookies, downing two of the three before Claire knew what was happening. "Anyway, I think I could do this a few days a week."

"Do this? What's *this*?"

Lifting the third and final cookie to her lips, Annie popped it into her mouth, whole. "Work here."

She resisted the urge to search high and low for a hidden camera and, instead, kept her focus on the girl hell-bent on eating her way through Claire's lunch. "Did you say w-work ? *Here*?"

Annie nodded. "Yah. Esther Miller stopped by the farm this morning and said you were looking for help at your store. She said I would have fun. She also said I would need to wear my boring clothes, but that is okay. I can wear both."

Then, without waiting for anything resembling a follow-up question, Annie lifted her dress to reveal an ultrashort skirt. "See?"

"Wow. That's really . . . uh, *short*." It was all she could think to say at the moment, but it fit, unlike the skirt.

Annie released the Amish dress from her hands and laughed. "That is what Rumspringa is for—to do as the English do."

"I don't wear skirts like that." Claire reached around Annie and liberated the sandwich from the counter before it, too, disappeared.

"You're old."

She had to laugh. "No, I'm not old, Annie. I just don't feel the need to showcase myself like that. Most English women don't."

A flash of something Claire couldn't quite identify skittered across Annie's face, disappearing as quickly as it had come. "Plenty do. I see them at the bridge. I see the attention they get from boys."

"It's the wrong attention, Annie. From the wrong boys." She took a bite and then brought her free hand to the side of the teenager's face. "The right boys see *this*, Annie. And your face is beautiful with nothing more than a smile. Remember that, okay?"

Annie stepped back, surprised. "You think I am beautiful?"

"You don't?"

"I am plain." Annie brushed at her dress like one might brush at an unwanted crumb. "Like these clothes."

Reluctantly, Claire lowered the sandwich back to the counter and, instead, reached for the small handheld mirror she'd bought for Esther's use whenever Eli's buggy appeared in the alleyway. She held it up in front of Annie. "Look at your eyes, Annie . How can you call them plain?"

"That is because I am on Rumspringa and I wear makeup."

"Smile, Annie. A real smile."

Annie made a face first, but finally did as she was told, her cheeks rising upward and igniting a sparkle deep inside her eyes.

"Do you see that sparkle? The way it makes your eyes dance? That's not makeup, Annie, that's you."

The chocolate brown of the girl's eyes disappeared

momentarily behind lashes clumped with too much mascara. "The Amish boys do not notice me. But, with makeup, the English boys do."

Claire tucked the mirror back on its original shelf beneath the register, shaking her head as she did. "I don't believe that, Annie. I really don't. You are far too pretty to go unnoticed. But you are also only, what? Fifteen? Sixteen?"

"Sixteen."

"Don't be in such a rush," Claire cautioned. "And stay true to yourself. It's the only way to be, and the only way to find the person who is truly right for you."

The girl fell silent for a moment, her demeanor softening for the first time since walking through the door. "Do you think I could?"

"Could . . ."

"Work here. In this shop. With you."

Claire's knee-jerk reaction was to say no. After all, she'd specifically told Esther she wasn't ready to hire anyone yet. But when she opened her mouth to say so, something made her hold back long enough to consider the many pluses and minuses of employing Annie Hershberger.

In the plus column, she'd have the help she knew she needed and the opportunity to come in a little late or leave a little early once or twice a week. By hiring someone, she would also have more time to make the candles and decorative picture frames she'd been unable to make with her crazy schedule the past three months. Being able to make those items again would increase her inventory and the dollar amount on her own bottom line.

In the minus column, she had a teenager who was obviously trying to find herself. That could have no negative impact on Claire and the shop at all, or it could come back to bite her in more ways than just unreliability. And to top it all off, Annie wasn't Esther.

"I could be a hard worker if that is what you need."

"That's exactly what I need, Annie." She crossed her arms in front of her chest and met the teenager's gaze head-on. "This place is quiet right now, but the reason that food was on the counter was because I hadn't had a chance to eat lunch yet."

"That was your lunch?" Annie whispered.

"I was working so hard all day, this was the first break I had." She reached again for her sandwich and finally took a bite, the ham lukewarm. "Some days are quiet around here. Others are like today—where there's a decent amount of customers to take care of and lots of tasks to get done, as well. Once spring and summer hit, the quiet days will be no more. Can you handle that?"

Annie took a moment to look around the store, her focus shifting rapidly from one gift display to the next, the nature of her thoughts difficult to guess.

"I need someone who will be here when they're supposed to be . . . doing the things I ask, and knowing what needs to be done if I'm too distracted to ask."

"And if there is quiet time like now?" Annie asked, returning her gaze to Claire's. "What is to happen then?"

"If everything is done, we eat."

"And talk?"

"Uh . . . if you want to."

When Annie said nothing, Claire took advantage of

the momentary lull in their back-and-forth to finish her sandwich and poke around in a nearby drawer for anything resembling a forgotten snack.

"Claire?"

She pushed aside a pad of paper and a handful of pens but found nothing. No snack-sized bag of pretzels, no mints, no edible cookie crumbs, no nothing.

Her stomach gurgled in disappointment.

"Claire?"

Pushing the drawer closed, she forced her attention back to Annie. "Yes?"

"I will work hard. You have my word."

Chapter 14

She located the bookmark beside her thigh and slipped it into the mystery novel she was simply too tired to keep reading. Try as she might, she couldn't absorb the comings and goings of the story's protagonist any longer.

Transferring the book to the end table, she peered across the parlor at her aunt. "I don't know how you seem to maintain your energy the way you do. I'm half your age and I can barely keep my eyes open past nine o'clock these days."

Diane tilted her head downward and peered at Claire from atop the upper frame of her reading glasses. "When I head upstairs at nine thirty each evening, I actually go to sleep. You, on the other hand, don't."

"Oh?" she asked, yawning.

"I'm in my sixties, Claire. I can no longer make it through the night without going to the bathroom at least once."

"And your point?"

"There's light coming from beneath your door at all hours of the night." Diane flipped her own book onto the armrest and stretched. "That's why you're running out of steam."

It was futile to argue, so she kept her mouth shut.

"What I can't figure out, though, is why. The financial issues at the shop that you kept from me throughout the fall have been resolved, yes?"

"Yes."

"You still get to see Esther even now that she's married, right?"

"I do."

"And you have an absolutely wonderful young man in your life who is positively smitten with you."

She laughed. "Positively smitten, eh?"

"Positively smitten," Diane repeated with conviction. "So why are you still awake at one, two, sometimes *three* in the morning?"

Why, indeed?

Swiveling her body to the left, she lifted her legs onto the couch and reclined her head against the armrest. "You know me, Aunt Diane. I worry. About *everything*."

"I know that. But there's nothing to worry about right now, dear."

She watched the flickering shadows from the fireplace dance on the ceiling and willed herself to relax, to let the peaceful setting work its magic on the tension she'd felt building for days. But she couldn't. "A girl's body was found next to a barn less than a mile and a half from here."

"And it's tragic, Claire, it really is. But staying up all hours of the night isn't going to change anything. Instead, it has you being tired before you ever even open your shop."

"Oh, that's right, I didn't tell you yet." She rolled onto her side and smiled at her father's only sister. "I hired some help this afternoon."

Diane clapped her hands. "Oh, Claire, how wonderful!"

"Let's wait and see if that's really the case, shall we?" She closed her eyes long enough to travel back to the moment she extended her hand in Annie's direction, virtually sealing a deal Esther had foisted on her in rather sneaky fashion. "This could turn out to be a disaster of a decision."

"Oh, stop it. How could having an extra pair of hands be a disaster?"

"Let me count the ways," she mumbled as she bypassed another glance at the ceiling in favor of the actual flames.

"What on earth are you talking about, dear?" Diane persisted.

"Well, my first impression of my new employee wasn't good. And I'm not sure that ever really changed convincingly enough to offer her a job."

"So why did you?"

"Because, at the last minute, I picked up a hint of genuine sincerity."

"And?"

"To put it bluntly, I caved."

Diane swung her legs over the lounge chair and stood, her sensible-soled shoes making soft padding sounds across the series of hand-hooked rugs that dotted the parlor's wood floor. "Don't go anywhere; I'll be right back."

Claire thought about protesting in light of the sleep she knew she needed, but she was too tired to give it words. Besides, Diane was right. She didn't sleep. At least here, in the parlor, she had someone to talk to, to share her worries with even when they weren't hers to worry about in the first place.

Five minutes and a few familiar sounds later, Diane reentered the room carrying a medium-sized tray with two mugs of hot chocolate and a plate of oatmeal scotchies. "Sit up! Sit up! I have sustenance!"

She looked from the plate of cookies to her aunt and back again, licking her lips as she did. "Yes you do . . ."

Diane set the tray in the center of the coffee table, divvied up the mugs and cookies, and then sat back down on the edge of her favorite chair. "I almost grabbed the last few chocolate chip cookies but then I remembered you packed them for lunch today."

"I packed them but I didn't eat them." She bit into the still-warm oatmeal cookie and savored the sweet taste added by the butterscotch chips. "Mmmm . . ."

"You passed on cookies?" Diane repeated in disbelief. "Are you feeling okay, dear?"

"Aside from being exhausted, I'm feeling fine."

Diane's left eyebrow arched upward.

"I didn't pass on the cookies because I didn't want them." She brushed a few cookie crumbs onto the napkin

Diane had placed beside her mug and then leaned forward to take a sip of her hot chocolate. "I didn't eat them because my new employee did."

"Tell me about her," Diane prompted as she, too, took a sip from her own mug.

Wrapping her hands around the cup of steaming liquid, she settled on a starting point for Diane's verbal introduction to Claire's new employee and potential nightmare. "She's sixteen, Amish, and wearing mini-skirts under her plain dress."

"Ahhh, she's on Rumspringa."

"Until the last few minutes before I caved, she was a girl who wanted to work at my shop for two reasons. The first being money, of course, and the second tied to the lack of customers when she walked through the door. She assumed, because of the latter, an employee of mine would have nothing to do except, perhaps, eat the best parts of my lunch."

A knowing smile made its way across Diane's thinning lips. "The cookies?"

"Yes, the cookies . . . The grapes . . . The crackers . . ."

The woman's soft laugh filled the distance between them and made Claire wish they were sitting side by side. If they were, maybe she could rest her head on Diane's shoulder the way she used to as a child. "And during the last few minutes?"

She took another, longer sip of the hot liquid and then returned it to the table in favor of another cookie. "The kid actually seemed like she wanted to work with me."

"That doesn't surprise me."

"Spoken like the incredibly biased, yet wonderful aunt that you are, Diane." She allowed herself to enjoy the light feeling before revealing the last noteworthy piece of news regarding Esther's replacement. "Her name is Annie. Annie Hershberger."

"As in Bishop Hershberger's youngest daughter?" Diane asked, her left eyebrow resuming its previous arch, with the right one quickly showing its solidarity.

Claire nodded.

"Hmmm."

"Is that a good hmmm, or a bad hmmm?" she asked between bites of her cookie without truly tasting the fruits of her labor.

Diane shrugged, then settled all the way back in her chair. "It's neither, really. I've just always been curious about what it's like to be an Amish bishop . . . or an Amish bishop's wife."

"I can't help you there but I suspect I'll be fairly well versed on the many trials and tribulations of being an Amish bishop's *daughter* before the end of the week." She reclaimed her mug for another few sips and then set it back on the tray along with her crumb-filled napkin.

"It'll work out fine, Claire, just you wait and see. Having Annie there will allow you to get back to making your candles. It'll also give you more time to visit Esther and maybe go out to lunch once in a while with a certain good-looking detective . . ."

There was no stopping the smile that raced across her face at mention of Jakob. Playing in the snow with him the previous day was the most fun she'd had in years if not her whole adult life. Yet as quickly as her daydream took off, reality came along to squash it in its tracks. "That certain good-looking detective of whom you speak has more important things to do right now than squire me off to lunch."

"Such as?"

"Such as figuring out how Sadie Lehman died and who, if anyone, was responsible for her death."

"That's where that journal Benjamin found will come in handy, right? It gives Jakob three distinct people to question."

"Two," she corrected.

"Two? But I thought you said Elizabeth mentioned three people."

She stood and wandered over to the first set of built-in bookcases that lined more than half of the room. Interspersed among the collection of hardcover and paperback books Diane had assembled over the years were framed pictures of Heavenly and its people, as well as pictures of Claire taken during countless summer visits as a kid. "Miriam Stoltzfus ran."

Diane's gasp mingled with the sound of firewood crackling in the hearth. "*Ran?* What do you mean *ran?*"

"I mean she was here one day and gone the next, her sudden destination someplace up north. Caring for a sick relative her own husband can't even name."

"Maybe it's an old friend. Maybe Jeremiah is too distracted by everything happening on his property that he doesn't remember the name his wife said," Diane offered.

Claire ran her finger down the edge of a black-and-white frame, the picture taken alongside one of her favorite roads on the Amish side of town. "Or maybe she was afraid Jakob's investigation into the discovery of Sadie's body would lead him to her door. And secrets she doesn't want to tell."

"Oh dear. I hope you're wrong."

"So do I, Aunt Diane, so do I." She dropped her hand to her side and continued meandering around the room.

"In the meantime, while he waits for Miriam to come back, Jakob can certainly see what Leroy Beiler remembers, can't he? Maybe he'll know something helpful."

She crossed to the large front window and parted the heavy drape at the center, her gaze drifting out over the darkened fields of Heavenly. "If Leroy Beiler knows what happened to Sadie, he's been keeping it a secret from her parents and his community for a very long time. And if that's the case, he's already proven his disinterest in being helpful."

"And let's not forget Mike O'Neil," Diane reminded. "He's another one who won't be terribly excited to be questioned about an unreported death that transpired in his midteens. Something like that could destroy his mayoral campaign."

Claire took in the fire one last time and then leaned forward to plant a kiss on her aunt's forehead. "I better try and get some sleep. I have to start training Annie tomorrow. Thank you for tonight, though. I needed it more than I realized."

"Annie will do fine, dear, you just watch and see." Diane beamed up at Claire before reaching for her book once again. "Having some time for yourself is a good thing, Claire. It lends itself to all sorts of new possibilities."

"I'll keep that in mind," she joked between yawns. Then, midway to the parlor door, she glanced back at her aunt. "Diane? When is the mayoral election?"

"The first Tuesday in April."

"April," she repeated as much for herself as the only other set of ears in the room. "Hmmm . . . Maybe with all my new me time, I can see what it's like to work on a political campaign during its last few weeks."

Chapter 15

Three hours into their first day together and Claire was hard-pressed to find one thing Annie had done wrong. In fact, if she was honest with herself, the teen-ager was an incredibly hard worker who seemed to have a real knack for interacting with customers.

When asked to stock a shelf, Annie not only stocked the shelf, she also arranged it in a way that was more eye-catching than its previous incarnation.

When asked to take the trash out to the Dumpster in the back of the alley, Annie not only did as she was told but also stopped to sweep the small hallway and shovel away a sliver of ice from the back stoop.

And when asked to help a customer while Claire assisted another, Annie invariably ended the interaction with a sale.

The girl was, in a word, a godsend, and it was time

Claire acknowledged her efforts with more than just a nod and a smile.

"Annie?" Claire dumped a new roll of quarters into the cash register and shut the drawer. "Can you come sit with me for a second?"

Annie jumped down off the step stool that had allowed her to stock a few new hand-carved trinket boxes on the shelf and stared at Claire, wide-eyed. "Did I make a mistake with the money?"

She glanced down at the register and then back up at Annie as the reason behind the baseless concern took root. "No . . . no, it's nothing like that. You've just been working hard these past few hours and I'd like you to come sit with me for a little while. If you brought a lunch, you're welcome to eat it now if you'd like."

"Isn't the store still open?" Annie asked as she carried the stool to its holding spot just inside the doorway to the back hall.

"It sure is. But if someone comes in, I'll take care of them. You need to eat."

Annie shrugged, disappeared into the hall, and then returned a few moments later with a small basket similar to the one Esther had used for lunch as well. When she reached the counter, the girl set the basket in front of Claire. "I hope you like cold chicken."

"Cold chicken? Annie, you don't have to bring me lunch."

"I ate yours yesterday; it is only right you eat mine, today." Annie reached around Claire and removed the piece of tan cloth that served as the basket's lid. "There is a piece of Eva's bread inside, too. It is good bread."

"Annie, I can't take your lunch," she repeated.

"It is the right thing to do." Annie backed into Esther's stool and then perched atop its floral cushion. "If I did not make a mistake with the money, what have I done poorly?"

Claire peeked inside at the contents of the basket and then held out a piece of chicken and bread to the girl. "I will only eat this if we share it."

Annie hesitated and then took the food from Claire's hand, biting into the chicken leg almost immediately. Claire started on the bread. "Mmmm. Annie, this bread is absolutely delicious."

"I can see why you were so hungry yesterday when I came in. It is hard work here at the store. There is much more to do than I knew."

"Oh, it's busy, that's for sure, but fun, too. The nicest people come in here, don't they?"

"Yah."

They talked about a few of their favorite customers that morning before Annie's earlier concern resurfaced in spades. "Please tell me what I have done wrong. I will make sure not to do it again."

It was hard not to shake her head over the differences between the girl who'd first walked into the shop the previous day, and the one sitting in front of Claire now. "You haven't done anything wrong, Annie. Quite the contrary, actually. You worked really hard this morning and I'm very impressed."

A flash of something resembling disbelief flitted across Annie's features before being pushed aside by a noticeable tension in everything from the way the girl ate to the way she fidgeted with her hands between bites.

"Annie? Is there something wrong?"

The girl pushed off the edge of the stool and wandered over to the trash can Claire kept hidden from the customers' sight. Carefully, she wiped any residual crumbs from her hands into the can and then turned to face Claire. "My dat was happy to hear of my new job. Knowing I am okay during the day takes away much of his worry."

"Your father is worried about you?" At the girl's emphatic nod, she quickly tacked on the next logical question. "Why?"

"I think because I am different. Different than my older brothers and sisters."

"How so?"

"I ask many questions. I do not just nod at his answers."

Claire, too, stood, her focus completely on Annie. "What kind of questions?"

"I ask about the things we do not have . . . like telephones and cars. He says we do not need such things, and, still I ask why. My brothers and sisters did not question. They have all been baptized and now have families, too. But I . . . I am not sure."

"You mean about being baptized?"

"Yah."

She gave the girl's words their due attention and then moved on to the sadness they held. "That's what Rumspringa is for, isn't it? To see how people like me live?"

"Yah."

"When did yours start?" she asked, curious.

"Last week."

She nibbled back the smile that started to form lest

her young employee think Claire was making light of her problems. "You have a long time to go, Annie."

"Dat found a cigarette in my pocket two nights ago. He was not happy."

"Smoking is bad for you, Annie," she cautioned. "People die from cigarettes."

Annie crossed to the window that overlooked the alley between Heavenly Treasures and Shoo Fly Bake Shoppe and rested her forehead against the cool glass. "He worries that will happen. Like it did for Sadie Lehman."

Claire grabbed hold of the countertop for support. "I . . . I'm not following. Your father worries that *what* will happen like it did for Sadie?"

"That I will die and he will not know."

"I would imagine that is a fear *many* parents share in the wake of a story like the one from the other night. Even Amish ones."

"But I am like her, Dat says."

Step-by-step, Claire slowly closed the gap between the counter and the window until she could see the side of Annie's face. "Like who?"

"Sadie. And her friend Elizabeth."

"You weren't even born when Sadie was alive. And you couldn't have been much more than a baby, if anything, when Elizabeth died. So I don't understand . . ."

Annie lifted her head from the windowpane and turned to face Claire. "My big sister, Eva, was a little younger than Sadie and Elizabeth but she remembers them. Dat, of course, does, too. He said they were good girls who did not know how to say no."

"No to whom?" she asked quickly.

"Miriam."

She tried to squelch the gasp, but it was too late. "Miriam Stoltzfus?"

"Yah. But she was a Hochstetler then." Annie covered her face with her hands and sighed. "Dat thinks Rebecca is the same way."

Bypassing the urge to learn more about Rebecca, Claire went straight to the part that had her antennae pinging loudest. "Is your father not fond of Miriam?"

Annie dropped her hands to her side and shook her head rapidly. "No. It is not like that now. It was when Miriam was my age."

"What was wrong with Miriam then?"

"She made friends with the English who knew of cigarettes and drinking. She talked Sadie and Elizabeth into trying such things with her. Now, Sadie is dead. Elizabeth, too."

She took a moment to assemble everything she'd heard thus far into some cohesive order. When she had something that made sense, Claire jumped back into the conversation. "And your father feels this Rebecca person is doing that with you?"

Annie bowed her head, nodding as she did. "Yah."

"*Is* she?"

Annie lifted her gaze to Claire's but said nothing.

Finding herself in uncharted territory, she reached out, took hold of the teenager's hand, and led her back to the stools. When the girl reclaimed her earlier seat, Claire did her best to be both supportive and wise. "One of the things about getting older, Annie, is the opportunity to see things with more clarity. To realize mistakes you made and lessons you learned. One of the lessons I've learned is to be true to myself. If I like to sing while I drive and someone thinks I'm silly because of that, it doesn't matter. I enjoy it, so I do it. The same goes for things I don't like—if I don't like something or it goes against what I want for myself, I don't do it. Even if everyone else around me, *does*."

"I am like that, too," Annie exclaimed. "I did not smoke that cigarette because Rebecca did. I did it because I wanted to know what it was like."

"And?" she prompted.

"It is not good."

She smiled. "Did you tell your dat that?"

"I did. But still he worries. He has visited the Lehman farm. He knows of the sadness Sadie's mamm and dat feel. He knows of the sadness Miriam holds in her heart at news of her old friend. Eva speaks of Leroy's quiet since Sadie's body was found."

Her head snapped up at the familiar name. "Leroy? As in Leroy Beiler?"

"Yah. He is Eva's husband."

Rewinding their conversation back a few minutes to try to make the names Annie spoke match in her memory, Claire asked, "And Eva is your sister, right?"

"Yah."

"And Leroy and Sadie were friends?"

"Yah."

She pulled her legs up to the first rung of the stool and positioned them in such a way as to allow her arms to rest atop her thighs. "What's Mr. Beiler like?"

Annie clenched and unclenched her hands atop her own lap before jumping to her feet once again. "I do not call him that. I call him Leroy. Mr. Beiler is Leroy's *dat*."

"Oh. Sorry." She made a mental note of the clarification and then moved on to finding a way to defuse Annie's sudden agitation. "What's Leroy like? Is he nice?"

"He is quiet and hardworking." Annie, herself, was quiet for a moment and then smiled ever so slightly as she continued to describe her brother-in-law. "He picks wildflowers for Eva in the summer. They are to have their sixth child soon."

"That's wonderful, Annie."

"Yah. That is what Dat wants for me, too. To be baptized. To marry a nice man. To have many children like Eva."

"And you don't want that, do you?" she asked in rhetorical summary.

"No. I do. When it is time."

"Then just tell him that, Annie. Hearing that from you will probably allay a lot of his worry."

"I try. But there are always knocks at the door."

"Knocks at the door?"

"If it is not The Pest, it is someone new. Like Benjamin Miller to tell of the body on Stoltzfus's farm. Or the policeman my father does not like to speak to who comes to ask questions about Sadie. Then it is Eva who speaks of Leroy's quiet. Knock, knock, knock . . . someone always has a problem to tell the bishop. But he is not just the bishop, he is my dat, too."

She'd never really thought of it that way, but now that Annie had put things in perspective, it made a lot of sense. Bishop Hershberger was, essentially, the go-to guy for everything that happened in his district. But he was also a father—a father Annie was desperate to connect with one way or the other.

"Can I give you a hug?" she asked.

At Annie's empathic nod, Claire slid off the stool and pulled the teenager close. "Growing up is hard on everyone—kids and parents alike. Maybe what your father needs more than anything is someone he can talk to who *doesn't* have a problem."

Chapter 16

She locked the back door of Heavenly Treasures and waved to Annie as the girl disappeared around the corner of the shop in a pair of bargain-basement blue jeans and an oversized long-sleeved shirt. Part of Claire wanted to call Annie back, wanted to demand the teenager switch back into the light blue dress and apron covering that fit more naturally than the newly donned evening wear, but she didn't.

Annie needed to experience the world from a slightly different vantage point than her father's buggy allowed. It was a rite of passage, a way to be sure.

Still, Claire worried. Despite the tough, I-don't-care attitude the girl had exhibited twenty-four hours earlier, Annie was fragile. Whether or not the girl was truly strong enough and savvy enough to stay away from the pitfalls of the English world remained to be seen.

"Hey there, I was hoping I'd catch you before you headed to the inn." Jakob half walked, half jogged up the alley to greet Claire with a warm hug. "How was your day?"

She stepped back, slipped the shop's keys into her coat pocket, and did her best to rustle up the smile he deserved. "I hired a new employee and I actually think she's going to work out just fine."

"Now that's fantastic news," he said before addressing the latter part of her sentence. "But you had doubts?"

"She's only sixteen. When she came into the shop asking about the job I'd told Esther I wasn't ready to fill, she didn't necessarily project the image of someone who wanted to do a whole lot of working. And her attitude? Not good."

"And today?"

"She worked hard all day long."

He fell into step alongside her as they turned and made their way down the alley and onto the sidewalk that lined Heavenly Treasures' side of Lighted Way. "And the attitude?"

"A ruse to get noticed."

"Sounds like a teenager," he joked. "What's her name?"

"Annie."

"A junior at Heavenly High School, I imagine?"

Stopping just shy of the road, Claire leaned against the clapboard exterior of her shop. "No. Annie is Amish."

Any momentary surprise she caught on Jakob's part vanished just as quickly. "Oh? Which family?"

"She's Bishop Hershberger's youngest daughter."

He walked a few feet away and then retraced his steps back to Claire, the tone of his voice difficult to read. "Then she won't be acknowledging me when I stop by the shop to see you, that's for sure."

It was a wrinkle she hadn't considered. Then again, maybe it wasn't . . . "She's on Rumspringa," she offered as a counterpoint.

"She's still Atlee's daughter."

"Which might be the exact reason she *does* speak to you," she mumbled before lifting up the bottom of her left boot and resting it against the shop.

"You lost me."

"Remember what I said a few minutes ago? About Annie's attitude being a ruse to get noticed?"

Jakob nodded, his gaze fixed firmly on hers.

"The person she's trying to get noticed by is her dat."

"Oh. That changes things . . ." Jakob turned and leaned against the building beside Claire. "Sounds like Miriam Hochstetler part two."

"Huh?"

He palmed his mouth then let his hand slip down his chin, slowly. "Before Bishop Hershberger, there was Bishop Hochstetler. He'd handed the reins to Atlee just a few weeks before I left, making me Hershberger's very first—and, I believe only—excommunication."

"So what does that have to do with Annie and Miriam?"

"Miriam saw her father's role as bishop as some sort of reason to be more rebellious during Rumspringa. And she tried her darnedest to entice Elizabeth and Sadie down the same road." Jakob cocked his head up until he had a view of the late-afternoon sun. "I always found it curious that the bishop's daughter would be the crazy one."

She pushed off the wall with her boot and turned to face Jakob, the day's discovery making it possible for her to shed light on the subject. "From what I was able to gather while talking with Annie today, an Amish bishop is a busy man."

"Without a doubt."

"When someone dies, he's called. When there is a problem to be solved, he's called. When something awful happens—like the discovery of Sadie's body the other night—he's called." At Jakob's slow nod, she continued. "He's oftentimes so busy attending to everyone's needs outside his home, he has no time for those that arise inside . . . like a Rumspringa-aged teenager who wants nothing more than to talk about life with her father."

Again, he brought his hand to his mouth, only this time he let it linger there a little longer as he absorbed Claire's words. "Wow. I guess I'd never really thought of it that way but . . . yeah . . . it makes a ton of sense. By acting out, by being the rebel, her father is almost forced to take notice."

She swept her focus across the street and to the snatch of Amish farmland visible through the matching alley on the other side of Lighted Way. There was no doubt the Amish lifestyle was less drama-filled than that of the English, but it was, by no means, without its own trials.

"I'm worried about her, Jakob."

"Who? Annie?"

"She's sweet. She really is. Thoughtful, too. But I'm afraid she's so intent on making her father see her that she's going to do something to really get herself hurt."

He reached for her hand and smiled broadly when she readily gave it in return. For a moment, she allowed herself to get caught up in the warmth of his skin and the caressing touch of his thumb, but it was his words and the love with which he shared them that spoke to her most. "I don't discount the need to be noticed by your parent, I really don't. I get that probably better than anyone else. But I also know that genuine affection and concern is genuine affection and concern no matter where it comes from. Getting a dose of that from you a few days a week might be exactly what she needs to keep her feet firmly on the ground."

"You really think so?" she whispered, looking up.

"Yeah. I really do."

She flipped her hand inside his and squeezed. "Thank you."

"My pleasure." He pulled her a step closer and brought his forehead to hers. "I've got something I've gotta do now, but I was hoping that maybe we could meet back up later this evening."

"Oh?" she teased.

"We could go for a drive . . . or maybe come back into town for a coffee or hot chocolate at Heavenly Brews. Or maybe we could even run out to Breeze Point and pick up a movie and some microwave popcorn and take it back to my place."

She allowed herself a moment to inhale, to revel in the shift that was taking place in their relationship. "All three of those sound good as long as they're with you," she whispered.

Zipping her coat all the way to the top, Claire turned and headed toward the inn, the surprisingly abrupt shift in temperatures reminding her of what the melted snow couldn't. Spring might be on its way, but it wasn't there yet. Suddenly, the winter coat that had been overkill when she stopped at the post office midday, was now sorely needed as were the gloves and hat she'd gone back to the shop to retrieve after parting ways with Jakob.

Still, there was something about knowing she'd be seeing him again that gave her feet a purpose beyond just merely getting home and out of the cold. One by one, she considered the suggestions he'd tossed out for their post-dinner evening together. The drive, while nice, would probably be better suited for a weekend or daylight saving time. The coffee at Heavenly Brews would give them time to talk in a datelike setting. And the movie at his place, while datelike in its own way, also carried a more intimate feel.

She glanced up at her fellow shopkeepers' front windows as she walked, each one's nod to spring dependent on their inventory. Ruth Miller's window showcased an assortment of desserts with floral touches—flower-shaped cookies, pastel iced cakes, and pies that boasted flower imprints across the top crust. Howard Glick's window boasted the kind of tools most heavily utilized in spring—trowels, garden rakes, pruning shears, and more.

At the end of the block she crossed the street and turned left, the remaining half mile or so of her walk promising blacktop rather than cobblestone, and knee-high political signs rather than quaint storefronts. She knew she should care more than she did about the upcoming election now that she was a local business owner, but she really didn't. To her, it didn't matter what color backdrop their name was scrawled across just so long as they cared about Heavenly and its people.

"Excuse me, miss?"

She stopped midstep and turned around to find a young man of about twenty holding out a pamphlet. "Yes?"

"I won't keep you. I just wanted to give you some literature on Mike O'Neil and his run for mayor of Heavenly."

"Mike O'Neil?" She took the pamphlet and peered down at the mayoral candidate who'd found his way into more than a few conversations with her aunt as of late. "Oh yes, of course, I've heard of him."

"That's wonderful. When you have a moment, I hope you'll read what Mike has to say about our town and his plans for its future. That way, come April, you can make an informed vote."

Holding the professional picture under the closest gas-powered lantern, she took a moment to really study the candidate. She knew, from stories she'd been told about his childhood and the time frame in which they'd happened, the former troublemaker was in his mid to late thirties. The almost too-youthful style with which he wore his burnished red hair was evened out by fine lines that started at the outer corners of his blue-green eyes and branched outward, hinting at a life that hadn't been as easy as his polished smile might have one believe.

"I'm glad you stopped me." She inhaled slowly, giving herself a little extra time to think through the untruth she was about to share. When she'd taken in as much air as she could, she let it out along with her story. "I know you've been working on Mr. O'Neil's campaign for quite some time and I know we're getting awfully close to the election, but I was wondering if maybe I could help a little."

"Seriously?"

At her nod, he broke out into a grin. "I take it you know him?"

She looked again at the pamphlet and the man it portrayed on the front cover. "Actually, no. I'm just fascinated by the"—she paused to choose her words carefully—"road he's traveled to get to this place."

"Me, too. So many folks think he's just doing it to follow in his father's footsteps . . . but he's not. He wants to make his own mark on this town."

Unsure of what to say, she merely nodded again.

"Hey, I'm Tim, by the way."

"Claire. Claire Weatherly."

He shook her hand, and then hooked his thumb in the direction of the empty storefront housed between the police station and the parade of park benches heavily utilized by tourists throughout daylight hours. "Our campaign headquarters just took up shop in this place last night and the electricity has been running inside nonstop ever since. Why don't you come on in for a few minutes and let me show you around."

She quickened her step as they neared their destination. "Do you expect Mike will be stopping by often? You know, to check on how everything is going?"

Tim reached for the door handle and nodded. "I absolutely think he'll be around every chance he gets. He's real hands-on in everything he does. Heck, he helped us move into this place last night and I'm not sure he's even gone home to change yet."

"He's inside now?"

"He sure is. Want to meet him?"

She refrained from pinching herself long enough to follow Tim through the door and into the hustle and bustle that was Mike O'Neil's campaign headquarters. A table off to her side was flanked by teenagers tasked with folding a stack of glossy colored printouts into the same brochure Tim had handed Claire. In between the folders were three telephones and three older volunteers who were in varying stages of campaign calls. One was dialing, one was in the throes of her pitch, and the other was answering questions.

Another table off to the left housed a variety of ages hovering around a pair of button-making machines. Each and every button they made found its way into a big box for distribution at a later date.

"I think it says a lot about a candidate when so many people are willing to give up their free time just to see him in office, you know?"

Before she could formulate a reply, he stepped forward and again motioned for her to follow. "I think he might be in the back room with his dad."

"His father was Heavenly's mayor for a long time,

wasn't he?" she asked as much to make conversation as for any other reason.

"Not long enough, from what my own dad has said." Tim headed through an open doorway in the back of the main room and stopped as he reached the other side. "But Mike's dad is the first one to say new blood is good if for no other reason than it makes you appreciate what you had. Once you do, it's easier to recognize it again in the future."

When she caught up, Tim poked his head into a room similar in size to Claire's office in her own storefront. "Excuse me, Mike? Do you have a minute?"

The younger of the two men stood and met them at the door, his blue-green eyes dancing between his campaign volunteer and Claire.

"Of course, Tim, how can I help you?"

"Claire Weatherly, here, would like to help with your campaign."

Mike reached for Claire's hand and shook it warmly. "Claire, I can't thank you enough for your support. It's knowing I have the support of people like you that keeps my head held high during what can be a rather grueling process."

"My pleasure," she said. "I love knowing you grew up in this town. I've only been here a little over a year myself, but I committed to it being my home for many years to come when I opened my own shop here on Lighted Way."

"Oh? Which one is yours?"

"Heavenly Treasures." Then, for clarity's sake, she put its location in perspective using the one shop everyone knew. "It's next to Shoo Fly Bake Shoppe."

The man laughed. "Ruth Miller's apple pie really is something else, isn't it?"

Movement just beyond the candidate's shoulder yielded a face similar to Mike's but older. The older man's handshake was just as warm. "You must be the niece Diane Weatherly is always talking about whenever I see her out and about, yes?"

"I am."

"I'm Ryan . . . Michael's father." The man jabbed his son in the side with his elbow while jutting his chin toward Claire. "Claire, here, lives at Sleep Heavenly with her aunt."

"For now," she interjected. "Eventually I hope to buy my own place in town."

"Where were you living before you moved to Heavenly?" Mike asked.

"New York City."

"Wow, that's quite a change." Michael reached around his father and liberated a familiar to-go box from the first of two rickety desks he'd managed to cram into the tiny space. "Would you like a cookie? They're from everyone's favorite bakery in town."

She helped herself to a small sugar cookie and took a bite. "Heavenly and New York City are as different as night and day. Here, I fit. There, I didn't."

"How so?" he asked as he returned the box to his desk and his undivided attention to Claire.

"If I had to boil it down to one thing, I'd say the quiet. Beyond that, it's the simple life led by the Amish that spreads itself outward to the rest of us."

Mike rubbed his thumb along the underside of his chin and nodded, the narrowing of his eyes letting her know he was truly absorbing her words. "I've lived here my whole life but have never really been able to put a finger on why I love it in such a clear and concise way. And you're right. Even though we live our lives very differently than the Amish, their simplicity, their work ethic, and their forgiving hearts have a way of rubbing off. Funny things is, it's almost ironic that a group of people who are such hard workers can also help the rest of us to slow down, you know?"

"Something we all need to do once in a while," she added.

"Agreed. In fact, it took some Amish friends in my teen years to make me really step back and look at all the things I thought were so important, but weren't."

At the wistful turn to his tone, she broached the subject that had propelled her to sign on as a volunteer for a candidate she'd never met. "You grew up with Leroy Beiler, Miriam Hochstetler, and Elizabeth Troyer, I believe."

He drew back in benign surprise. "I did, indeed. How did you—"

"Sadie Lehman, the girl whose body was likely recovered last week, was part of your group of friends, too, wasn't she?"

She didn't need better lighting to notice the way Mike's face paled at the mention of Sadie, nor did she need a psychology degree to pick out the genuine sadness that revealed and highlighted the same facial lines she'd seen in his campaign brochure.

What she did need, however, was a muzzle to mute her audible gasp as the elder O'Neil grabbed hold of his son's arm, propelled him through the doorway, and instructed Claire to leave her name and number in the very unlikely event the campaign needed more volunteers.

Chapter 17

Claire lifted her face to the noon sun and allowed it to warm her from the outside in. All morning long she'd been saddled with an inexplicable chill she couldn't quite shake or accurately attribute to any one particular thing.

Sure, it had been chilly when she walked to work that morning. But in the grand scheme of things, she'd contended with far colder mornings during the months of January and February.

The heat had been on the fritz when she first arrived at the shop, but a call to her fellow shopkeeper and landlord, Al Gussman, had gotten things under control and back to a pleasant temperature within an hour of opening.

She'd tried to keep her shivering to a minimum as she attended to customers and various tasks around the shop, but when Annie offered to hold down the fort while

Claire took a break to warm up, she knew she'd been unsuccessful.

A pulsing vibration just beside her hip made her jump and Claire reached into her pocket for her phone. A quick check of the display screen ignited the chill all over again.

For a moment, she considered letting it go to voice mail, but knew she couldn't. Not if she wanted answers, anyway.

Flipping the phone open, she held it to her ear, the chill that had permeated her body all morning successfully moving into her voice. "Good afternoon, Jakob. What can I do for you?"

A long hesitation was broken first by a gargled noise, and then a worried plea. "Oh no. Please tell me you got the message last night."

"No. No message."

The initial gargled noise turned into a frustrated groan. "I called your cell, Claire. I left a message telling you my meeting went longer than I expected and that I wanted to reschedule for tonight. If you're free, of course."

The sun cleared the top of Shoo Fly Bake Shoppe and bathed the alley in blink-worthy brightness. More than anything, she wanted to chalk up his unexplained no-show the previous evening to a misunderstanding, but something inside her made her falter, and she hated it.

She *knew* Jakob. She *knew* what kind of man he was— his decent ways and his unshakable integrity. Just because her ex-husband had made a sport out of standing her up didn't mean Jakob was destined to do the same.

Still, she had to be sure . . .

"Hold on a second," she murmured as she pulled the phone from her ear and looked down at the screen. Shielding the sun from her eyes with her left hand, she went into her message panel and scrolled down to the line dedicated to voice mails. Sure enough, a number one was listed beside the appropriate icon, yet nothing next to the missed-call category. Slowly, she lifted the device back to her ear. "I'm sorry, Jakob. I . . . I never heard the call or noticed the message."

"You thought I stood you up, didn't you?"

She nodded, only to realize her mistake and correct it with her verbal assent.

"I can assure you, right now, that I will never stand you up without a darn good reason—like police business. And even then, with the exception of a complete emergency, I will always let you know that I'm not coming and why."

She swallowed over the sudden tightness in her throat and found the words she needed to say. "I'm sorry, Jakob. I'm sorry for assuming something about you because of the actions of someone else. I really should have known better."

"Hurt at the hands of people we love and trust cuts deeper than even we realize, sometimes. I get that." She heard a squeak in the background and knew he was calling from his desk chair, the image of the handsome detective in his office birthing her first true smile of the day. "So, since you didn't get to listen to the message, I should probably bring you up to speed on why I had to put our evening on hold."

"You don't owe me any explanation, Jakob. Just knowing you tried to call is enough."

"No, it's not." He paused momentarily before filling in the blanks as quickly and succinctly as possible. "When I saw you just after closing last night, I was on my way out to Ben's place."

"You went to Benjamin's house? Why?"

"I wanted to talk to him directly, to see if he could shed light on Elizabeth's mood and demeanor the last few weeks of her life—things that now, in the wake of finding her journal, might be noteworthy."

"Okay . . ." she prompted, intrigued.

"At first, the meeting was rather stilted. I asked basic questions and Ben gave one- and two-word answers. But as we began to revisit the past by way of my questions, we found that there was a lot to say about a lot of things. Some, of course, related directly to my reason for being there, and some didn't, but the overall conversation ended up going much, much later than I'd originally thought."

Suddenly, it didn't matter that she'd spent most of the night staring up at the ceiling, berating herself for trusting another man. It didn't matter that she'd moved around the store that morning in a complete funk with a side order of incessant shivering. And it didn't matter that all of it had been for naught. What *did* matter was that two men who'd once been friends had found a way to communicate with each other despite decades of bitterness and a belief system that only furthered that divide.

"I'm glad you stayed with Benjamin. I'm glad the two of you worked out your differences . . ."

"For the first time since I was probably eight years

old, I realized that my father's preference for Ben wasn't Ben's fault. He didn't seek to make me look bad by building a really good chicken coop or chopping more wood than I did. And it wasn't his fault that Elizabeth was interested in him instead of me. It just was. *I'm* the one who chose to blame my problems with my father on Ben. *I'm* the one who chose to see Elizabeth's choice as some sort of final betrayal on his part. *I'm* the one who destroyed our friendship, not him."

She leaned against the shop's side door and sent up a silent prayer of praise for bringing a man like Jakob into her life—a man who had the maturity to open his eyes and truly *see*.

Still, she rushed to remove at least some of the weight he now shouldered. "Even if none of that had happened, the Ordnung is the reason you can't be friends, now."

"True. But the Ordnung wasn't responsible for the anger I've carried in my heart toward Ben all these years. That's on me . . . and it was wrong. My father's hang-ups were his alone."

A telltale *clip-clop* at the entrance to the alley forced her eyes open and her attention to the approaching buggy, the hatted man seated behind the trusted horse acknowledging Claire with a quick nod and an even quicker smile. "Speaking of Ben, he just pulled up for the Miller brothers' noon check on their sister."

"I'll let you go so you can say hi. But before I do, will you consider giving me another shot at our date tonight?"

"There's nothing to consider. I'm looking forward to it very much." She heard the breathless excitement in her voice and knew he heard it, too.

"Any thoughts on whether you'd prefer the drive, the coffee, or the movie?" he asked via a smile she didn't need to see to know was there.

"I think the movie sounds most fun."

"Me, too. I'll pick you up at seven, okay?"

"I'll be ready." She flipped the phone closed, held it to her face for an extra minute, and then slipped it back into her pocket as she stood to greet Benjamin. "While I always love seeing your brother, Eli, it sure is nice to see you around here again."

Ben crossed in front of his horse with an unfamiliar gait and an even more unfamiliar pair of dark circles rimming his lackluster blue eyes. "Claire."

"You look awful. What's wrong?" Then, realizing how she sounded, she hurried to explain. "You look like you haven't slept in days. Did something happen?"

"I slept last night. For a few hours. But it was the first time since I found Elizabeth's notebook."

She lowered herself back to the step she'd inhabited while talking to Jakob and patted the top one for Ben. He remained standing, his eyes now hooded. "Was it a special memory of Elizabeth that finally enabled you to relax and sleep?" she asked.

"I have many memories. On many, many days. Her smile. Her laugh. But, most of all, I cannot forget the way she stared into the fields like she was waiting for something." He pulled a sugar cube from his pocket and offered it to his horse, the animal as pleased with his owner's gentle touch as he was with the treat. "When I would ask her, she would wipe at her face and then go back to her chores, saying all was fine. Now, because of her written words, I know that she wiped tears she did not want me to see."

Oh, how she wanted to argue, to make up some sort of excuse that would remove the anguish from her friend's heart, but she couldn't. From everything she'd heard from Ben, Elizabeth had been a troubled woman her last few years on earth, a fact underscored by the Amish woman's own written words. But just as Jakob had come to realize Ben was not responsible for his father's actions, Ben was also not responsible for Elizabeth's.

How to say that, though, was the hard part.

Benjamin had loved his wife. He'd asked for her hand in marriage and committed his life to her. Knowing, after the fact, that she had been tormented by a secret she never should have kept, had to be torturous in its own right.

"But Jakob helped me to see that her step was lighter her last day."

"Her step was lighter?" she repeated, confused. "I don't know what you mean."

Again, Ben stroked his horse, his back to Claire. "It is there, on the last page of her notebook. She was going to tell. To know that she would soon be free of her secret would give her peace." His hand dropped to his side and he turned until his gaze was on no one but Claire. "Before the notebook, I knew her death was God's will and that she died content. After the notebook, I feared she died troubled. Now, because of Jakob, I believe she died with peace."

Unsure of what to say, she seized on the mention of a man she knew they both treasured. "I'm glad you and Jakob were able to talk last night. It's apparent you both helped each other accept something that needed to be accepted in order for each of you to find peace, as well."

"Jakob is a good man."

This time when her throat tightened, she didn't fight the feeling so fast. Instead, she let herself mull over the many precipitating reasons for her reaction, not the least of which was the obvious thawing that was beginning to take place between two childhood friends and the hope it brought to her own heart.

"Now it is time for Zebediah and Waneta to know peace," Ben said as he looked up at the sky.

"You mean Sadie's parents?"

"Yah. It is as Jakob said. To know the truth is to be at peace."

Chapter 18

"To know the truth is to be at peace," Claire repeated beneath her breath as she stepped through the back door of Heavenly Treasures and cocked her ear toward the front room. From the snippets of conversation she could make out, Annie was wrapping up a transaction with a customer with such ease Claire couldn't help but be impressed by the teenager's work ethic all over again.

Suddenly, because of Annie, Claire had options again. No longer did she have to work open to close, seven days a week. No longer did she have to eat her lunch between customers or forgo it completely in order to get her list of daily tasks completed in a somewhat timely fashion.

And she had Esther to thank for it—Esther and her ability to know what Claire needed even when Claire didn't.

"Sitting in the sunlight surely agreed with you, yah?"

Startled, she looked toward the showroom doorway

to find Annie staring at her with an openly amused expression.

"I, uh—"

"You look as I feel after I have sat in the sun with Smokey."

"Who's Smokey?" she asked.

"He is the barn cat. When I am tired when I should not be, or I am sad about something, I like to walk into the field next to our barn and lie down in the sun. Sometimes I do not know Smokey has followed me until he climbs on my stomach and begins to purr. Soon, I feel better."

"Thanks for suggesting the break, Annie. I guess I didn't realize how badly I needed one."

"You are happy now?"

She thought back to her conversation with Jakob, the smile spawned by the memory stretching her mouth wide. "Yes, I am happy—"

The jingle of the front door had barely registered in her conscious thought when she heard an oddly familiar voice calling her name. "Miss Weatherly? Are you here?"

"I'll be right with you," she called before returning her focus to Annie. "Your lunch is in the office, right?" At Annie's nod, she crossed to the doorway, patting the teenager's shoulder as she passed. "You've put in a really solid morning, Annie. Why don't you take your lunch outside on the stoop and enjoy a little sun yourself."

"Are you sure?" Annie asked.

"I'm sure." She walked into the showroom only to stop, midstep, as the man behind the voice materialized in the flesh. "Mr. O'Neil?"

"Please, call me Mike." The mayoral candidate stood

awkwardly beside the paneled upright and shifted from foot to foot, periodically swiping his thick hand through his close-cropped hair. "I was hoping I'd find you in today."

"Oh?"

"I wanted to apologize for the abrupt end to our conversation last night and assure you I am grateful for any assistance you're willing and able to give to my campaign."

She stopped herself midnod and, instead, took the direct approach. After all, one of the three people capable of divulging the truth behind Sadie Lehman's fate was standing in front of her of his own accord. Maybe, if she played her cards right, she could learn something that would be of help to Jakob and his investigation. "I got the distinct impression your father doesn't share your sentiment."

He dropped his hand to his side and crossed the storeroom seemingly to examine a hand-painted milk can, but, when he got there, his shoulders sagged along with his voice. "I guess for you to understand my father's abruptness last night, you have to understand my father."

"Okay . . ."

"My dad was born in Heavenly just as his dad and his grandfather before him were. Back when my grandfather was growing up here, the town was pretty much the way you see it now—at least on the Amish side, anyway. The Amish lived in their farmhouses, tended their fields, and kept to themselves."

Intrigued, she leaned against the counter. "And the English side?"

"It pretty much consisted of the house my grandpa grew up in and a few large farms. My great-grandfather was the first official mayor of Heavenly—a job that was probably pretty easy on account of the fact there wasn't much going on around here. But, over time, that changed. Slowly but surely, the English farmers began to parcel up and sell off their land—some to newly married Amish, and some to people who knew a thing or two about home construction.

"By the time my grandfather was elected into the office, a smaller town just south of here was essentially picked apart by Heavenly and other neighboring towns. With the annex of new land, came more homes and more property tax money. Eventually, my father won the same mayoral seat my grandfather and great-grandfather had once held and he became a huge factor in Heavenly becoming the tourism attraction it is today. It was during his stint that Lighted Way went from being simply a link between the English and Amish to being an almost living, breathing celebration of both."

"He did an amazing job," she admitted. "I'm sure his father would be proud."

"You'd certainly think so, but I often wonder how much of that pride was about what my father accomplished and how much was simply because he'd followed in the footsteps of his elders."

"And now, here you are, years later, running for the same office," she mused.

Mike roamed the outer edge of the shop, occasionally stopping to look at a homemade item but mostly just pacing. "You make it sound like I have a choice."

"You don't *want* to be mayor?" She instantly regretted

the shock she heard in her voice as it seemed to pull the man out of his almost trancelike state.

He turned widened eyes in her direction. "I . . . I didn't say that."

She scrambled to regroup and get them back on the original path, a path that held far more promise than the one her big mouth threatened to yield. "I'm sorry. I guess I—"

"All you have to do is walk through town hall and look at the photographs of past mayors to know why I need to do this. It's a legacy my father has groomed me to continue since the day I was born."

"Sounds like a lot of pressure to me," she said honestly.

He half snorted, half laughed. "That's putting it mildly."

She tried to think of something to say, something to serve as the probe she needed to go deeper, but she was at a loss.

Fortunately, he continued, unprompted. "The day I started kindergarten, I was told to be nice to my classmates because they might be the voters who put me into office one day. When I started in sports, I was the one who always had the end-of-the-year parties. So my fellow teammates would remember me as generous and kind. And when I was a teenager, I was badgered to toe the line on a daily basis. When I didn't, my actions were quickly swept under the carpet before any sort of blemish on my record could take hold."

"The latter must have made you feel invincible."

This time, his laugh was accompanied by a downward tilt of his head. "Did it ever. I could essentially do whatever I wanted and know that my father would make it magically disappear.

"If I hit a guardrail with my car because I was drinking, a more sympathy-inducing story would be disseminated through my father's handpicked channels. Suddenly the story became about me swerving to avoid a deer, or my brakes malfunctioning, that sort of thing."

"Wow." It was a way of life she could only imagine.

"Before you think it was a cakewalk for me, you have to know that my peers weren't stupid. They saw what was going on, heard the creative spin that always followed, and began to resent me. Which is why, when I was about sixteen, I went looking for a different group of friends—kids who knew what it was like to grow up with a set of expectations that had nothing to do with them and everything to do with a way of life virtually handpicked for them generations earlier."

"You're talking about the Amish now, aren't you?"

"They didn't care that I was or wasn't the mayor's son. They just thought my car was cool, my clothes were cool, and *I* was cool. And I knew they weren't going to go home telling stories about me that would eventually make their way back to my father."

She hung on everything he said and the holes he helped fill. "So that's how you knew Leroy Beiler, Miriam Hochstetler, Elizabeth Troyer, and Sadie Lehman, right?"

He turned his back to her and stared out the window. "They were in that yearlong thing where they get to be bad, essentially. They can smoke if they want to, even *drink* if they want to. But mostly they just get to be un-Amish for a little while. And they looked to me to help them be un-Amish. Funny thing is, I think I learned as much from them as they ever did from me."

"Friends have a way of teaching us all sorts of things, don't they?" she said softly.

For a moment, she wasn't sure he'd heard her, but just as she was about to repeat herself, he nodded, the anguish her words caused evident in his hushed yet raspy response. "Especially when you realize they're the only true ones you've ever had."

She gasped. "That was nearly twenty years ago, Mike. Surely you've had friends since then."

"No, not like those four, I haven't."

"How do you mean?"

He slumped against the window, shoved his hands into the front pockets of his pants, and stared up at the ceiling as if searching for something. After several long moments, he sighed and allowed his gaze to drift slowly back to her face. "They looked up to me like I was something special. They trusted *me* in a way no one had ever trusted me before." He stopped, cleared his throat, and then added, "In a way no one has trusted me since."

She teed her hands in the air. "I have to stop you on that last one. Because, based on what I saw in your campaign headquarters last night, there's a whole bunch of people trusting you at the moment."

He thumped the back of his head against the glass pane behind him and squeezed his eyes shut temporarily. "I'm aware."

"And that's a bad thing?" At his emphatic nod, she dug a bit deeper. "For whom? *You?*"

"No. For them."

She stepped forward, then backward, unsure of how to react to the man's self-deprecation. Did she pat his back and tell him he was too hard on himself? Did she bombard him with questions designed to unearth the reason for his obvious self-loathing? Or did she try to get the conversation back where she needed it to be?

Before she could settle on a plan of action, Michael spoke again. "It seems as if I have a real gift for betraying those who trust me."

"I—"

Michael pulled his left hand from his pocket, held his index finger in the air between them, and then pulled his right hand out to reveal a vibrating phone. Looking down at the caller ID screen, he released a muted groan. "I don't know how he does it, I really don't."

"How who does what?"

"How my father seems to know when I'm about to—" He stopped, shook his head, and then brought the phone to the side of his face. "Hey, Dad. What's up?"

She watched as the man's jaw ran the gamut from tight to slack and everything in between before he was finally given an opportunity to speak. "Yes, Dad, I know how important this kind of media coverage is to you . . . Yes, you're right . . . How important this kind of media coverage is to *me* . . . I guess I just don't understand why I have to do the interview outside Grandfather's old house . . . Yes, Dad . . . Yes, I know . . . Okay, okay, I'm on my way."

Slowly, he dropped the phone to his side, his head hung low. "I've gotta go." Then, lifting his head, he established eye contact just long enough to apologize. "I didn't come here intending to bend your ear, I really didn't. But I felt bad about the way my father cut our conversation short yesterday, and even worse about the fact I just let it happen. Again. But, as you probably saw just now on the phone, I don't really have a spine where my father is concerned. Never have."

She resisted the urge to nod and, instead, offered what she hoped was thoughtful if not insightful commiseration. "I don't have children myself, but I guess maybe it's hard for some parents to ever fully see their offspring as independent adults capable of living their own life. All you can do, I guess, is talk to him, tell him how you feel."

He sidestepped Claire and headed for the door, his footfalls heavy with an invisible weight. "I wish it were that simple."

"Why can't it be?"

When he reached the door, he turned, his blue-green eyes shrouded in pain. "Because if I'd taken the reins of my own life the way she wanted me to years ago, I'd have destroyed my father and his legacy."

Claire stared at Mike. *"She?"*

If he heard her request for clarification, he gave no indication, his words, his focus somewhere else entirely. "Lately, though, I have to wonder if it was my *father* I was truly worried about . . . or *myself*."

Chapter 19

Looking back, Claire knew Peter's premarital apart-ment should have been a clue as to his priorities in life, but as a young twenty-something, she hadn't made the connection. At the time, she'd seen the sparse personal touches as an indicator he needed a woman in his life—someone who could help him create a real home. Sadly, as their marriage fizzled to an end, she'd come to realize the sterile feel of her then husband's surroundings wasn't a cry for help but, rather, a crystal clear snapshot of the man himself.

Emotionless . . .

One-dimensional . . .

Money oriented . . .

And utterly clueless as to what makes a life worth living.

She shook off the memory and willed herself to focus

on Jakob and everything his surroundings were poised to say about him.

"Now remember, I've only been renting this place for seven months so it's still lacking in some respects." Jakob jiggled his key in the lock and turned it, his hand sweeping her inward as he did. "But it'll do for now."

She preceded him into the tiny foyer and stopped, her audible intake of air making him laugh.

"Or . . . maybe it won't," he quipped.

Pulling her gaze from the bits and pieces of the living room she could make out, she tried to focus on her host, his quiet laughter making it apparent she'd missed a joke. "Is something wrong?"

"I didn't think so, but after that gasp of yours just now, it's rather obvious I've been deluding myself." He helped her out of her coat then hung it in the hall closet beside his own. "Maybe you could make some decorating suggestions? I'm a pretty quick study with most things."

"Are you kidding me?" she asked as she inched closer to the living room for a better view. On the far side of the room was a stone fireplace, an evening's worth of wood stacked neatly beside it in a brass holder while a handful of picture frames lined its mantel from left to right. Across from the hearth, yet angled to enjoy its cozy warmth and charm, was an oversized couch with a homemade Amish quilt draped over the back. A stack of books—mostly thriller novels—was within easy reach while the remotes for the television were tucked neatly beside the DVD player on the tastefully simple entertainment cabinet. "I'd say you're doing just fine all on your own."

Anxious to get a closer look at the pictures, she

wiggled out of her boots and tiptoed across the old-fashioned wood-planked floor, Jakob's laugh soliciting a smile of her own. "What?" she asked without stopping. "What's so funny?"

"Nothing. I'm just happy, I guess. Happy that you're here, happy I suggested we watch a movie here, and happy you actually said yes."

"How could I not?" It was an honest reply and one she hoped felt as good to hear as it did to say. She slowed as she approached the mantel, the familiar frame, dead center, prompting her to look in disbelief over her shoulder at the detective. "You still have this?"

He answered her shock with his own. "Why wouldn't I? It's one of the prettiest pictures I've ever seen of Lighted Way in the snow."

She returned to the photograph and studied it critically. "I'd tried to capture the way the sun glinted off the snow-encrusted streetlamps, but I didn't quite get it. Not completely, anyway."

"I think it's perfect just the way it is."

Something about his voice and his sudden nearness made her swallow nervously. "I . . . I'm just surprised you actually put it up."

"For a long time, it was the only thing that made this place feel like home." At her unrestrained surprise, he continued. "I'll never forget the moment I first saw you in the lobby of the police department with that blue-and-green-striped gift bag in your hand. I was so blown away by your presence it took a few minutes to register that you were there to see *me*."

"I wanted to welcome you to Heavenly."

"Everyone else to that point had simply waved, or, in the case of my family, turned their backs. But you not only took the time to seek me out, you also put a little bit of yourself into a gift bag and gave it to me." He reached out, traced the edges of the frame with his index finger, and then cleared his throat of the emotion that threatened to choke his words. "I still have the candles you made, too."

She followed his index finger to the far side of the mantel and the royal blue and teal candles she'd made especially for him. "I . . . I know you thanked me numerous times that day, and even mentioned putting everything up inside your home, but . . ." She let the words disappear from her lips as she became all too aware of Jakob's proximity and his hand, now gently caressing her cheek.

"I was—and am—hooked. On you."

She tilted her chin upward with the pressure of his fingertips and gave in to the kiss that had been building for quite some time, the warmth and hope she found there sending an unexpected tingle down her spine.

When they finally stepped apart, he pulled the quilt off the sofa and wrapped it around her shoulders with such love and tenderness she had to blink back tears. "Sometimes, I have to wonder if all of this is some sort of dream."

"It is." He dropped into a squat and added two fresh logs to the fire, the accompanying crackles and pops merely intensifying the coziness of the room. "The dreams that happen when your eyes are open are always the best kind, in my opinion."

"Agreed." She pulled the quilt more tightly against her body and shifted her focus to the rest of the frames displayed atop the mantel. To the immediate left of hers, was a picture of the hidden swimming hole Jakob frequented as a young Amish boy. "I know how special your memories are of that pond. Makes me wish I could transport myself back just to see you and Martha laughing and having fun."

He poked at the fire a few times and then returned the metal pole to its holder on the far side of the fireplace. "I couldn't have asked for a better sister than Martha. She made growing up Amish the treasured memory it will always be for me. But that's not all I think about when I look at that picture."

"It's not?"

Slowly he rose to face her once again. "I also remember putting my arms around you for the very first time so I could teach you how to skip rocks."

She couldn't help but smile at the memory as she, too, found herself recalling the jolt of awareness that had come from the feel of his arms—an awareness she'd pushed aside at that time purely out of fear and confusion. "Thanks to you, I've become quite the little rock skipper, if I must say so myself."

His laugh warmed her as quickly and completely as the restoked fire, and she moved on to the picture of intertwined hands. "Is one of those yours?"

"That's Esther's and Eli's hands on their wedding day. I know I probably shouldn't have taken it, but I thought it would be a nice memory."

"Did they know you took it?" She heard the surprise in her voice and rushed to explain it. "I just know the Amish don't like to have their photos taken."

"I know. It's why I almost left the camera at home before

I picked you up that day. But, in the end, I couldn't help myself. Then, at some point when I was walking around, giving myself a tour of Martha's home and grounds, I saw the two of them holding hands. I pulled out my phone and snapped a picture. I'm pretty sure Eli saw me because he turned their hands just enough to give me a clear shot."

"It's beautiful," she said in awe.

"I put that one in a frame to remind me there's always a chance."

She pulled the quilt from around her shoulders and tucked it under her arm instead. "A chance?"

"When I moved back here, I fully expected my sister and my brother would pretend as if I didn't exist. I dared to hope I was wrong, of course, but I was Amish once, too. I knew the drill." He took the quilt and her hand and led her to the couch. "Within days of being here, I met you. And before I could fully bask in that good fortune, you and your shop gave me a place where I could at least *see* my sister and my niece. Five months later, I'm at her wedding. Granted, I was only there as your guest, and not a single solitary Amish person gave me the time of day, including my own family, but, still . . . What matters is that I *did* get to watch Esther get married and I know my being there meant something to her and Martha even if they could never show that in front of Bishop Hershberger or any other member of the Amish community."

"I'm glad you were there with me that day," she said honestly. "In fact, I was proud to have you as my date."

"The feeling was mutual." He reached across the end table closest to him and retrieved a stack of DVDs she hadn't noticed. Holding them out like playing cards, he smiled. "Okay, so what sounds good to you? I tried to make sure all genres were represented—documentary, mystery, a missing person drama, comedy, and even a so-called chick flick."

She looked from title to title and then shrugged. "How about I narrow it down to the drama and the comedy, and you make the final decision?"

"Hmmm. Okay, let's go with the comedy. The way I see it, Miriam Hochstetler's vanishing act this week is enough of a missing person drama all on its own, don't you agree?" He deposited the remaining movie cases back on the end table and opened the one he'd selected. "I'll pop this in and then head into the kitchen to make some popcorn. What can I get you to drink?"

The last thing in the world she wanted to do at that moment was think about Sadie Lehman and her long-buried body. But ever since Mike O'Neil's visit to Heavenly Treasures that afternoon, she'd been able to think of little else.

"Claire?"

Something about the tone in which Jakob said her name had her reaching for the quilt all over again. "I know this is probably the last thing you want to talk about right now but . . ." She stopped, swallowed, and then started again, all hesitancy falling by the wayside as she thought, again, about the town's newest mayoral candidate and the disdain he seemed to have for himself. "I was wondering if you've been able to reach Miriam yet."

If he was bothered by the unexpected detour her question brought to their evening, he didn't let it show beyond a raised eyebrow and a momentary pause. "She's Amish.

She left to care for an Amish friend in upstate New York. I can't call her because she doesn't have a phone. And I can't solicit the help of the appropriate law enforcement agency in the area where she's gone because even Jeremiah seems at a loss for where, exactly, his wife went, and which friend she has gone off to care for."

"So now you move on, right? To one of the other names mentioned in Elizabeth's journal?"

"If all goes well, Bishop Hershberger will have some information for me on Miriam and her whereabouts very, very soon."

"Bishop Hershberger?" she echoed, shocked. "I thought he refused to even acknowledge you as a human being."

He held his hand up, quieting her words. "As a former member of the community, he will not speak to me. But, as the police detective assigned to finding out what happened to Sadie Lehman, he will. Zebediah and Waneta deserve answers about their daughter's death. They deserve to know how she died and why someone would bury her on their former property and never tell them."

"I know this, and you know this, but does *Bishop Hershberger* know this? Especially when tracking down this information invariably means having contact with you?"

"Yes." Jakob's hand came down on hers and held it, warmly. "I know it bothers you the way the Amish treat me, Claire, and your loyalty in that regard is one of many things I love about you. But you have to understand I made the choice to leave after baptism. I knew the repercussions of that decision. You can't hold them accountable for my choice."

She tried to accept his reality, but it was hard. "I guess

I just really struggle with the hypocrisy of a group that will turn the other cheek for someone who commits a horrible crime against them, yet can't do the same for someone who's only so-called crime is becoming a police officer."

"It's not that I became a police officer, Claire. It's that I did it after being baptized."

She stared down at his hand atop hers and took a steadying breath. No amount of bemoaning the Amish rules of excommunication was going to change anything. All she could do was support the people she loved— regardless of where they fell on the Amish/English spectrum.

"So who's next?"

"You mean in terms of the investigation?"

She nodded.

"Besides Miriam, I've got to interview Leroy Beiler and Mike O'Neil."

"When will that be?" she prodded.

"By week's end, I hope. Leroy's wife, Eva, is due to deliver their sixth child anytime now and Ben asked me to wait. Since Leroy isn't the type to cut and run, I agreed. But, as an added precaution, I've asked one officer from each shift to keep watch outside Beiler's farm."

"And Mike?"

"That's one I have to take slowly. His father has a lot of pull in this town."

"I know. I've heard."

He spun the chosen DVD case around in his hands before bringing it to a stop on the edge of his knee. "Is there something you aren't telling me, Claire?"

She felt the hitch to her breath as she looked from the fire he'd carefully set to the DVD he was eager for them to watch together. More than anything, she wanted a date with Jakob, wanted an opportunity to kick back and get to know him even better. But if she shrugged off his question and smiled herself back into date mode, it wouldn't be with the same undivided attention he deserved.

"How much can a former mayor actually sweep under a carpet?"

He stopped, stared at her for what seemed like an eternity, and then finally spoke, his eyes fixed on hers. "What are you trying to get at, Claire?"

More than anything she wished she'd kept her mouth shut. If she had, they'd be cuddled up with one another on the couch by now, laughing at the antics on the screen. But she hadn't. She couldn't . . .

"He knows what happened to Sadie. I'm positive of it," she finally said. "And I think it claws at his soul in much the same way it did Elizabeth's."

"You think *who* knows?" Jakob asked.

"Mike O'Neil."

Jakob looked up at the ceiling and released a pent-up burst of air. "If you're right, his candidacy for mayor is o-v-e-r."

Chapter 20

Claire didn't need history with Annie to know the girl was upset. It was obvious in everything from the not-so-subtle twist of her lips to the heavy-handed way she arranged the latest influx of Amish dolls.

But in true teenager style, each inquiry Claire made was met with the same terse brush-off. After the tenth rote reply, she ushered Annie to a stool.

"Look, kiddo, you keep telling me, 'it is nothing,' but there are twenty brand-new dolls sitting on that shelf over there who would beg to differ." She pointed toward the pyramid shelf Ben had designed especially for the doll display. "They're *soft* dolls, Annie . . . yet, somehow, each and every one you added to the shelf made an actual *thump* sound."

Annie's brown eyes cast downward in shame.

"I'm not trying to guilt you, Annie. I'm not trying to reprimand you, either. I just want you to tell me what's got you so worked up." Claire reached for the second stool and pulled it close enough to perch against its cushioned edge. "Sometimes talking out a problem has a way of making a person feel a little better."

Balling her hands together, Annie bounced them against her lap, the anger she'd displayed all morning clearly at odds with the tears she rushed to wipe away. "I would not know. He does not have time to listen."

The split second of confusion stirred by the teen's words was pushed right out of Claire's thoughts by the memory of a two-day-old discussion. "You're talking about your dat, aren't you?"

For a moment, Annie said nothing, the only indication she'd even heard Claire coming via a watery eye roll. Then, after a second swipe at even more tears, she lowered her nodding head into her hands.

"Aw, sweetie, I'm sure your father isn't trying to hurt you. It's just that he—he has such an important role in your community." She hurried to Annie's side and wrapped her arms around the crying girl. "I'm sure if you just tell him how you're feeling, he will make more of an effort to carve out time for you."

"I *did* try. He did not have time."

Her heart ached for the girl whose shoulders hitched with each sob. "I imagine your mother's passing has been hard on both of you," she mused softly. "I'm sure you both miss her terribly."

"Dat does not speak of Mamm often, but I know he

189

thinks of her as I do," Annie said between sniffs. "I miss her, Claire. But I miss Dat, too. He has not passed but he is busy—too busy for me."

Claire reached out, pushed a wisp of hair off Annie's forehead and back inside her kapp. "I know the days are busy for the Amish, but isn't the time before bed about being together as a family?"

"Yah. But when there is something wrong, when someone has a problem that must be discussed, they come to the bishop, like I told you. Last night was such a night. I wanted to tell him about my job, about the things that I do here, and about you. But when I started to tell, the knocking started.

"First, it was that policeman."

"Policeman?"

"Yah. The one that was Esther's uncle."

"You mean the one that *is* Esther's uncle?" Claire corrected, firmly.

"Yah."

"His name is Jakob and he is a detective with the Heavenly Police Department. He's investigating the discovery of Sadie Lehman's body on the Stoltzfus property last week. He *has* to talk to your father in order to find the truth about what happened. It's his job."

Annie recoiled as if she'd been slapped, prompting Claire to temper the rest of her statement with some much-needed understanding. "Don't get me wrong, I would imagine having to share your parent—particularly your only parent—with other people all the time has to be hard. But maybe if you can find a way to tell him how you're feeling, he will realize you have needs every bit as important as the people in his district."

"I see Dat. I see him troubled by things others do. I do not want to trouble him. I just want to talk to him. I want him to smile at me, to nod his head when I speak of my new job and the customers I have met."

"I get that. But I know Jakob didn't stay all night because he was back at his home by seven o'clock." She heard the slight catch to her voice and knew it was a reflection of the disappointment she still harbored at the way she'd single-handedly derailed her first movie date with Jakob. Pushing aside the avalanche of self-recrimination that was sure to start next, she forced herself back to the topic at hand. "Did you try to talk to him after Jakob left?"

"The next knock came before Jakob left."

"And who was that?" she asked.

Annie's face contorted in disgust. "It was who it always is—The Pest."

She felt awful laughing in the face of Annie's obvious angst, but there wasn't much she could do. The girl's facial expression, theatrical tone change, and chosen nickname for her father's second visitor was nothing if not entertaining. "The Pest?" she repeated.

"Yah," Annie said, firmly. "He is a pest. I do not think a night goes by when he does not knock on our door. If there is a fire, he is the one to tell. If there is a new baby, he is the one to tell. If someone is to be shunned, he is the one to tell."

"The English have folks like that, too, Annie. Only we call them busybodies."

191

"Mamm used to say it started when Leroy and Eva were courting. Back then, he came with only good news. After the wedding, he would bring bad news, too."

"Wait. I don't understand what this person has to do with your sister and her husband."

"The Pest is Leroy's dat."

"Okay . . ."

"Leroy courted my sister. Leroy's dat courted my dat."

"And when they got married?" Claire prompted, intrigued.

"He is at my house each night as if he is my family. As if he is my dat's"—Annie's brow scrunched—"oh, I cannot think of the word right now . . ."

"Assistant?"

"Yah!" Annie jumped down off her stool and smoothed her hand down the front of her aproned mint green dress. "Last night he came to tell Dat Eva's baby would be here soon. She is my sister and Dat's daughter. Of course we know the baby will be here soon."

"Sounds like your nickname for Mr. Beiler fits."

Annie wrung her hands together and then wandered over to the register, the slump of her shoulders and the absentminded way she began to trace the number on each button a clear indication her sudden swell of irritation was taking a backseat to sadness once again. "I want people to see him as my dat. Not someone . . . *special*."

"Have you ever talked to your sister about this? Since she, too, grew up a bishop's daughter?"

"Dat did not become bishop until Eva was baptized. After that, she was courted by Leroy. Mamm was alive, too."

Claire nodded. "So then your sister had lots of people to talk to in her life, yes?"

"Yah." Annie turned from the register and sighed. "For me, there is no Mamm, anymore. I am not court-ing . . . yet. Eva is busy with her own family. I only have Dat and Dat's many knocks."

Claire held her hand out and waited for Annie to take it. "I know this is only your third day here, but you have *me* now, too. I'm happy to listen whenever you want."

The bell over the door jingled loudly and prevented Annie from putting any words to the resurgence of tears she valiantly tried to blink away. Instead, she offered a smile constructed from trembling lips that vanished from her face the moment she looked past Claire.

Confused, Claire turned toward the door, the five foot eight Amish man standing just beneath the string of bells, unfamiliar. "Good morning. Welcome to Heavenly Trea-sures. How can I help—"

Annie stepped around Claire, clearly fidgeting as she did. "Mr. Beiler," Annie croaked. "Is—is everything . . . okay?"

"It is time."

"Why did my dat not come?"

"I told him I would collect you and bring you."

"I will get my things." Annie glanced at Claire over her shoulder with large, unreadable eyes. "Claire, I must go. My sister is to have her sixth child and I must help. Mr. Beiler will take me in his buggy."

Claire nodded politely at the man, then brought her lips within whisper distance of Annie's ears. "I take it that's The Pest?"

Annie nodded.

"Are you okay going with him?"

A momentary hesitation was followed by another, slower nod as Annie returned to the counter and the lunch pail housed on the other side. "Eva needs me. I must go."

"Okay, kiddo. Take as long as you need and just come back when you're ready, okay?"

Annie set the pail on top of the stool and came around the counter to accept Claire's waiting hug. "I hope you do not give this job to another person. I will work hard when I come back."

Claire stepped back, tapped a finger to Annie's nose, and offered what she hoped was a reassuring smile. "Don't you worry, Annie, this job is yours."

And then Annie was gone, her ankle-high lace-up boots barely making a sound as she followed Leroy Beiler's father out the door. Claire moved closer to the front window and watched as Annie climbed onto the seat of the waiting buggy.

"Claire?"

Startled, she spun around to find Ben and Eli's sister, Ruth, standing in the back of the shop with a plated brownie in her hand.

"I did not mean to frighten you, Claire. I just wanted to bring you this brownie before more customers come."

Claire tried to quiet the answering rumble of her stomach with her hand but it was too late. Ruth had heard the ruckus from across the room.

"Perhaps I should have brought a sandwich, too?" Ruth added.

"No, I brought something to . . ." Her reply fizzled

away as she glanced toward the counter and the simple metal pail sitting atop the stool. "Oh no . . ." She trotted over to the stool, grabbed the lunch pail, and ran back to the front window, only to find Annie and The Pest gone.

"Is something wrong?"

She looked down at the pail and then over her shoulder at Ruth. "It's not a big deal, I guess. But Annie Hershberger just left to help her sister with the arrival of baby number six and she forgot her lunch."

"I could bring it to her when I close. Or, perhaps, Eli could bring it to her after his noon visit."

She considered both options and subsequently discarded each one. "Thank you, Ruth, but I think I will bring it out to Annie, myself. That way I can say hi and make sure she's doing okay."

Chapter 21

Claire lowered her window halfway and reveled in the promise of spring and its not-so-gentle response to Sunday's late-season snowfall. All around her, snow was continuing to melt—on the cobblestoned street that was Lighted Way, on the gravel road that linked the popular thoroughfare with the Amish side of town, and on the two-inch-high stalks that marched like soldiers across the fields to her left and to her right.

She knew, from her first spring in Heavenly, that the yellowish-brownish stalks would soon turn a vibrant green as the wheat, rye, and barley crops began to really grow. Come June, soybeans, oats, and tobacco would be planted in neighboring fields to ensure maturity in time for the harvest season.

Sometimes, when she drove along these roads, she couldn't help but feel as if the pages of her calendar had drifted backward a hundred years to a simpler time when life was governed by people rather than technology. It was as if the world was passing the Amish by in so many ways, yet they didn't care.

For them, an open-top wagon or a gray-topped buggy was all the transportation they desired.

For them, an inexpensive bolt of durable fabric and a sewing machine were all they needed to clothe their families.

For them, communication with friends and family came not through social media and cell phones but, rather, with face-to-face visits.

For them, mates weren't found with the help of Internet dating sites. No, they were found across the room at church, or during a Sunday afternoon hymn sing or volleyball game.

For them, helping a neighbor through tragedy meant rolling up one's sleeves and doing whatever it took to get someone back on their feet.

She turned the wheel with the subtle curve of the road, her thoughts mentally ticking off the family name of each farm that she passed—King, Lapp, Stoltzfus, Lehman . . .

Lehman. Sadie Lehman.

Ever since Jakob had placed odds on the discovered remains being those of Sadie Lehman, Claire found herself trying to put faces to the young woman's parents—Zebediah and Waneta. She vaguely remembered their names from Esther's wedding to Eli, but which couple they'd been out of the nearly two hundred and fifty people she'd been introduced to that day, was the true question.

Yet, somewhere in her not-so-good-with-names-and-faces memory, snatches of one woman's face kept resurfacing each night as Claire laid her head down to sleep. The woman she recalled had been nice—friendly, even. But her eyes had stood out to Claire for their hollowness—as if whatever joy could be mustered to create a smile, burned out before it could ever reach her eyes.

She tried to imagine the other people she'd met that day, tried to see if anyone else jumped out as a possibility, but she always came back to the same woman.

And it made sense.

Claire didn't need to be a mother to be able to imagine the torment one would feel if their child simply up and disappeared without a single word. It was an experience she prayed she'd never have to know, and hoped no one would ever have to face again.

But even worse than having that child run off, would be learning that they'd never really run off at all. That the whole time you were thinking one thing, your child's body was buried within sight of your kitchen window. Suddenly, any hope you might have had for a reunion was gone, ripped from your world along with the good-bye you never got to say.

It was too much to even try to fathom. Too painful to try to put herself in Waneta Lehman's shoes. All she could do was hope for truth and justice for Sadie and her family . . .

She passed her favorite turnoff in all of Heavenly and continued on even as her thoughts opted to take the turn, climb the hill, cross the covered bridge, and settle on a particular rock with its breathtaking view of Heavenly's

Amish country below and its promise of a brilliant star-filled sky above.

At the next dirt-and-gravel driveway, she continued ticking off land in the order Ruth had schooled her—Hochstetler, another Lapp, Hershberger, heavily wooded area, and, finally, Beiler. If she kept going, she knew she'd pass the large wooded area that separated the Beilers from the first of three farms owned by a Miller on the remaining stretch of Amish road.

Ben's parents and sister . . .

Ben, himself . . .

And, eventually, Eli and Esther . . .

Other farmers were sprinkled around between them, but those farms belonged to families she didn't know, with names she hoped to learn in the years to come.

She veered onto the shoulder to allow a rare car to pass and then turned up the lane that would lead to Leroy and Eva Beiler's farmhouse. To her right stood a large barn open to the mild day. She could just make out a horse in one stall and a pair of barn cats meandering out of another.

Up ahead, and to the left, was the farmhouse, its two-story white exterior like so many of its neighbors to the east and west. Any notion the home might be owned by an English farmer was quickly squelched by the presence of dark green shades in the windows, a pair of clothes-lines, and the trio of buggies parked under a grove of trees.

She slowed to a stop, shifted into park, and cut the engine. Then, armed with Annie's forgotten lunch pail, she stepped from the car and headed toward the farmhouse and the five hatted towheads that stretched across the front stoop like a second set of stairs.

"Mamm just had a baby," said the tallest step—a boy Claire guessed to be about ten, maybe eleven. "His name is Melvin, Dat says."

"How exciting!" Claire stopped at the base of the steps and smiled at each one of the children, with the youngest of the group—a girl—not much more than two years old. "And who are all of you?"

The oldest spoke again, his finger moving from himself to the rest of the stair steps that were his brothers and sisters. "I'm Samuel. That's Mark, Joshua, Mary, and Katie at the end."

"It's very nice to meet all of you. I'm Claire."

Mary, the second to last stair step and the one Claire guessed to be about four, pointed at Claire's left hand, her eyes wide. "That is Annie's pail."

"You're exactly right, Mary. She left it at work and I came out here to make sure she gets it back."

"Annie makes good lunch!"

Claire shifted her focus to the right and the little boy with the gap-toothed smile. "You know what? I like her chicken, myself."

"Yum! Yum!"

She took a step back and viewed the children as a whole, their wide eyes, cheerful smiles, and plain dress stirring something inside her she couldn't deny. One day, when the time was right, she wanted children of her own. They might not dress like the youngsters in front of her, but she'd do everything in her power to make sure they were just as sweet and happy.

"What are you five talking about out here?" Annie pushed open the screen door, stepped onto the porch, and stopped. "Oh. Claire. I did not hear you come."

The teenager scurried across the porch to the top step, with a brown sack in one hand and a pair of baby bottles in the other. Crouching down, she handed the sack to Samuel and the bottles to Mark. "Samuel, take Joshua and Katie with you to feed the chickens. Mark, you take Mary to feed the new calves." Then, looking up, she flashed a half smile at Claire. "One of Leroy's cows and one of his horses just had babies this morning, too. All boys. All will stay except the calf. He will be going to another farm soon."

"They don't keep male cows?"

Annie laughed. "Not on a dairy farm, they don't," she said before officially shooing her nieces and nephews in the direction of the barn on the other side of the driveway. When they were out of sight, she sunk onto the step previously inhabited by the children and invited Claire to sit, too. "I see that you brought my lunch pail. That was not necessary."

Claire placed the pail between them and gave in to a laugh of her own. "If I hadn't, I wouldn't have had the pleasure of meeting your sister's adorable crew."

"You should see the new one. He looks just like the rest of them."

"His name is Melvin, right?"

Annie nodded in surprise. "How did you know?"

"Samuel filled me in." She closed her eyes for a moment and drank in Katie's and Mary's squeals as they helped feed their assigned animals alongside their older brothers. Something about their innocent joy was mesmerizing. "So how does it feel to be an aunt for the sixth time?"

"Melvin makes twenty for me."

"Tw-twenty?" she stammered in disbelief. "Are you serious?"

"Yah. My brother Luke has seven. My other brother John also has seven."

"Wow," she whispered. "Just wow."

"I do not see Luke and John and their families often. They live fifty miles from here. But when we are all together, there is much noise."

"It sounds wonderful." And it did. Especially to someone like Claire who'd been an only child with older parents. "So how is Eva doing? Everything go okay with her?"

Annie reached up, loosened the ties on her kapp, and leaned against the corner of the closest upright. "She makes it all look so easy—giving birth, raising children, helping Leroy. She is a good mamm."

Claire studied her young friend closely, the uncertainty she saw on Annie's face understandable. "You still have time, you know. You're only sixteen."

"I do not know if I will do a good job. Eva had Mamm to show her how. I do not."

Claire reached across the pail and gently tugged one of Annie's dangling kapp strings. "Hey, of course you'll do a great job when the time comes . . . how could you not?"

When Annie said nothing, Claire continued. "I saw the way those kids looked at you just now when you came out. They adore you—the *you* that you are because of your mamm, your dat, your sister, your brothers, and *yourself*."

Annie lifted her eyes to meet Claire's. "You think that is so?"

"I *know* it's so."

The screen door banged shut behind them and Annie leapt to her feet with such force the lunch pail tumbled down the steps to the dirt path below.

"I'll get—"

"Tie your kapp, Annie!"

Claire missed the handle of the pail as she turned toward the voice behind Annie's initial reaction and the subsequent shame with which the teenager now rushed to fix her infraction. There, standing not more than three feet away, was the same bearded man who'd collected Annie from Heavenly Treasures earlier that day, his emotionless expression on the heels of becoming a grandfather again stoking a sudden and irrefutable protective streak inside Claire.

"She didn't untie it, she just loosened it."

Annie waved Claire off only to be reprimanded for that, as well.

"Respect your elders!"

The screen door banged shut a second time to reveal a taller, younger version of the man still staring at Annie. "Dat, I will take care of Annie. It is time for you to check on Mamm and bring her news of Melvin."

"I must first stop at the bishop's home." The older man lifted a single finger in Annie's direction as he passed her on the steps, the silent gesture and its accompanying glare of disapproval making the reason for his stated itinerary change clear.

When his feet left the last step, he turned toward his

buggy, climbed onto his seat, and urged his horse down the driveway and onto the main road. Claire continued to stare at the empty driveway left in the elder Beiler's wake for several long minutes, the residual fallout from the man's lingering presence still heavy in the air.

"Leroy, I am sorry. I did not mean to loosen my kapp in front of your dat," Annie pleaded.

Claire looked back onto the porch and allowed herself a moment to soak up Annie's brother-in-law. Like the elder Beiler, Leroy's face was narrow, his brows thick. The shape and color of their eyes was the same, too, but, thankfully, in Leroy's she saw only kindness.

"Do not worry, Annie. Your dat will understand. It has been a busy day for you, for Eva, for all of us."

"What on earth was that about?" Claire finally asked as she looked from Annie to Leroy and back again, the cessation of happy squeals from the barn making the thump of her heart sound even louder in her ears.

Leroy stepped forward and extended his hand to Claire. "I feel as if we have met before but, in case I am wrong, I am Leroy Beiler."

"And I'm Claire Weatherly."

"Claire Weatherly," he repeated slowly. "You are the Englisher who was at Eli and Esther's wedding, yah?"

"Yes, that was me."

"We work together in town," Annie interjected in a tone that could best be described as wounded. "It is Claire's shop—Heavenly Treasures—where I work. I left my lunch pail at the shop this morning when your dat came to fetch me. Claire was kind to bring it to me."

"Can I ask why your father was so hard on Annie just

now?" she asked, determined to understand. "I know her strings are to be tied, but his anger was over the top."

Annie's head sunk low, her voice still lower. "Please, Claire. It is I who was wrong."

"You loosened your kapp strings, Annie . . . you didn't hurt someone or steal something."

"Kapp strings are to be tied, Miss Weatherly," Leroy explained, not unkindly. "My father wants Amish to be Amish."

She assembled a protest in her thoughts but stopped short of verbalizing it aloud. Arguing with the man's son accomplished nothing. Still, it couldn't hurt to let Leroy know how she felt about Annie. "Annie has worked with me just three days now and she is a hard worker. Perhaps I should make a point of stopping by her father's home to tell him *that*."

"I am sure Atlee would welcome such news," Leroy said as he crossed to the step and sat down. "She was a big help with Eva today, as well."

"The children are in the barn looking after the chickens and the calves. I should go inside and check on Eva and the baby, see that they do not need anything before I go home." Annie stepped off the porch, lifted her lunch pail from the ground, and then retraced her steps, continuing on to the door before stopping to offer Claire a half nod, half smile. "Thank you for bringing this to me. I am sorry I was so forgetful."

"It's fine, Annie. You had a lot on your mind when you left."

She saw the answering flash of relief and gratitude that crossed Annie's face but knew it stopped short of being able to undo the hurt and worry ushered in by Leroy's father.

"Annie will be fine," Leroy said in a quiet voice when they were alone on the porch. "My father only seeks to teach."

"There are far more patient ways to teach than yelling." She pulled her gloves from the pockets of her coat and slipped them on in an effort to combat the evening chill that was officially beginning to roll in.

"And it is with that patience that I teach my own children. But I am not my father and it is not for me to judge his ways."

"He isn't Annie's father, either," Claire reminded him before opting to change the subject. "I met your little ones when I arrived. They are adorable."

"Do you have children, Miss Weatherly?"

"No. But one day, I hope."

"Yah."

If he thought it was odd that she continued to stand there long after Annie had taken her lunch pail and gone inside, it didn't show. Instead, there was something so natural about his ensuing silence that made her feel almost welcome.

"Sometimes, when I look at your world, I see such peace and joy that I'm almost envious. But then, I realize that the Amish world is not immune to sadness, either. Bad things happen here, too."

"I do not understand."

"Here, in your home, there is much happiness over a new life. Yet, just five farms from here, Waneta and Zebediah Lehman mourn the loss of *their* child—a child that has likely been dead for more years than Annie has been alive." She cast a glance in Leroy's direction and tried to make out his expression in the gathering dusk. "And they didn't even *know*."

The steps creaked beneath Leroy's body as he shifted forward, his hands leaving his beard in favor of fidgeting with his suspenders.

"I can't imagine that, can you?" she continued, casting the net still further.

The shifting and fidgeting continued for several long minutes before Leroy finally spoke, his words, his tone, his meaning rendering her coat and gloves completely ineffectual. "Back then, as Dat's son, I did not want to imagine. But now that I am a dat, too, I cannot stop."

She stared at him, waiting.

For what, though, she wasn't exactly sure.

"I should have listened to Elizabeth." He struggled to his feet, calling for his children as he did. When they flocked to his side, he herded them up the steps and toward the door, glancing back at Claire as they disappeared inside. "We *all* should have listened to Elizabeth."

Chapter 22

She was just filling the coin slots in the register when she heard the jingle of the front door and the footsteps she'd all but memorized over the past few months. It was a sound she'd come to equate with the kind of inner happiness capable of transcending even the craziest of days.

"Good morning, Claire. I got your message just now and figured I'd stop by before the day got away with me." Jakob met her in the middle of the room and pulled her in for a warm hug and an even warmer kiss. When he stepped back, he gave her a stern, yet playful look. "That said, you *can* call my cell phone, you know . . ."

"It wasn't really a personal call."

"Should I be crushed?" he teased before pausing to take in her powder blue blouse and gray dress slacks. "Wow. You look great."

"Don't look too hard, kind sir. Makeup can only go so far in covering a lousy night's sleep."

Instantly, all sense of humor disappeared from his eyes, claiming his dimples as collateral as it did. "Is everything okay?"

"Define 'everything.'"

"You . . . Diane . . ."

She nodded quickly then wandered over to the front window and its view of the still-quiet morning on Lighted Way. "I'm fine, Jakob. So is Diane."

"Then what's up?"

She took a moment to compose her thoughts and Leroy's words in such a way as to not waste too much of the detective's time—time she knew was about to be stretched in far too many directions.

"Claire?" he asked as he inched in her direction. "Did I do something wrong?"

"I was out at Leroy Beiler's house last night."

His right eyebrow lifted. "Oh?"

"Eva had her baby yesterday afternoon and I had to bring something out to her sister, Annie." She took a deep breath and counted to ten in her head, the information she'd all but verified destined to shake Heavenly's Amish community to its very core. "After Annie went inside to look in on Eva, Leroy and I started talking."

When Jakob said nothing, she got to the only point that truly mattered. "I mentioned Sadie. Or, to be more specific, the worry her parents must have felt over their daughter's unexpected disappearance, and the absolute anguish they must feel *now* to realize she's been dead this whole time."

"And?"

"He definitely knows what happened to Sadie."

His eyes bored into hers as he took hold of her hands and held them tightly. "Did he give you details?"

"No, but—"

"I will tell now . . . as I should have told nineteen years ago."

Pulling her hands from Jakob's loosening grasp, she turned to see Leroy Beiler standing just below the string of bells neither she nor Jakob had heard.

"Le-Leroy?" she faltered. "I didn't hear you come in."

"Leroy, it's been a long time." Jakob stepped around Claire and extended his hand to the Amish man. "In fact, when I left, I think you were, what, seventeen? Maybe, eighteen?"

"I know that I was old enough to know right from wrong. Still, I chose to do wrong."

Jakob responded with a slow but deliberate nod. "Why don't we step across the street to my office? We can talk in private, there."

"I would like to speak my piece here, in front of Miss Weatherly." Leroy took three more steps into the shop and then stopped as if he'd stepped in glue. "Fourteen years ago, someone wanted me to speak the truth, but I did not. Now, because of Miss Weatherly, I am ready to do what I should have done then."

"Are you talking about Elizabeth Troyer—I mean, Elizabeth Miller?" Jakob pulled a small notebook and pen from his shirt pocket and prepared to record Leroy's answers to the first of many questions that were sure to follow.

Claire listened for the answer even as she made a mental note of the remaining twenty minutes that stood between them and the standard opening time noted on the shop's front door.

"Yah."

"This involves Sadie Lehman, doesn't it?" Jakob asked.

"Yah."

"Do you know who killed her?"

"It was all of us."

Jakob dropped his pen atop his notebook and held up his hand. "Wait. I have to encourage you to get an attorney before you say anything else."

"I do not need an attorney. It is time to speak a truth God already knows."

"Are you sure?"

"Yah."

Jakob exhaled against his open palm before letting it slip back down to reclaim his pen. "Why did you kill her?"

Leroy's face paled. "We did not set out to kill Sadie. One minute we were talking, laughing, and . . . some of us were drinking."

"Where did you get the alcohol?" Jakob queried.

"I do not know. It was just on the rocks below the bridge when we met there."

"Who is 'we'?" Claire asked before rushing to apologize for her interruption.

"There were five. Sadie, Elizabeth, Miriam, me, and Michael—an Englisher." Leroy stood ramrod straight as he traveled back nineteen years with Jakob and Claire as his captive companions. "Sadie and Elizabeth did not drink."

"You mean that night?"

"They did not drink at all."

Jakob filled the first two pages of his pad with notes and then flipped to a new page. "Why were they with you if they weren't drinking?"

"Miriam made them feel bad if they did not come."

"Feel bad?" Claire repeated.

"She told them they had to go, that it was part of Rumspringa to go to the bridge. When that did not work, she would tell Sadie that Michael liked her."

Jakob's head snapped up. "Michael and Sadie had a relationship?"

"I do not think so. But it made her smile to hear Miriam speak such things."

"What happened next? After the five of you were"—Jakob flipped back to the first page and read what he'd written—"talking and laughing . . . and you, Miriam, and Michael were drinking?"

"Michael pulled out a bag of candy and passed it around the circle. We all took some."

"All?" Jakob clarified.

Leroy nodded. "Yah. All."

"Go on . . ."

"We sat under the bridge, eating candy and talking. Miriam talked silly and did not make sense in the way drink can do. I talked about Eva and how I was going to marry her one day. Elizabeth suggested ways I could get Eva to notice me. The Englisher tapped his foot against the bridge and sang songs with the radio. Some of the songs I liked, some I did not."

Claire silently ran through the names Leroy had mentioned and came up with the only one he hadn't. "And Sadie? What was she doing?"

"She tried to tap her hand to the music, too, but she did not know the songs. After one or two, she stopped and just ate candy." Leroy wiped a bead of sweat from his brow and continued, his voice raspy, yet firm. "Soon, I heard a thump. Then scream."

"Who screamed?" Jakob asked.

"Elizabeth."

"Why did Elizabeth scream?"

"Sadie was on the ground and touching *here*"—Leroy demonstrated on his own throat. "She did not speak. She did not cry. She just closed her eyes."

"Did anyone touch her?"

Leroy looked at Claire. "When she closed her eyes, yes. Before she closed her eyes, no."

"Then what?"

"Michael, the English one, put his ear to Sadie's mouth. Then he put his hands here"—again, he demonstrated, but this time he pointed to his chest instead of his throat. "He pushed and pushed. Miriam tried to make Elizabeth stop crying but she could not."

"And you?" Jakob prodded. "What did you do, Leroy?"

Leroy's head dipped downward until all Claire could see of him was the top of his hat, his beard, and his body. His face was hidden in shame. "I did nothing. I did not help, I did not pray, I did not comfort. I just stood and watched."

"Why didn't you do anything, Leroy?"

Slowly, solemnly, the Amish man lifted his chin once again, his gaze finding and holding Jakob's with palpable sadness. "I was afraid."

Jakob ditched his pen on top of his notepad and reached into the front pocket of his pants to reveal a buzzing cell phone inside his palm. A quick check of the screen had him stepping away from Claire and Leroy to take the call.

While they waited for the detective to return, she tried to think of something to say to ease Leroy's pain, but everything she came up with seemed grossly inadequate. Fortunately, though, Leroy took care of the silence.

"Last night, you spoke of Zebediah and Waneta. As a young boy, I did not know what it meant to be a parent. I did not think of the hurt such a secret would bring them. I worried only about what my dat would say.

"Today, I do not worry about what Dat will say. I worry only about Eva and the children and how they will get along when I am in English jail."

Jakob came up behind them, his phone no longer in his hand. "That was the station just now. Seems Miriam and Bishop Hershberger are waiting for me in my office." He took a moment to give Leroy a thorough once-over and then placed his notepad and pen back into his shirt pocket. "I'm going to have to ask you to come with me, Leroy. I suspect I'm going to have a lot more questions after I speak with Miriam."

"Atlee is there?"

At Jakob's nod, Leroy closed his eyes just long enough to take in a fortifying breath and straighten his hat. When he was done, he returned Jakob's nod, gave a second and slower one to Claire, and then followed the detective to the door.

To see a buggy parked along Lighted Way wasn't really something out of the ordinary. In fact, with the exception of Sundays, and a smattering of Tuesdays and Thursdays during wedding season, their presence was as normal for the tourist-friendly shopping district as their more modern counterparts.

Some of the buggies were owned by Claire's fellow shopkeepers, others by those who supplied the English-owned shops with authentic Amish food and wares. And, from time to time, they belonged to shoppers themselves, with Amish women purchasing sewing supplies at the Heavenly Stitchery, or their husbands picking up a needed implement at Glick's Tools 'n More.

But as surely as the hatted and unhatted commingled along Lighted Way on a near-daily basis, there was one building the Amish avoided at all costs.

From the exterior, the Heavenly Police Department looked like every other shop and restaurant that lined the busy street. It boasted the same clapboard siding, the same wide front porch, and the same tastefully written sign above the front door. But, inside, there were no Amish. No Amish in the waiting room, no Amish talking to the dispatcher, no Amish arguing a speeding ticket with the chief.

The reason for the group's aversion to men in blue was hard to nail down completely, but from what Claire had been able to gather from her aunt and Jakob, it came down to their refusal to use force in any situation. For the deeply religious group, those who employed violence under any circumstance refuted Jesus's command to turn the other cheek. As a result, even when victims of crime themselves, the Amish tended to steer clear of the police—opting to let things like burglary, road rage, and even home invasions go unreported.

So even though she knew the why behind the two buggies parked outside the station, Claire still couldn't help making periodic checks out her window. On the one hand, she was glad Miriam and Leroy were finally ready to talk about what happened to Sadie Lehman nineteen years earlier. On the other hand, though, she couldn't keep from thinking about all the new casualties from such a confession.

In particular, the five smiling towheads who'd claimed her heart the previous evening—five towheads and one brand-new baby who needed their father.

Although she knew very little about Miriam Stoltzfus, she did know the woman was a parent—one who, by all accounts, had emerged from her own rebellious Rum-springa stage a different person.

She stepped to the left in the hopes of gaining a slightly better view of the bishop's buggy but it made no difference. An empty buggy was an empty buggy. Changing positions didn't change that fact any more than watching a pot made it boil faster.

Whatever was happening inside the walls of the

Heavenly Police Department would remain a mystery whether she lingered at the window doing nothing or actually made an effort to cross off a few tasks on her daily to-do list. However, if she focused on the latter, time would go faster and she'd have less hanging over her head when Jakob finally did break free of his interrogation.

Her mind made up, she crossed to the clipboard she'd all but ignored to that point and reacquainted herself with the first two tasks . . .

1. Create a new themed sale event for both April and May.

2. Make a list of needed inventory for Martha, Esther, and Eli.

Making a mental note to pick Annie's brain for ideas on the first, Claire moved on to the second task, the first two items for Martha's list the same as always—painted milk cans and painted wooden spoons. Only this time, she'd specifically request spring and summer scenes for both.

For Esther's list, there were more Amish dolls, simple shawls in pastel colors, and the wildly popular place mats Claire was having difficulty keeping stocked.

Eli's list was easy, too. Basically anything he crafted out of wood was a veritable hit, with children's footstools and fold-up booster seats beginning to rival the always-sought-after blanket chests.

"It's three minutes past five, Claire. Mind if I steal the fourth?"

She smiled at the familiar voice even as she continued

to write one more item for Eli. "You can have the fourth *and* the fifth, Howard. But that's just because I like you so much."

"The feeling is mutual." The balding and plump hardware store owner ambled through the doorway of the gift shop and made a beeline for the front window. "Did you happen to notice the pair of buggies that have been parked outside the police station since before noon?"

She considered feigning surprise but knew it wouldn't fly around the self-proclaimed, yet lovable busybody of Lighted Way. "I did."

"Did you happen to see who got out of them?"

Since she hadn't witnessed the disembarking of the buggies at their current location, she was able to shake her head without too much guilt.

"I couldn't make out who the tall man from the second buggy was, or even the woman in the first one . . . but I'm certain that the man who escorted her inside was Bishop Hershberger." Howard patted his stomach and nodded as if he was in conversation with himself as much as Claire. "Now, I'm not a betting man, but if I was, I'd bet it has something to do with those bones they found out at Jeremiah Stoltzfus's place last week."

"Oh?" She closed the space between them with several easy strides. When she reached the window, she satisfied her own continued curiosity by taking another look. Sure enough, both buggies remained. "What makes you think that?"

"I always thought something was fishy about that young girl's sudden disappearance. I didn't know the Lehmans personally, but I used to see them around from time to time. That little girl never seemed the type to just take off on her mamma like that." He clicked his tongue against his teeth and peered at Claire atop the reading glasses he'd failed to remove from the bridge of his nose when he left his shop. "No, sirree. Those two were close. Like two peas in a pod, if you ask me."

"If that was the case, why didn't the cops follow it up back then?"

"Because her parents never filed a missing person report. They just took the word of Sadie's friends when they said she ran off to be a star." Howard lifted his chin, took off his glasses, and scrunched his brow in disbelief. "Me? I never quite bought it. Just like I never bought that whole story about the way *his*"—he hooked his thumb over his shoulder—"wife died, neither."

She took a moment to catch up with Howard's train of thought but realized, fairly quickly, she'd gotten off a stop or two prematurely. "I'm sorry, Howard, I really am. I was following you all along until the last sentence or two. Whose wife are you talking about and what story are you not buying about her death?"

Again he used his thumb to point over his shoulder, only this time he clarified its target with words. "You know, Ruth's brother."

She drew back, both startled and confused. "You mean, *Ben*?"

"Yes, yes, Benjamin. How could I forget?" He brushed away the question with his hand. "I'll tell you, Claire, this getting-old stuff is for the birds—the birds, I tell you!

"My latest trick in the forgetful department is to come up with a great idea for a do-it-yourself project at the store and then forget what it is before I've finished gathering up all the necessary tools." Howard's belly jiggled as he laughed at himself. "Before long, I'll be tying a to-do list around my finger so I don't forget the supplies I need for the project I can't remember I'm doing anyway."

This time it was Claire's turn to wave a hand or two in the air. "Wait. Go back to what we were just talking about."

"Tools?"

Worry pushed aside curiosity only to recede as the jovial man winked and laughed. "Gotcha, didn't I?"

She resisted the urge to roll her eyes and, instead, found the smile she knew he needed for his comical efforts. "You got me, alright."

"Okay, so what *were* we really talking about?" He rubbed the day-old stubble on his rounded chin, taking one last look out Claire's front window as he did. "That's right—Benjamin Miller's late wife. I think her name was . . ."

When it became apparent he wasn't going to get to the point without filling in the blank, she supplied the sought-after name. "Elizabeth."

At his nod, she moved on. "You don't believe she was killed by a stray bullet from a hunting rifle?"

"I believe *half* of that statement." Howard surveyed the various shelves and displays he could see from his vantage point before eyeing the clock on the wall above the register and subsequently hightailing it back across the shop. "I've got to go, Claire. The missus will have my head if I'm not home when her famous chicken potpie comes out of the oven."

She chased after him, determined to get at least some

sort of clarification for his comment about Elizabeth. "Please. Before you go . . . Which half of my statement about Elizabeth *do* you believe?"

"That she was killed by a hunting rifle."

"And the part you *don't* believe?"

"That it was a stray bullet."

Chapter 23

"You were awful quiet at dinner tonight, dear. Is everything okay?"

Claire placed a medium-sized log into the fireplace and watched as its initial catch point grew into a roaring fire capable of heating the parlor and the entryway with ease. Yet, even as she sat there, waiting, she knew its warmth didn't stand a chance against the chill Howard's parting words had ushered into her heart more than three hours earlier.

She'd wanted nothing more than to convince her fellow shopkeeper to stay long enough to explain his troubling hypothesis. But the promise of Mrs. Glick's chicken potpie had proven to be an impossible challenger in the fight for Howard's time and attention.

Now, all she could do was replay his words in her mind and wonder at the basis on which they'd been formed.

Was he right?

Had Ben's wife, Elizabeth, been murdered?

And if so, by whom?

They were the same three questions that accompanied her on her walk home from work, as she helped prepare dinner in the kitchen, as she served guests in the dining room, and at that very moment as she contemplated adding a second piece of wood to the hungry flames.

"Claire?"

She glanced over her shoulder and then stood, her aunt's sudden appearance making it easy to postpone her decision about the additional log. "Have the guests all retired to their rooms for the evening?"

"They have."

"This new round of folks seems to be very nice." Claire crossed to the couch and the paperback mystery she'd placed at her spot before tending the fire. "They sure hit it off with one another, wouldn't you say?"

"I was a bit more focused on you this evening."

"Me?" She dropped onto her favorite corner of the couch and nestled in with her book. "Why? What did I do?"

"It's not what you *did*, dear, it's what you *didn't* do." Diane stood with her back to the room's main window and its view of the moon-drenched Amish countryside, an uncharacteristic frown on her gently lined face.

"Did I forget a side dish?" Claire asked.

"No."

She gripped the edge of her still-closed book and leaned forward. "Oh no, please tell me I didn't forget someone's food allergy . . ."

"No. You did everything right concerning dinner and the guests."

Relief allowed her to sink back against the corner of the couch and release a much-needed breath. "Phew. Okay, so what *didn't* I do?"

"You didn't speak more than a few monosyllables here and a few monosyllables there while we were preparing the meal and cleaning it up." Diane swiveled to the left just long enough to pull the heavy drapes closed on yet another day. "And that's not like you."

"Are you saying I talk too much on a normal basis?" she teased.

"I'm saying I missed hearing about your day and the customers who came into the shop." Diane came around the back of her favorite lounge chair and slowly lowered herself onto the seat. "You didn't talk about Annie, or the smells coming out of Ruth's bake shop, or any of your usual topics."

Claire freed the book from her hands and allowed her head to loll against the back of the couch as she contemplated the best way to address her aunt's obvious concern. "I'm fine. Truly. I guess it's just one of those days when you live inside your head more than you probably should."

"You're not thinking about Peter, are you?"

She smacked a hand over her answering snort and then laughed away her aunt's question. "No. It's become a rare day when I actually think of that man."

"Good." Diane scooted back on her chair until she was sitting tall with her feet outstretched. "Is Annie working out okay?"

"Annie is working out marvelously. I couldn't ask for

better, actually. But she wasn't around for the bulk of yesterday or any of today."

"Oh? Why not?"

"Her sister, Eva, had her sixth child yesterday afternoon and Annie was summoned by Leroy's father to help with the delivery and the other children."

"Oh . . . how wonderful," Diane exclaimed. "What did she have?"

"A little boy. His name is Melvin." She pulled her legs onto the couch and tucked them into the narrow space between the back end of the cushions and the frame. "I didn't see the baby, but I did get to see Annie and the other five children. They were so sweet and smiley."

"Which is exactly how I picture the little ones you and Jakob will have."

"Diane!" she scolded. "Jakob and I are just barely dating. You can't keep talking like that."

"Of course I can." Diane stuck out her tongue in playful defiance and then got back to the original topic. "Has Josiah softened any as a grandfather?"

Still distracted by her aunt's prediction for her future with Jakob, Claire caught only bits and pieces of the question lobbed in her direction. "I'm sorry, you asked something about a Josiah? I don't know anyone by that name."

"Oh, I just assumed, because you mentioned him, that you'd actually met Leroy's father." Diane wiggled her socked toes to the front and back in what was destined to be the first of many stretching exercises the woman did on a near-nightly basis.

"Wait. I did meet Leroy's father, I just didn't know his

first name." She thought back to the previous evening and the man's harsh treatment of one very tired teenager, her head beginning to shake in disgust before she'd even completed her mental tour of the memory. "That man is rather wound up."

Diane moved on to her ankles by tilting her feet up and back and all around. "So I guess the answer to my question about whether he's softened as a grandfather would be no, then . . ."

"*Soft* is not a word I'd use in any form where Josiah Beiler is concerned, that's for sure. But, then again, in all fairness, I never actually saw him interact with the little ones . . . just Annie." She bent her head forward just enough to check the status of the fire and then leaned it back against the couch once again. "You should have heard the way he railed at her for loosening her kapp strings, Aunt Diane. You'd have thought she'd done something truly awful if you'd been within earshot to hear his tone."

"That's Josiah for you. He's fanatical about being Amish. Just ask Jakob."

She snapped her head off the couch and turned to face Diane. "Jakob? What does Jakob have to do with Josiah Beiler?"

Diane lifted her left leg up, then her right leg, the agile way in which she did more than a little impressive. "From the way I understand it, Josiah Beiler is the one who led the charge against Jakob seventeen years ago."

"You mean when he left to become a police officer?"

"When he first *talked* about leaving," Diane corrected. "If you'll remember, it was John Zook's then-unsolved murder that got Jakob actually thinking about becoming a police officer, himself . . . so he could help solve the crime. He'd been fascinated with the profession before that, of course, but it was the murder in his own community that took that fascination into a realm where he uttered the thought aloud.

"Oftentimes, I've wondered if it was Josiah's taking it to the new bishop and thereby calling Jakob out that made Jakob feel as if he had to go through with it."

Claire nodded as a few more pieces of the puzzle that comprised Heavenly's Amish community fell into place. "Oh, I get it. Miriam's father was bishop up until a few months before Jakob left, right?"

"Bishop Hochstetler, yes. His health was failing rapidly and that's when Atlee Hershberger took over. What Atlee doesn't see or know about, is delivered to his door by way of his son-in-law's father, Josiah."

She took it all in, pondering each new addition on its own merits. "Do you think that's *because* of the Leroy connection?"

"Maybe," Diane said mid–leg lift. "But I think Josiah is just like that. Knowing his son is married to the bishop's daughter probably just adds to his unusual sense of self-importance."

"Does it? In terms of the Amish community as a group?"

Diane lowered her leg to the cushion while simultaneously searching the closest end table for her current read. "There's no elevating of anyone within the Amish community. Not in the way the English world does with its people, anyway. There are some members who are looked to with greater respect than others, certainly, but any feeling of elevation would be an individual thing inside one's heart—and it would be something they'd never admit aloud."

"Okay . . ." She stopped, regrouped, and revisited a conversation from earlier in the week with someone who, essentially, shored up Diane's conjecture. "Annie said she has a hard time knowing if her peers like her for her or because she's the bishop's daughter. I guess if that can happen at the teenage level, it can happen at the adult level, too, yes?"

"I imagine it happens far less with the Amish, but I don't believe they're completely immune. They *are* human, after all. They cry and hurt and mess up like the rest of us from time to time."

Claire stood and crossed back to the fire, the diminishing flames and cooling temperature in the room mandating the addition of two new logs. When they were safely added and arranged with the poker, she remained seated on one of the few sections of the wood-planked floor that wasn't covered by a hooked rug.

"I know you're right. I know they're human. But there's something about the way they try so hard to live a simple life that makes any hardship they face more difficult to witness, you know?"

"I know. I feel the same way. Always have."

She continued to stare at the flames even as a very different image took front and center in her thoughts. "I'm afraid a whole bunch of them are about to hurt in unbelievable ways very, very soon and there's nothing anyone can do to stop it."

Diane's gasp brought Claire's focus back to the parlor and the growing fire within arm's reach.

"Does this have something to do with Sadie's body being found on the Lehmans' former property last week?"

Oh, how she wished she could shake her head.

But she couldn't. Not after everything Leroy had said in her shop that morning. Not after everything she suspected he and Miriam were still telling Jakob when she passed their buggies nearly six hours after they'd been hitched to poles outside the police station.

"Claire?"

She thought, too, about Howard's comment and the unsettling feeling his guess kept igniting in her own head.

If Howard was right and Elizabeth's death hadn't been an accident, could it be related to what happened to Sadie? Had someone known Elizabeth was about to tell? Had someone tried to stop her?

"Claire? Please. Talk to me. Tell me what's on your mind."

She shook the troubling thought from her head long enough to frame an answer that wouldn't be too premature to share with her aunt. "It seems as if Elizabeth's journal was right and four people *did* know the truth behind Sadie Lehman's fate. Three of them are still alive and facing—or, about to face—the consequences for whatever happened that night."

"Like Leroy's five little children," Diane mumbled just loud enough for Claire to hear.

"Six, now, but yes . . . And Miriam's brood, too. And whatever life Michael has going for himself beyond just his run for an office he'll never be elected to now."

Diane's second gasp was followed by a distinctive clucking sound that succeeded in guiding Claire away from the fire and back to her spot on the couch. "What are you thinking, Aunt Diane?"

The clucking eventually stopped only to be replaced by a slow, almost methodical shake of the woman's head. "Unlike Josiah, who is fanatical about being Amish, Ryan O'Neil is fanatical about his son and their legacy in this town. He has whitewashed that young man's life every step of the way just to get him to this point."

"And what point is that?" Claire asked.

"A veritable shoo-in as Heavenly's next mayor."

Chapter 24

Claire didn't have to look far to see the vast differences between her old life in New York City and her new life in Heavenly, Pennsylvania.

They were there each morning as she came down to breakfast, her aunt's cheerful "good morning" a stark contrast to the precoffee silent treatment that had ruled her mornings with Peter.

They were there each day as she unlocked the front door of her very own dream instead of always waiting to be included in someone else's.

They were there when people stopped on the sidewalk just to say hi, rather than elbow past with nary an upward glance.

They were there when the dinner she helped make for eight was actually eaten by eight, instead of the countless candlelit dinners for two that had been eaten by one.

And they were there when she climbed into bed at the end of the day and the light peeking around her shade came from the moon and stars rather than the roof rack of a passing emergency vehicle.

Yet, as much as she loved Heavenly and everything about her life in the quaint town, worry, stress, and uncertainty still crept into her heart. Sometimes, that worry was for a troubled friend or her often-overworked aunt. Sometimes, the stress rolled in on the heels of a lackluster week at the shop, when bad weather kept customers and their wallets at home. Sometimes, the uncertainty that had affected her faith in herself through much of her former marriage reared its head and made her second-guess whatever was building between her and Jakob.

But that night, as she stared up at the ceiling and tried to summon sleep, it was a combination of all three that threatened the success of her efforts.

She'd always been a worrier. It was in her blood. It didn't matter that she'd known Annie less than a week, and the teenager's brother-in-law and his children even less than that. Just knowing that their lives were about to change in drastic ways had her worrying about everything from trickle-down effect on her teenage employee, to the despair six innocent children were about to know, firsthand.

The stress was easy to pinpoint, too. Benjamin was her friend and she cared about him very much. And while she hadn't known him at the time, she was well aware of the hurt he still carried over the sudden and tragic death of his young wife—a death Howard had called out as questionable and now had Claire considering a very real and very disturbing scenario that made all too much sense.

As for the uncertainty, well, that came into play over what, if anything, she should say regarding Elizabeth. And to whom she should say it.

Did she raise the subject with Ben? And if she did, and it proved accurate, what would that do to him all these years later?

Did she raise the subject with Jakob? And if she did, would he be offended at the suggestion his fellow officers had failed to do their job fourteen years earlier, or would he see her as some sort of wacky conspiracy theorist who could never just relax?

So many times during the course of her marriage, she'd posed work-related thoughts and suggestions to Peter, only to get shut down each time with a roll of his eyes or a dismissive turn of his head.

Did she really want to put herself on the line like that with Jakob? Especially now that their friendship was blossoming into something deeper?

She pulled the covers all the way up to her chin and then flipped onto her side, the lack of light seeping around the edges of her shade a by-product of the clouds that had started rolling into town, midday. With Leroy's latest circumstances and Eva's new baby, the likelihood Annie would be helping around the store the next day was slim to none. A night of limited sleep added to the mix would only make her Saturday even harder.

Still, she couldn't clear her mind and couldn't make her eyes close for more than a fleeting second. Instead, all she could do was come back to the same terrifying certainty that had played with her thoughts all evening long . . .

Had someone killed Elizabeth to ensure she didn't disclose Sadie's fate?

And if so, who?

She knew the likely candidates would be found among those who shared the same secret—Miriam, Leroy, and Michael.

She also knew that to go to the extreme measure of murder to safeguard a secret, the expected fallout from that secret had to be significant.

Rolling back to her starting position, Claire flung the covers off her upper body and lifted herself into a sitting position with the headboard as her support. Thanks to Elizabeth's journal, they knew exactly who the remaining living players were . . .

Miriam Hochstetler, now Stoltzfus.

Leroy Beiler.

And Michael O'Neil.

Three very different people, with three very different demeanors and backgrounds.

Miriam, by several accounts, had been a rebel during her Rumspringa years. She'd also been the daughter of the then bishop. The latter certainly provided motive for keeping the secret to start with, but would it be a powerful enough motive to kill a friend years later?

Then again, the woman had, essentially, ran off within days of Sadie's body being found. Surely that didn't bode well for her innocence.

Leroy, by his own admission that very morning, had been scared when Sadie died. He'd been drinking, he was Amish, and he was smitten with a young girl he desperately wanted to marry. But was any of that reason for him to murder a friend? Particularly when said murder happened after he and Eva were officially married?

It was hard to know, hard to digest. But one thing was for sure, Miriam and Leroy had finally come forward to talk about Sadie Lehman. Would someone who was guilty of an offshoot crime do that? She didn't think so.

And then there was Michael O'Neil—the son, grandson, and great-grandson of three of Heavenly's past mayors. A son whom Diane had described as being virtually groomed for the local seat from the day he was born. On one hand, if Michael's mistakes were always wiped clean thanks to his father's long arms, why would he think whatever happened to Sadie would be any different? And if his father could make things go away, why would Michael need to kill Elizabeth just to keep the original secret?

It was a question that came down to the power of a mayor in a small town like Heavenly—a power Jakob had insisted wouldn't stretch to murder . . .

But was he right?

She glanced at the nightstand and the outline of her cell phone beside its base. There was a part of her that wanted nothing more than to pick up the phone, dial Jakob's number, and unleash all of her thoughts and fears into his always-listening ear. But just as she reached for the phone to actually place the call, she chickened out.

Everything that was preventing her from sleeping was pure conjecture. Conjecture that had haunted her thoughts from the moment Howard had uttered his suspicion aloud.

She liked Howard, she really did. He was kind, thoughtful, giving of his knowledge and experience, and smart.

But he was also a busybody who liked to know everyone's business and then spread it around to everyone else.

Elizabeth's death more than a decade earlier was old news to everyone in Heavenly except Claire. Maybe the only basis for Howard's comment was simply to have something to say. Maybe his theory was more a case of "what if?" than anything else.

If either of those reasons had, in fact, spawned Howard's comment, she'd look ridiculous taking it to Jakob.

But if *it* didn't . . . and *she* didn't . . . a killer who'd already been allowed to walk free for more than a decade would continue to do so for countless more.

Was her pride really worth that much?

This time, when she reached for her phone, she didn't stop. If she was wrong about Elizabeth, then she was wrong. It was a chance she was willing to take.

Glancing down at the screen, she swallowed.

Eleven forty-five P.M.

It was too late to call.

Even if he was awake, which she doubted, she wanted him clearheaded when she shared her thoughts with him.

No, it would have to wait until morning. Or, rather, tomorrow evening when she closed her shop for the day. Maybe then, over coffee and hot chocolate at Heavenly Brews, they could talk.

If he was available . . .

She peeked at the time once more and then pressed the message icon on the upper left-hand corner of her phone. It was too late for a phone call, but maybe a text would be okay.

If he was awake and heard the message come in, he'd respond.

If he wasn't, then he'd at least be aware of her request and better able to work it into his schedule.

But what did she say?

Did she say she thought Elizabeth was murdered?

Did she tell him she had an idea about the Lehman case she wanted to run by him?

"Why don't you just come right out and tell him you want to stick your nose in where it doesn't belong and see how long it takes before he stops coming around completely?" she hissed beneath her breath. "Yeah, that's the one, idiot . . ."

She stared down at the blank screen for a moment and then simply handed the choice over to her tired fingers.

Hi there.

Been thinking about a few things tonight. Hoping I can share them with you tomorrow? Any chance we can grab a hot choc at Heavenly Brews tomorrow evening after I close? My treat.

Claire

Glancing back through the message, she opted to spell out chocolate and add a smiley face icon beside her name before finally pressing send.

And then she waited.

One minute.

• Two minutes.

"He must be—"

The answering buzz of her phone cut her observation

short and made her sit up even taller. She opened the message, the words a bit blurry to her sleep-deprived eyes.

Claire,

Doesn't look good 4 a hot choc 2moro.

Busy.

Rain check?

Jakob

She didn't need daylight and a mirror to know her face had fallen along with her shoulders. And it wasn't just because she couldn't play Watson to Jakob's Holmes. No, she also wanted to spend time with him—time she'd all but ruined at his house the other night.

"Who are you kidding? A hot-chocolate date would go the same way as the movie date . . ." She let her head drift back against the headboard with a faint *thud* as she pondered her situation and the fact that her aunt's periodic coughing from the next room followed each and every self-recrimination Claire uttered aloud.

She contemplated answering Jakob's message with something fun and flirty, but she had nothing to offer in either department. And if she went the honest route, her disappointment stood a good chance of coming across as whiny.

Instead, she simply shut her phone off and returned it to her nightstand, another sleepless night now a veritable given.

Chapter 25

She was just reaching for the pitcher of orange juice when she heard the gentle tapping at the inn's back door. Closing the refrigerator, she answered her aunt's wide brown eyes with her index finger.

"Keep going with the pancakes. I'll see who that is." Claire set her glass back down on the counter and headed across the kitchen. "Are you expecting a delivery this morning? Or maybe some new guests who are trying to access the wrong door?"

"No. And there won't be anyone new checking in until tomorrow."

"Okay. I'll take care of it." She stepped into the tiny foyer, crossed its cozily scarred floor, and pushed aside the simple curtain panel that hung from a thin rod over the top third of the back door. "Jakob?"

Clearly able to read lips, he smiled in return and then

held up two large to-go cups imprinted with the Heavenly Brews logo.

She unlocked the door and pulled it open, the chill it ushered in no match for the warmth of the detective's presence. "Come in, come in before you freeze."

"It's not so bad when you get used to it," he said as he stepped through the door and handed her one of the cups. "I took a chance and got you a caramel hot chocolate. If that's not good, you can have this one"—he held up the second cup—"which is your basic hot chocolate."

She couldn't help but smile—at his presence, his sweetness, or anything else about the man standing less than a foot away. "I thought you were more of a coffee guy."

"I am. But since I couldn't be sure on the caramel flavor, I figured I'd go with a regular hot chocolate just in case."

"You didn't have to do that," she protested.

He shrugged and then peeked into the kitchen. "Good morning, Diane. It sure smells good in here."

"I'm making pancakes. Would you care to stay and have some?"

He smiled at Diane but allowed his gaze to roam its way back to Claire. "Well, I was kind of hoping I could drive your niece to work this morning if you don't need her here to help you with breakfast."

Diane waved her hand. "I don't need her at all."

"Gee, thanks," Claire mumbled loudly enough for her aunt to hear.

"Now, dear, I always *need* you . . . but I don't need you *this morning*. You've already done the things I needed help with, anyway."

She felt her face warm under the weight of Jakob's wink and did her best to remain focused on the woman flipping pancakes just inside the kitchen. "Are you sure?"

"I'm sure. Now off with the two of you before I get sidetracked from what I'm supposed to be doing and end up having to serve my guests burned pancakes."

"As if that would ever happen," she teased back before setting her cup down long enough to wiggle into her coat and gloves and grab her purse from the shelf beside the door. "Okay, I guess I'm all set."

He held the door open for her and then joined her on the stretch of grass that separated the Victorian home's back entrance from the small but well-maintained parking area. "I'm sorry I couldn't commit to meeting you this evening when you texted last night, but I'm kind of expecting today to shake out a lot like yesterday."

"Which was . . ." she prodded.

"Totally and completely nuts."

They fell in step with each other as they maneuvered around the last of the almost-melted snow piles and headed toward his car. When they were settled in their seats, he started the engine, turned on the heat, and left the car in park. "I wanted to stop out here last night and bring you up to speed on what began in your shop yesterday morning and continued for nearly eight more hours in my office, but the night got away with me."

"So what happened?"

"I talked to Leroy, Miriam, Atlee, Sadie's parents, and the district attorney. When all of that was done, and I released Miriam and Leroy to go back to their respective homes for the night, I had a mountain of reports to write."

She traced her gloved finger around the lid of her to-go cup and leaned her head against the seat back. "I woke you with that text I sent, didn't I?"

"I wish." He swiveled his body to face her as he took a sip of his drink. "No, I was actually still in the office, talking to the chief when your text came in. It was a bright spot, I'll tell you."

"Phew," she sighed. "That's a relief."

He stopped midsip and furrowed his brow. "Were you really that worried you woke me? Because if you were, you shouldn't have been. I actually think it would be nice to wake up to a message from you. Even nicer if I got to hear your voice in my ear."

At a loss for what to say in response, she took a sip of her own hot chocolate and used those extra few seconds to consider her next step. When she finally lowered the cup to her lap, she brought the subject back to something he'd already mentioned. "So Leroy and Miriam got to go home last night?"

"They did."

"I guess I'm a little surprised by that. I kind of figured that maybe you'd have to arrest them."

He shifted his body against the door and propped his left elbow and forearm against the top of the steering wheel. "Early on, as things were just getting started, I kind of assumed it would come to that, as well. But after running through the story again with Leroy, listening to Miriam's take on the same event, and, finally, Zebediah and Waneta's input on how it all fit in relation to their daughter, it became apparent that jail time wasn't really applicable in this case. At least not for the two of them, anyway."

"But Sadie is dead! And they buried her on her parents' property and said nothing for nineteen years! And, let's be honest, the only reason they're speaking now is because the body was found and they knew you were onto them," she protested. "How could there *not* be jail time?"

She heard the outrage in her voice and stopped herself short. Less than nine hours earlier, she was worrying about Leroy's children if he went to jail. Now, she was single-handedly leading the charge to lock him up?

Gripping her cup tightly with both hands, she turned her focus to Jakob. "I'm sorry. I have no right to question how you do your job. Will you forgive me?"

He leaned forward, tugged her closest hand from its death grip on her cup, and captured it inside his own. "Forgive you for what? Wanting justice for a dead girl and her parents? There's nothing to forgive about that, Claire. I was feeling exactly the same way when this all started . . . and still do on many levels."

"Then what's changed?"

"In the beginning, I was on a quest for justice. Now I know the way this shakes out within the parameters of the law."

She looked down at her hand inside his and then back up at him. "Meaning?"

"Leroy and Miriam didn't commit a crime."

"They didn't commit a crime?" she repeated, stunned. "How can you say that?"

He inhaled deeply then let the same breath release slowly through his nose. "After talking to Zebediah, Waneta, and Sadie's now-retired doctor, it appears as if Sadie had an allergy to peanuts. They never made a big deal out of it because, well, the Amish don't make a big deal out of anything and they simply refrained from having anything with nuts in their home."

"Go on."

"Remember the candy bars Leroy said they ate that last night?"

"Yes."

"The doctor believes, and I have to agree, the likely cause of death was an allergic reaction to something in the candy. I showed Miriam and Leroy a variety of candy at the station and they each pointed to the same kind as being one of the ones they ate that fateful night."

"It had peanuts, didn't it?" she whispered.

He answered by way of a nod. "The way both parties described Sadie in her final moments only served to shore up that theory."

"Why didn't they say anything? Why didn't they go running for help?"

"Because they were kids—fifteen- and sixteen-year-old kids. And they were scared."

She pulled her hand from his and brought it to her forehead. "Scared of what? They didn't do anything wrong."

For the first time since he took her hand, Jakob swung his gaze off her and onto the parts of Heavenly he could see through the front windshield of his car. "They didn't know that, Claire. They only knew that they were doing things the Amish don't do—like drinking, telling dirty jokes, and listening to loud music."

"They were on Rumspringa," she protested.

"Rumspringa or not, they still knew they were doing things their parents and the bishop wouldn't condone."

He lifted his hand, raked it through his hair, and then let it drop down onto the steering wheel. "And while they're sitting there, doing these things, one of their friends falls over and dies. They don't know what to think. They don't know if people will think they've done something to her. And then, on top of all of that, their ages and their unfamiliarity with the things they're doing make it so they're not a hundred percent sure that they haven't done something wrong."

She took a moment to process everything she was hearing and to examine it from all angles. When she was done, she reclaimed his hand from the top of the steering wheel. "Okay, so they didn't harm her . . . and they didn't say anything at the time because they were afraid. But to stay silent for nineteen years? To allow Sadie's mother to believe Sadie was alive somewhere and intentionally staying away? Surely it's a crime to stay silent, isn't it?"

"You'd think so, wouldn't you?" He flipped his wrist so they could be palm to palm, and then used his thumb to gently massage the back of her hand as he filled in the rest of the gaps. "Concealing the death of a child is a first-degree misdemeanor in the state of Pennsylvania. But it only applies to the parents of the dead child."

"Who didn't know their child was dead," she interjected.

"Exactly. If the kids had been questioned by officials as to Sadie's whereabouts and they lied to them, they could be charged with unsworn falsification—a *second*-degree misdemeanor. But, since Zebediah and Waneta didn't involve the police in their concerns about their daughter's whereabouts, we never opened an investigation."

"So you're saying they didn't do anything wrong?" She heard the shrillness in her voice and tried to call it back, but it was no use.

"*I'm* not saying they didn't do anything wrong. *They're* not even saying they didn't do anything wrong. But the wrongness of their actions is a moral issue, not a legal one." He squeezed her hands, bringing her focus back on him. "There is no doubt in my mind that Leroy and Miriam have led a very tortured existence these past nineteen years. They will never forgive themselves for what happened that night or the unbearable pain their actions heaped on a family who had the right to know."

"But to give these people *hope* . . . when they knew there was none? I . . . I just can't fathom that. And I can't fathom the notion that, in the eyes of the law, none of them did anything illegal in all of this."

"One of them did."

"One of them did?" She shot up tall in her seat. "What are you talking about?"

"Sadie's body. It was buried on the grounds of her own home. Without a casket. Without a service."

"Okay . . ."

"It is a crime to abuse a corpse."

Again, she jerked her hand away. "They abused her body?"

"No. No. Not in the way you're thinking." Jakob reached into his backseat and retrieved a fairly new, yet beat-up file folder and opened it on his lap. After shuffling through a few papers, he began to read. "'Except as authorized by law, a person who treats a corpse in a way that he knows would outrage ordinary family sensibilities commits a misdemeanor of the second degree.'"

After asking him to read the statute again, she did her best to apply it to Sadie. "So, because she was buried in a way her family would not have wanted, it could be considered abuse of a corpse?"

"That's right."

She let everything soak in and then moved on to the next most obvious issue. "Does it matter that it happened nineteen years ago?"

"Maybe, maybe not." He shuffled a few more papers. "The statute of limitations—42 PA CS 5552—is for two years. But there's a *chance* the prosecuting attorney could make a case for the clock starting at the moment the crime was known, which didn't start until the body was discovered last week."

"So who buried her?" she asked

"Michael O'Neil."

She closed her eyes. "How did they get her back to her property?"

"Michael's car."

"Did the rest of them help?"

When she opened her eyes again, he was watching her closely. "According to Leroy and Miriam, no. They were too scared. But I'll know more once I sit down with Michael and hear his account of things."

"And when will that be?"

"Once I get everything ready to go."

"I don't understand. Can't you just go out to his house and pick him up?"

"If he was the average joe, sure. But there's an awful

lot of people in this town who have been conditioned to protect this guy. And if I don't have everything I need when I call him in for questioning, he, too, could wiggle out from under this abomination."

It was the part of small-town politics she knew nothing about. To pretend otherwise would only make her look foolish.

She pointed at the dashboard clock and then reached around her right shoulder for her seat belt. "I've got to get to the shop. I'm supposed to open in ten minutes."

He, too, took in the time and then turned to buckle his own restraint. "I promise we'll have a real date soon, okay?"

"The other night? At your house?" she said by way of reminder. "*I* was the one who threw the monkey wrench in that one. And today? I wanted to hear what was going on every bit as much as you wanted to share it."

He steered the car out of the lot and toward the main road. "We did okay with the snow date, though, didn't we?"

"We did awesome with that one." She allowed the momentary memory of their special day to relax her body as they drove the short distance to Lighted Way, the sight of the picturesque shopping district chasing the last of the morning chill from her body. But as they officially left pavement in favor of cobblestone, she couldn't help but swing her attention to the police station on the left-hand side of the street. "Jakob? Can I ask you a question?"

"Of course."

"What happens if some of those people who have been conditioned to protect Michael O'Neil are inside your own department? What happens if they give him a heads-up and he runs? What then?"

"The only one who knows anything of consequence is the chief and he's got no allegiance to Michael's father."

"And the district attorney? Or Sadie's now-retired doctor? Any connections there?"

"All I can do is hope there isn't."

He slowed the car as they approached Glick's Tools 'n More and Shoo Fly Bake Shoppe, and then pulled into a spot directly in front of Heavenly Treasures. "How's this for rock star parking?"

She looked from the clock, to her shop, and, finally, to Jakob. "I know you've got a lot on your plate right now. I really do. But I think you should look at whatever files your department has on Elizabeth's accident."

He drew back, eyes wide. "You mean, *Ben's* Elizabeth?"

She answered by way of a half-nod, half-shrug combination.

"Why?"

She took a moment to muster up the courage she needed to dump her Howard-born theory on Jakob. Sure, she was still afraid he'd think she was a lunatic, but she simply couldn't keep it to herself any longer. "Because there's no getting around the fact the timing is suspect."

"Timing?"

"Think about it, Jakob. She was killed on her way to tell the truth about Sadie. A truth three other people were desperate to keep secret."

Chapter 26

Claire was just dragging the spring sale sign through the alley and down to the sidewalk when Annie came walking up, the girl's smile rivaling the sun that had yet to completely chase away the chill left by her conversation with Jakob.

"Well, look who's back." She released her hold on the tent sign long enough to pull the teenager in for a quick hug. "You worked here for just two and a half days, left for a day and a half, and I'm already at a loss around the shop without you."

A slow smile spread across Annie's face only to disappear in short order. "I am sorry I could not work yesterday. Eva needed me to help with the children when Leroy came to town and did not come back until very, very late."

She tried not to react to the mention of Annie's brother-in-law and, instead, focused on the only part of the girl's words that mattered at that exact moment. "First, I'm glad you spent time helping your sister—that's what family does for one another. And second, I didn't say what I said to make you feel bad. I said it because you're a hard worker and I'm blessed to have you working here with me."

Annie cast her eyes downward but not before Claire caught sight of the noticeable reddening of the teenager's cheeks. "I am happy to work here."

"So how is the new baby?" she asked as she continued lugging the sign toward its final destination.

"Hungry."

She laughed, positioned the sign so as to be seen by people approaching the store from either direction, and then motioned Annie to follow her inside. "Since it's your first Saturday, I should probably warn you that we'll see more customers than we do during the week. That won't necessarily be the case as the spring tourism season kicks off, but for now, it is."

"I understand."

"As a result, you won't see any tasks listed on the clipboard that will have either of us needing to be in the back room—unless we're retrieving a particular item for a customer. Today is really all about being on the floor, answering questions, and ringing up purchases."

"That is my favorite part," Annie confessed. "I like to talk to the customers. I like to see what they wear and hear how they speak."

"And from what I saw on Tuesday and Wednesday, the customers love you, too." She grabbed a cloth from a bin just inside the back room and wiped the counter thoroughly. When she was done, she tucked the cloth underneath and double-checked the register to make sure they had the proper change to make it through the rest of the day.

"You made an impression on little Mary."

She closed the register drawer and tilted her head. "Little Mar—wait. You mean your niece, right?"

"Yah. She was pleased to tell me that you like my chicken lunches."

"Because I do." She raised up on tiptoes in an effort to see through the room and out onto the sidewalk where their temporary lack in customers was guaranteed for at least a little while longer. "So Leroy got home late last night?"

"Yah. Eva was worried. Leroy is always home for supper."

"Were you there when he finally returned home?"

"Yah."

She waffled at the notion of asking more questions but, in the end, she couldn't resist. "How did he seem?"

"Quiet. Tired."

"Did he say where he'd gone? Or why he was late?"

"I do not know." Annie stopped reorganizing the pile of embroidered table napkins and raised a quizzical eyebrow. "Why do you ask such questions?"

She made herself stop and breathe. It was not her place to share Leroy's secret. It was his. To Annie, she merely shrugged. "I don't know. Just making conversation, I guess."

The jingle above the front door propelled her out from behind the counter and saved her from any further inquiries regarding her ill-conceived fishing expedition. "Good morning. Welcome to Heavenly Treasures . . ."

The rest of her greeting petered off as the identity of her first customer registered in her head.

"Uh . . . Mike . . . Hi. It's nice to see you again."

The tall, lanky candidate hesitated just inside the doorway, his greenish blue eyes dulled by something that looked a lot like worry. The fact that he barely lifted his feet en route to meet Claire in the middle of the room simply backed up her assessment.

He knew.

Of that, she was virtually certain.

But how? Had Jakob reached out to him in the thirty minutes that had passed between dropping her off and that very moment?

No. If he had, Mike wouldn't be standing here right now . . .

"What can I do for you, Mike?"

"I'm not sure. I'm not even sure why I came in here instead of going straight to the police department the way I intended. But maybe it's because you're new here and you're the first person I've met in a long time who didn't have preconceived notions about me—good or bad."

She shifted her weight from one foot to the other before turning to address Annie. "Can you hold down the fort out here for just a little while? I think Mr. O'Neil and I could use a little time to talk privately in my office."

"Of course," Annie said. "I will take good care of the customers."

"I know you will. Thanks, kiddo." She motioned for Mike to follow her toward the back of the room and the small hallway that led to her office. "If you need me, Annie, just give me a shout."

Any hesitation Mike may have shown at the thought of sitting down to talk disappeared the second they entered her office and she unfolded a chair for his use. When he was seated, she leaned against the edge of her desk and gave him her full attention.

"I don't know what you've heard, if anything, but I'm well aware of how fast news can travel in this town. Heck, even when I was a teenager and my father thought he was squashing things, they still made their way around this place like wildfire."

Something inside her told her to play dumb and she took its advice. "I'm not sure what you're talking about."

"You will," he mumbled. "My father thinks he can wipe this one away, too, but even if he could, I don't want him to. What I did was wrong. I didn't do it to be malicious, mind you . . . but it was still wrong."

Easing to the side, she slowly lowered herself to her actual desk chair and hoped its ear-piercing screech didn't break whatever spell had the man unburdening his soul to a practical stranger. "*What* was wrong?"

"Burying that poor girl the way I did." Without looking up, he continued, his eyes, his mouth, his words angled to the floor. "Sadie Lehman. That Amish girl whose body just turned up last week. I could have told you it was there because I'm the one who put it there nineteen years ago."

"But why? Why didn't you say something back then?"

"Because even though I wasn't sure what happened to her that night, I knew it was something bigger than even my dad could cover up. And as much as I griped and groaned about having to follow my father's legacy back then, I guess there was a part of me that didn't want to be the one who messed it up, either."

Once he started talking, he seemed incapable of closing the floodgates on the nineteen-year-old secret that flowed from his mouth. "I also didn't want to see the rest of them get in trouble on account of me."

"The rest of them?"

"For starters, the Amish kids. The ones who actually seemed to like me for who *I* was, instead of liking or not liking me because of who *my father* was."

She was vaguely aware of the tickle his words unleashed on her subconscious but opted to keep things moving rather than try to figure out why. That was something she could do later, when Michael was gone. "Why were you so worried about them?"

"Because they were my friends."

"Sadie, too?"

He flung his head back and stared up at the ceiling. "I actually liked her best. She was sweet and kind and laughed at my jokes even when I knew she didn't have a clue what half of them meant." His Adam's apple bobbed a few times before he slowly lowered his chin enough to afford Claire an uninhibited view of his eyes—the worry she'd seen there previously now replaced with raw pain. "Sometimes, when she'd talk about her family, I'd think what it would be like to be part of it—to work all day and then sit together after dinner and talk."

"Yours wasn't like that?" she asked.

"Sometimes it was. On holidays, I guess."

She weighed the possibility of continuing to play dumb against her desire to know more and opted for the latter. If Mike noticed the shift, though, he gave no indication. "So how did you find out the police know about your involvement in what happened to Sadie nineteen years ago?"

"One of my father's moles inside the county called the house last night. I was there, working on my campaign, and answered. I don't think the guy on the other end knew it was me because he started in right away. He said two different Amish people had come clean about the events leading up to Sadie's body being buried where it was." He studied his hands as if they were foreign objects, his thoughts clearly somewhere far away from Claire's office. "And I knew right away it was Leroy and Miriam. It couldn't have been anyone else. Elizabeth has been dead for more than ten years."

She searched his face, his mannerisms, his breathing pattern for any tells when he mentioned Elizabeth's name, but there were none.

"I imagine you were scared, yes?"

He looked up. "When I was sixteen and sitting next to a dead body, wondering what the heck happened? Yeah, I was scared."

"I was talking more about last night," she clarified, "when you took that call."

Silence filled the space between them as he leaned back in his chair and brought his right ankle across his left knee. "I think I was shocked at first. Maybe a little scared, too, I guess. But not for the reason you probably suspect."

"Oh?"

"I knew I had to tell my father that the news was out.

That what my Amish friends and I did that night wasn't a secret anymore."

She started to ask another question but stopped as his explanation took root. "Wait a minute. You knew you had to tell your father that *the news was out*?"

He nodded, once, twice.

"But you say that like he's known what you did all along."

"Because I thought he did."

"And now you don't?" she asked, her curiosity at an all-time high.

"No. I saw his face when I sat him down and told him the cops knew. He stared at me like I had six heads. So then I got more specific. You know, about Sadie dying and me burying her body. When he heard that, I swear I thought he was going to have a heart attack right there in front of me." He slumped back against the edge of the wall that cleared his chair, and let out a half-laugh, half-cry combination. "And that's when all the fear I've been carrying around the past fourteen years or so finally faded into relief."

"Relief?"

"Yeah, because now I know he holds no part in destroying my great-grandfather's legacy in this town the way I thought he had. Knowing that makes all of this a whole lot easier to bear."

She tried to make sense of what he was saying but wasn't entirely sure she was succeeding. "You were afraid he'd be held accountable for looking the other way?"

"No. I was afraid he would be held accountable for something much, much worse."

His ominous words kicked off a shiver that started at the top of her spine and traveled all the way to the bottom, taking her breath with it as it went. "I . . . I don't understand."

"For nineteen years, I've carried around the secret of what I did that night. For nearly fourteen of those years, I've also lived with the absolute certainty that my actions resulted in the death of someone who was only trying to do the right thing.

"I may still have to live with that certainty, mind you, but at least now I don't have to keep believing it was my own father who did it."

Chapter 27

So many evenings back when Claire used to watch Esther turn and head off in the direction of Amish country at the end of a long workday, she wished she could go, too. It wasn't that she didn't love living at the inn, because she did. The guests were always interesting, the food unbelievable, and Aunt Diane was, well, *Aunt Diane*. But when it came to pure tranquility, the western side of Heavenly had it over its eastern counterpart in spades.

On the English side of town, the end of the day meant more cars on the road as people traveled home from their jobs during the week, and to and from whatever sporting event or outing claimed their weekends. Inside their homes, television programs came on, home computers whirred to life, and phone calls were returned.

On the Amish side of town, the end of the day meant quiet fields and rare buggy sightings. Inside their homes, families gathered around the dinner table to eat, share tidbits from their day, and listen to stories from the Bible as dusk enveloped their homes in a blanket of peace.

It was a distinction that was hard not to envy at times. Yet tonight, as Annie waved good-bye and turned west to her east, Claire was glad not to follow.

All afternoon, she'd found herself thinking about Miriam and Leroy and the way their lives would surely change once they came clean about their secret to more than just the police. She wondered whether they would be shunned by their brethren during the next church service. She wondered if they would lose friends they'd had their whole lives. And she wondered if trust with their previously unknowing spouses would be irrevocably broken.

She tried not to think of Leroy and Eva's children and the impact such tension would undoubtedly have on their sweet, innocent smiles. She tried not to think of the new baby whose arrival into the world would be forever linked to the unveiling of a secret that never should have been kept and a family who'd been allowed to hope for a reunion that would never transpire.

With one last glance in Annie's direction, Claire crossed the street and began walking, her feet well versed in the route that would have her arriving home in just enough time to help her aunt with any last-minute dinner preparations. She knew, from the menu that had been placed on the table at the bottom of the stairs that morning, that pot roast and noodles was the dinner of the day. A childhood favorite of hers, Claire couldn't wait to get home in time to do a little behind-the-scenes sampling before the platters were brought out to the guests.

She glanced in the front window of the Heavenly Police Department as she passed and wondered what was going on inside. Had Jakob finished interviewing Mike? Would Mike face charges for abuse of a corpse, as Jakob had mused? And had Jakob been able to steal away a little time to look into the details surrounding the tragic death of his once crush and Ben's late wife?

She continued walking, her gait slowing as she reached the building being utilized as Michael O'Neil's campaign headquarters. This time, the posters that had covered nearly every square inch of window space only four days earlier were gone, their absence giving passersby a ringside seat to a pile of tables that had been dismantled and stacked in a far corner of the room. Next to the tables was a stack of boxes Claire recognized as once housing campaign buttons and pamphlets.

"You look as blindsided as the rest of us."

Startled, she turned to find a familiar face eyeing her from the alleyway next to the campaign headquarters. "Oh. Hi. *Tim*, right?"

The twenty-year-old nodded across the box he was holding, his face void of the smile he'd sported the first time they met. "And you're Claire, right?"

"Good memory." She hooked her thumb in the direction of the building. "What's going on in there? The election is still a month away."

"The election might still be a month away, but our candidate is done. From this race or any other race."

Not sure how to play the situation, she opted for surprise in the hopes she'd net something of interest. "Oh?"

"Yeah. Late last night, when most of the volunteers

had already gone home, Mike and his dad came in to tell those of us who still remained that it was over."

"Did they say why?"

"Mr. O'Neil didn't want to give any details. He just wanted to thank us for our time and send us on our way. But Mike was having none of that. He sat us down and told us that he'd likely be going to jail for a while . . . for worrying about his own neck for far too long. He didn't get into any real specifics, but when a person is talking jail time, they must have done *something*, you know?"

Sadly, she did know.

And so did Zebediah and Waneta Lehman.

"I know how disappointing this must be, especially in light of how much time you obviously put in on his campaign."

Tim shrugged. "It's like my dad said when I got home last night: 'Welcome to politics . . . you'd better get used to it.'" He repositioned the box in his arms and used his chin to gesture toward the car parked just on the other side of Claire. "So maybe I'll see you around on a different campaign sometime."

"Yeah, maybe you will." She continued toward the inn, her own shoulders beginning to droop with a disappointment she couldn't quite isolate. Sure, she'd always been sensitive to the plight of others, but Mike had committed a crime. The fact that nineteen years had passed didn't make it okay. Especially when his nearly two-decade-long silence only made things harder on Sadie's loved ones in the end.

And if that same underlying secret led someone to take Elizabeth Miller's life five years later . . .

She stopped midstep and groaned. Off and on, throughout the afternoon, she'd revisited her conversation with the disgraced candidate. To believe, for fourteen years, that his father had committed murder to protect *him* had to have been awful. Yet, after hearing about the great lengths to which the elder O'Neil had always gone in order to protect his son's image, she could understand why Mike had been worried.

Mumbling under her breath, she continued walking, her thoughts ricocheting between Jakob and Michael, Leroy and Eva, Miriam and Jeremiah, and finally, Howard and Elizabeth . . .

If Elizabeth *had* been murdered as Howard suggested, the only reason that made any sense was to keep her from telling the truth. And since her journal gave them every reason to believe she was heading to Zebediah and Waneta's home to do just that, the only real suspects that still remained were Leroy Beiler and Miriam Hochstetler, now Stoltzfus.

To murder someone simply to keep them from exposing a secret meant the culprit had to feel as if the fallout from their secret would be tremendous. If they didn't, why would they risk being caught?

Because they knew her murder could be passed off as an accident.

Hence, the hunting connection . . .

But even as she found herself considering both Leroy and Miriam for a murder no one had any reason to believe was a murder, she found herself hitting on the same repetitive conclusion with each suspect.

Why kill?

"Why, indeed?" she mumbled just before the answer

livened her tone along with her steps. "Because they still thought they'd committed a crime the first time. Against Sadie . . ."

A vibration against her hip made her jump and she reached into her jacket pocket to retrieve her phone. A quick check of the caller ID screen led her to a nearby park bench and a break she hadn't realized she needed.

"Hi, Jakob."

"Did I catch you at the shop? Or the inn?"

She turned her head to the left to survey the road she'd already traveled, and then to the right to take note of what was still left before she finally leaned back against the bench. "I'd say you caught me just shy of midway."

"Pavement?"

"Nope. The park benches near the end of the cobble-stones."

"Okay, I know where you are." A funny sound on the other end of the phone made her guess he was sitting at his desk, head tilted against his own seat back. "So, if I wasn't nose-deep in reports right now, I might have been able to see you as you walked by the station about two minutes ago?"

"More like ten or twelve. I got sidetracked by one of Mike O'Neil's former campaign folks along the way. He was carrying a box out to his car."

"I'm not surprised. Mike came in all on his own just before noon. His story matches up with everything we've heard from Miriam and Leroy." A squeak in the back-ground suggested he was changing positions. "And it doesn't look like he's going to face any jail time, either."

She tightened her grip on her phone as she, too, shifted positions. "Wait a minute. I thought you said he committed a misdemeanor of the second degree when he buried Sadie the way he did."

"And he did. Nineteen years ago. But according to the prosecuting attorney, he was free and clear of that charge seventeen years ago."

She heard the frustration in his voice and knew it matched her own feelings at that moment. "But no one knew what he did seventeen years ago!"

"Apparently, that doesn't matter. Statute of limitations in Pennsylvania starts at the moment the crime is committed. Only certain extenuating circumstances have the ability to change that, and none of those exist in this case."

"Wow."

"I know. But I still stand by what I said earlier," Jakob said. "The hell these three have lived with the past nineteen years is at least *some* punishment. And that's before the backlash from their family and friends kicks in."

"Somehow, that doesn't really seem like enough, does it?" When he said nothing, she continued on. "Annie came back today. I'm becoming very fond of that young girl."

When there was still no response, she pulled the phone from her cheek and checked the connection.

"Jakob? Are you still there?"

"Uh . . . yeah . . . can you give me a second? One of my coworkers is in my doorway . . ."

"Sure." She glanced back down the sidewalk toward Mike's former campaign building and watched as Tim made yet another trip out to his car. This time, he carried three boxes and was followed by a box-holding helper.

"Okay, so that was my coworker, Doug. He stopped by to let me know there is no file on Elizabeth's death."

She sucked in a breath. "You took what I said *seriously*?"

"Why wouldn't I? You're a smart woman with great instincts. You've more than proven that a time or two over the past seven or so months I've known you."

She didn't know what to say so she simply stayed silent. Waiting.

"But there's no file, no record of her death in the station."

"Why?" she asked, stunned.

"I don't know. But I do know some things from Ben. Like the fact that it happened on December fifth, which is important."

"Oh?"

"Hunting is legal in this county from December second until December fourteenth. She was also struck and killed on the outer edges of a piece of land widely known to be used for hunting on the Amish side of town."

"I'm surprised to learn the Amish hunt at all. It doesn't sound like something they'd condone."

"The Amish believe in nonresistance, which prevents them from using force against another human being. That's why they're so against what I do. But just because they won't serve in the military or on a police force doesn't mean they're shy about using firearms when it comes to putting food on the family's table."

Claire lifted her left shoulder in an effort to block the ever-decreasing evening temperatures from her exposed ear as she continued to concentrate on everything Jakob was saying. "Do *all* Amish men hunt?"

"No. And not all of them set aside a portion of their

land specifically for hunting, either. In fact, Josiah is the only one I can think of that still does."

She pushed off the bench and continued east, Jakob's voice just as good of a companion for walking purposes as it was for sitting. "I imagine tonight will be another paperwork kind of night, huh?"

"Probably. But I'll set it aside for a while to speak to Ben when he gets here."

"You asked Ben to stop by the station?"

"I did. I want to get his read on this notion of Elizabeth's death being linked to her intentions that day."

She shivered harder than the early-evening temperatures called for. "Uh, Jakob? Do you really think that's wise? I mean, it's hard enough to think you lost your spouse in such a tragic way as he's believed these past fourteen years. But to have someone suggest it wasn't an accident after all this time seems a bit harsh."

"Claire, if I was Ben and someone suspected something like this about *you*, I'd want to know."

Her feet transitioned to pavement at the same time his words sank in. "Jakob, I'm not your wife. There's no way you can compare the two."

"It doesn't mean I can't imagine myself in his shoes, with you as the woman I lost."

She willed herself to breathe in, breathe out, breathe in, breathe out . . . When she was steady enough to speak, she took control of the conversation before her mind started traveling through bridal magazines. "And if it turned out to be nothing? And what you'd always believed proved to be right in the end?"

"Then nothing really changed."

Chapter 28

Claire tried not to think of the smell of her aunt's famed pot roast as she drove down the driveway and back onto Lighted Way. The pull to stay and sample had been strong, but, in the end, the need to get behind the wheel for a little alone time had been stronger.

From the moment she'd hung up the phone with Jakob she'd been gripped by an anxiety she hadn't been able to pinpoint. She'd tried several times to figure it out, but short of little things here and little things there, nothing justified her unease.

There was no doubt the lack of punishment for Miriam, Leroy, and Michael ate at her insides. It wasn't that she had a burning desire to see them live out their remaining days in a jail cell, because she really didn't. Not when she considered the pain and suffering such a sentence would inflict on their family members—people who were no more deserving of pain than Sadie's parents and siblings. But she couldn't shake the feeling that they needed some sort of punishment for deciding what a young girl's family should and shouldn't know.

And then there was the whole thing about Elizabeth . . .

She hated the thought of Jakob tossing a theory like murder into Ben's lap fourteen years after the fact. Somehow, it seemed almost cruel, like prying open a thinly scabbed wound just to pour a tablespoon of salt inside.

If the salt was needed, that would be different. But until they knew whether Elizabeth was murdered for sure, she just didn't think it was worth telling Ben.

Turning west, she headed through town, the gas lanterns along Lighted Way guiding her past Heavenly Treasures and its neighboring shops. A fine spray of gravel shot up from her tires as she piloted the car onto the road that would wind her through Amish country. Where she was going, she had no idea. She just knew she needed some time away, time to clear her head.

The road curved every so often as it traversed trees and fields. She turned the steering wheel with each bend and mentally ticked off the Amish farms that she passed. It was a silly thing to do, really, but it had become a routine.

King.

Lapp.

Stoltzfus.

Lehman.

Hochstetler.

Another Lapp.

Hersh—

She shifted her foot to the brake as she came around the corner and spied a familiar outfit moving along the edge of the dusk-filled road.

Annie . . .

Pushing the button on her door handle, Claire lowered the passenger-side window and pulled to a stop beside the teenager. "Hey, Annie, want a lift the rest of the way?"

"Yah, I would enjoy that very much." Annie pulled the car door open and sat in the seat, her smile wide but tired. "Some days that is a very long walk."

"Mine is less than half as long and sometimes *I'm* tired by the time I get home." She waited as Annie fastened her seat belt before pulling onto the road once again. "Sorry I didn't come along before you were this close to home."

"That is okay. I do not mind. It is still less walking."

"That it is," she said, laughing. She turned the wheel to the right and followed Annie's driveway as it bumped along between a line of trees.

A quick gasp from Annie's side of the car was followed by a hand on Claire's upper arm. "Could you turn, please? I . . . I should stop at Eva's house. To check on the baby . . . and the other children, too."

Claire stopped the car halfway up the driveway and turned to look at Annie, the girl's sudden stiffness and lackluster eyes a study in extremes compared to her demeanor less than three minutes earlier. Confused, Claire took in the farmhouse and the single buggy waiting outside. "Is that your father?"

"No. He is not home yet."

"Then who is that man sitting in that buggy?" she asked.

"The Pest."

"Ahhh. Say no more." She K-turned her way back out of the driveway and turned west again, their new destination little more than a quarter of a mile ahead on the right.

As they passed the heavily wooded lot that separated Annie's home from her sister's, Claire stole a glance in the teenager's direction. Annie was sitting ramrod straight in her seat with her head turned toward the trees. "I do not know why he cannot stay on his own land. I do not know why he must always come one way or the other."

"Who? Leroy's father?"

"Yah."

"Where does he live?" she asked.

Annie answered with the point of her finger, the gesture guiding Claire's focus off her employee and toward the woods. "He lives in the woods?"

"He has fields, too. But you must first drive through trees to get to his house." Shifting her finger left, Annie indicated a narrow gravel lane Claire had never noticed. "I do not know why he has a house when he is always at mine . . . or Eva's."

They drove on, Annie's body noticeably relaxing as her sister's driveway grew nearer. "You really don't like that man, do you?"

"I try not to have such feelings. I know it is not right. But I cannot help it. He is a mean man. He tries to do Dat's job but he does not do it well." Annie's voice broke off only to pick back up with a shrillness that hinted at impending tears. "Sometimes, I think he forgets that we live in *God's* world."

"How do you mean?"

"When I do not tie my kapp strings, I do not answer to Josiah. I answer to God."

"But I thought that was how the Amish do things. That shunning or excommunication or whatever is carried out by the Amish themselves."

"By *everyone*, yah. Not by one man," Annie whispered fiercely. "Josiah judges alone."

Claire pulled her right hand from the steering wheel long enough to find and squeeze one of Annie's. "Let's not give that man another thought for the rest of the evening, okay?"

"I will try." When the car left the main road and turned up Eva's drive, Annie brightened. "You should come inside, Claire. Eva would like to meet you, and the baby is very sweet."

"I'd love to." Five towheads came running from their various locations around the yard as Claire parked beneath the same tree she had the first time. "I think you should go inside and check though, okay? Just in case your sister is tired or the baby is sleeping."

"If the baby is sleeping, he will sleep. That is not a reason to stay outside."

She smiled at Annie. "Just check, okay?"

Annie began to protest but stopped, shrugged, and stepped from the car. "You do not have to stay in the car while I check. That would be silly."

"We can't have that, now, can we?" Claire dropped

the car key into her purse and pushed open the door to find five smiling Amish children lined up to greet her. "Well, hello there. It's very nice to see you all again." Then, with a concerted effort to put the right name to the right little face, she extended her hand to each and every child from tallest to smallest. "Samuel . . . Mark . . . Joshua . . . Mary . . . and Katie."

Mary's smile widened and was quickly followed by a slight jump and a finger that pointed toward the barn door. "And that is Dat!"

Leroy's hand rose into the air in a wave before turning into more of a shooing gesture directed at his brood. "It is time to go inside and wash up for dinner. Tell your mamm I will be along soon."

She watched as each child spun around on bare feet and made a beeline for the farmhouse, their exuberance and joy as evident as it had been two days earlier. "They're precious, Leroy. Absolutely precious."

"Please. Come. Let us talk." He jerked his hatted head toward the inside of the barn and waited for Claire to join him. When she did, he led her toward the horse stalls in the back. "I thank you for listening yesterday. I should not have kept that secret. It was wrong."

She met his gaze and held it. "Yes. It was."

"I shared with Eva what I have done. I told her while the children slept last night. She cried."

"I'm sure it was a shock to hear after all these years."

He nodded. "That is what she said."

"And your father? How did he react?"

Leroy's jaw tightened. "He will know tomorrow. When I repent at church."

"Will you be shunned?"

"I will ask for forgiveness for I know I have done wrong. I know this now, as I knew then. But now I am older. I am a father. I understand in different ways now."

Unsure of what to say, she nodded and then pointed to a baby horse in the corner of a nearby stall. "That makes two babies on the farm, I see."

"Three, actually. There is a cow, too. But the horse and the cow are much bigger than Melvin."

Her answering laugh went a long way in dispelling any tension between them and she was glad. She didn't agree with what Leroy had done or the apparent lack of justice for his part in what happened to Sadie, but there was no getting around the fact she liked the man. He was kind and gentle.

"What is his name?" She wandered over to the waist-high pen and took a moment to soak up every detail of the colt—his wide eyes, his long lashes, and his spindly legs.

Leroy came and stood beside her, prompting the colt to approach. "Samuel thinks we should call him Trip. Because that is what he did when he was born."

"Trip is cute."

"But Katie calls him *Big* Baby."

"Big Baby, huh?" She leaned her upper body over the wall and tried to pet the colt, but the animal jumped back. "Oh . . . hey . . . I'm sorry, baby. I didn't mean to frighten you."

"You would like to pet the horse?"

"I'd love to but I think he is afraid of me."

"He will come back." Leroy said quietly. "He is curious and thinks we are all like him."

For several long minutes they simply stood there, watching the colt as he nuzzled his mother and stopped, periodically, to peek at them. Eventually, he took a step closer to them, his eyes inquisitive.

"Now, hold out your hand. He will nuzzle you. Perhaps he will even move his mouth on you as he does his mother."

She did as she was told and allowed Leroy to fine-tune her positioning. "Okay . . ."

"Now, hold still and wait. He will want to see and smell."

Sure enough, the horse's ears pricked up, his nose lifted, and he took a few tentative steps in Claire's direction. "Ohhh, he's coming," she whispered.

"Keep holding. Do not move."

The colt brought his mouth down to Claire's hand and, sure enough, sniffed and suckled at her fingers. After a moment, Leroy took hold of the underside of her hand and guided her palm to the side of the colt's head. Together, they petted him.

"He is so soft . . . so sweet."

A cough from the front of the barn made her glance over her shoulder. "Oh, hi, Annie. I just got to pet a baby horse for my very first time."

Annie stared down at the toes of her boots but said nothing.

"Annie?"

"It is time for dinner, Leroy."

She looked at the horse one last time and then hurried across the barn as Leroy double-checked the colt's stall door. "Annie? Are you okay?"

"I did something wrong but I do not know what," Annie murmured.

"What are you talking about?"

"The Pest. He was just here. Standing right there." Annie pointed to a spot on the drive not far from where they stood. "His back was to me when I came out of the house. I thought it was Leroy who was looking into the barn, but it was not. It was The Pest."

"Did he say something to upset you again?"

"He said nothing."

Claire guided the girl's chin upward until their eyes met. "Then I don't understand."

"When he heard me on the porch steps, he turned and looked at me. He was angry, very very angry." Annie's hands flew up to her kapp and its strings, and then moved nervously down the front and sides of her dress and apron. "I have never seen such anger. Such"—she stopped, swallowed, and tried again, her voice muted by fear—"such *hate*."

"Where is he now?"

"Look close. His buggy is almost to the road."

Claire stepped around the corner of the barn in time to see Josiah Beiler turn left onto the main road, his horse and its buggy moving at a good clip.

"He didn't say anything to you?"

"He did not have to. His eyes said enough."

She returned to Annie and pulled her in for a hug. "Based on what I saw Thursday night, if he'd had something to say to you, he would have said it. So put him out of your mind and enjoy your dinner with your sister and Leroy and the children."

"Will you come see the baby?"

She glanced between Leroy in the barn and the open doorway of the farmhouse and politely declined. "Another time. When you're not getting ready to sit down to eat."

"Please. Eva will be upset if you do not come inside. I will set a plate at the table and you can join us for dinner."

Chapter 29

Despite the lack of lights, Claire could still discern the outline of five little children in her rearview mirror. She couldn't make out each individual face, but she could tell Annie's nieces and nephews were waving as she drove down the driveway toward the main road.

"You have a really special family, Annie," she said as she took one last peek in the mirror. "Your nieces and nephews are absolutely adorable . . . and so smart."

Annie nestled into the bucket-style passenger seat and resituated the plate of bread atop her lap. "I like to eat with Eva and Leroy often. It reminds me of what it was like when Mamm was still with us and my brothers were still home. Sometimes Eva and Leroy would come to our house with Samuel and Mark. There would be much talking and laughing."

She looked both ways when they reached the main

road but waited a few moments to make the turn. "It's quiet at home alone with your father, isn't it?"

"Yah."

"I remember dinners like that."

Annie met Claire's eyes across the center console and pulled back just a little. "You lived with just your dat, too?"

"No. But I did share a home with just one person for many years. Most nights he did not come home for dinner and I ate alone." She leaned her head against the seat back and chose, instead, to savor the memory she'd just made. Sitting around the dinner table with Annie and her sister's family had been akin to some of Claire's favorite Thanksgivings growing up. The food had been good, of course, but it had really just served as a side dish to the conversation and merriment of the evening. It was everything she wanted for her own life one day.

"I am sorry to hear of that." Annie crossed her feet at the ankles and looked down at the bread. "Do you think you will marry one day? Perhaps have children of your own?"

She felt the smile even before it crossed her lips and knew what her answer would be just as surely as she knew her own name. "If you'd asked me that question six months ago, kiddo, I'd have told you no. But I've come to realize hearts can heal with time. And if you're willing to open your eyes to all that is good, your heart will follow."

"Eva says that you will marry Jakob."

"Eva says that?" she echoed.

"Yah. She is friends with Esther."

"Ahhh."

Six months ago, six weeks ago, even six *days* ago she'd have protested Esther and Eva's claim. But suddenly, that protest was gone.

She didn't know if she'd marry Jakob.

She didn't even know for certain if they'd ever have another date.

But there was something special about the detective. Something special about the way they interacted with each other. She'd be a fool to discount that.

"Is it true?"

"Is what true, Annie?"

"That you will marry the policeman?" Annie fidgeted with the edges of the plate as she waited for Claire to answer.

"I think we'll need to see what God has in store for Jakob and me."

"God is good."

She reached across the space between their seats and patted Annie's hand. "Yes, He is, Annie. Just look at that wonderful family we just left. How blessed you are to have them and how blessed we all are to have you."

"You are blessed to have *me*?" Annie whispered.

"Beyond words, Annie. Beyond words." Looking to the left and right a second time, Claire finally pulled onto the main road, her throat tight with emotion. "Five days ago, I was adamant that I wasn't ready to hire a replacement for Esther yet. And now, I can't imagine not knowing you."

She brightened her headlights but kept the speed low in an effort to give them as much time together as possible. "I think that alone has taught me the importance of being open."

They fell silent as they passed onto the stretch of road bordered by thick woods on the south and farmland on the north. She wondered what Annie was thinking but didn't ask. Sometimes it was okay to simply sit quietly and reflect . . .

"Whoa, what do we have here?" she mumbled as her lights trained on a familiar orange triangle ahead and to the right. Slowing the car to a crawl, she turned to look more closely at the slow-moving vehicle sign and the buggy it marked, its abandoned horse tethered to a tree. "Looks like someone's buggy might have broken down."

Annie leaned her forehead against her window for a closer look. "You are right. It is missing a wheel."

"Do you know whose buggy it is?" Claire pulled onto the shoulder just in front of the horse and shifted into park.

"If Dat were here, he could tell you who goes with that buggy. But I only know when I see who is sitting on the seat."

"Which doesn't do us much good when there's no one there, does it?" she teased. Then, reaching past her cell phone in the built-in cup holder, she popped open her aunt's glove compartment and retrieved the flashlight Claire herself had put there several months earlier. "I'm going to get out and look around. Just to make sure no one is sitting out here alone in the dark, okay?"

"Do you want me to come?"

"No. You wait here. I'll take a quick look on both sides of the road and then come right back."

She pushed her door open and stepped onto the finely graveled road, the lack of any real moonlight making her grateful for the four or five feet of illumination granted by her flashlight. Swinging the light toward the back end of her car, she was immediately struck by the size difference between the tethered buggy horse and Leroy's new colt. Both animals were beautiful, but what she saw in their eyes was much different.

The colt was full of wonder as he gazed at the world from behind the safety of his mother. The buggy horse looked tired and maybe even a little confused as to why he was standing on the side of a road all by himself.

"Hello?" she called out as she cleared the horse and shined her light onto the empty buggy seat. When no one emerged from the area behind the seat, she moved the beam into the empty field. Aside from sprouts of rye and barley, there was nothing.

She walked back to the horse and gently stroked the side of its head the way Leroy had taught her, the animal's initial rebuke soon followed by a soft whinny. "I can't believe someone would just leave you out here like this. It doesn't make sense . . ."

A distant but audible moan sent her light skittering across the street and moving from one narrow gap in the trees to the next. "Hello? Is anyone there? Are you hurt?"

"Yah. I . . . am hurt. Please come. Please help."

The light from her flashlight bobbed up and down as she ran across the street and into the first gap she could find. "Where are you?" she called.

"Keep walking. I am here. In the woods."

She moved the light to the left and walked in the

direction of the male voice, the snap of twigs and branches beneath her feet little match for the *thump* of her heart in her ears. "Should I go back to my car and call for help?"

"No! I will be fine with your help. Please. Do not leave. I knew you would come, knew you would try to help."

With careful steps, she walked farther into the woods, her progress thwarted from time to time by the pull of a branch on her clothes or a stumble on an unexpected rock or fallen tree. Twice she fell all the way to the ground and twice she picked herself back up.

The third time she fell and struggled to her feet, she heard it.

It was fast and it was faint but the metal-on-metal sound was unmistakable.

"Do not move!"

The voice that spoke was the same as it had been from the start. But now, instead of pleading, it was commanding.

Slowly, she moved her light to the right and then the left, trees and branches disappearing amid the fear of what she knew she would find.

Inch by terrifying inch she scanned the thick woods in front of her until she saw it—the long narrow shaft of steel trained on her chest. She wanted to turn, wanted to run faster than she'd ever run in her life, but she knew it wouldn't matter. Her only chance at that moment was to stand perfectly still.

Lifting the beam upward, all moisture that remained in her mouth drained straight through to her hands as the identity of the man holding the rifle became crystal clear.

"Josiah? What are you doing?"

"I am doing what needs to be done!"

"What are you talking about?" She heard the heightened pitch to her voice and did her best to keep it under control. The last thing she needed to do was escalate the situation with her emotions. "What needs to be done?"

"The Amish do not do these things!"

"What things?" she shouted back.

"I must rid my son of such temptation!"

"What are you talking about? What does Leroy have to do with any of this?"

"I know why you hired Annie! I know it was so you could have excuses to come to Leroy's farm."

"Come to Leroy's farm?" she echoed, confused. "No, I hired Annie because I needed help!"

"I saw you with Leroy in his barn not more than two hours ago! I saw his hand on yours! It is not right!"

"You saw Leroy's hand on mine?" she repeated even as her thoughts traveled back to Leroy's farm . . . to the dinner . . . to playing with the baby horse . . .

And then she knew.

Josiah hadn't been upset at Annie when she came out of the house. He'd been upset at Claire. At what he thought he was seeing between her and his son in the barn.

"Josiah, you misunderstood! Leroy and I weren't doing anything wrong! He was just introducing me to the new horse!"

"He was holding your hand!"

She stepped forward only to recover her step the moment the rifle inched upward toward her face. "He— he wasn't *holding* my hand! He was *guiding* it!"

"My son is married! To the bishop's daughter! I did not allow that behavior before! I will not allow that behavior now!"

"What are you talking about?" she shrieked. "We weren't doing anything wrong! He was just helping me!"

"If I do not stop this, it will continue. One help will turn into two helps . . . and then three. This time I will not wait for three!"

"This time you won't—"

She heard the echo of her gasp as reality struck with a punch to her gut that left her breathless.

Howard was right.

Elizabeth hadn't been killed by a stray hunting bullet.

She'd been killed by one specifically earmarked just for her.

By Josiah Beiler.

"You killed Elizabeth Miller, didn't you?"

"It was God's will!"

"God didn't pull that trigger . . . you did!" she shouted back.

"She was at my son's farm. Again and again, she was there! Talking to him . . . walking with him. She did not care that he was to marry in two weeks."

"Because Leroy and Elizabeth were friends! That's all!"

"He held her hand! He wiped her tears!" Josiah thundered. "He held her in his arms!"

She resisted the urge to drop to her knees and sob. She had to keep him talking, had to hope Annie would come looking when Claire didn't return to the car.

Annie . . .

No, Annie, don't come looking for me . . .

"He held her in his arms because she was scared," Claire protested. "She was trying to convince Leroy to tell the truth."

"He was to marry Eva! That was the only truth!"

The snap of a twig somewhere off to her right brought a momentary stop to the *thud* in her ears. If Josiah heard it, though, he gave it no due, opting instead to pull his arms and the rifle closer to his own body.

A methodical tapping from somewhere behind Josiah caught his attention and he turned, momentarily removing the crosshairs from her body. Before she could react, before she could even think, Jakob burst out of the trees to her right, his duty weapon aimed at Josiah's back. "Police! Drop the weapon or I'll shoot."

Chapter 30

She opened her eyes to a popping and crackling that was at first startling and then comforting as she slowly acclimated to her surroundings. Across the room, beneath the oddly familiar pictures and knickknacks, a fire roared. An afghan in varying shades of blue was tucked around her body from her feet to her shoulders.

"I guess Diane was right after all. You did need sleep more than you needed a movie date." Jakob perched on the edge of the sofa and stroked the side of her face, his touch both comforting and exciting all at the same time.

She struggled up on her elbow only to comply with the gentle pressure of his hand on her shoulder. "Please. I wanted to come. I really did. But I guess I didn't really feel safe enough to sleep until I sat down on your couch."

"You *are* safe, Claire. Josiah isn't going to hurt you or anyone else ever again. You have my word on that."

"How did you know to come? How did you know what was happening?" she asked as moments from the previous evening came flooding into her thoughts.

The disabled buggy . . .

The dark woods . . .

The deep voice . . .

The desire to help . . .

The click of steel . . .

The end of a rifle . . .

The pounding of her heart . . .

And fear like she'd never felt before.

"Ben came to my office yesterday evening like I asked. We talked about Elizabeth's journal, I filled him in on what really happened the night Sadie died, and I asked about Elizabeth's death."

She held her breath and waited, her concern for Ben dispelling the lingering fog in her head.

"From what I was able to surmise from Ben last night, the reason we didn't have any information on Elizabeth was because it was never reported. Ben and the rest of the members of his community believed her death to be a tragic accident—a simple case of being in the wrong place at the wrong time.

"The director of the funeral home who embalmed the body was days away from retiring and had no reason to believe her death was anything other than what he was told. As a result, he felt no need to file a report with us, either."

"*Should* he have?" she asked.

"When someone dies of a bullet to the head? Absolutely. But since he died of natural causes about five years ago, that doesn't really matter now."

"Oh."

"Since there was nothing to look at in any file, I began asking Ben questions—where it happened, time of day, that sort of thing. At first, nothing jumped out. I already knew, from an earlier conversation with him, that her death coincided with the legal hunting dates in Lancaster County and that it happened on property purchased and used for hunting."

"By Josiah," she finished.

His confirmation came via a nod and a squeeze of her hand. "So I started asking questions about Josiah and Leroy. At first, it was like pulling teeth to get Ben to say anything. The Amish do not engage in gossip. It's not their way. But, after a while, he began to mention little oddities about Josiah—his bent toward judgment, his belief that Leroy's marriage to the bishop's daughter somehow came with a position of power for him, and the near-daily visits to Bishop Hershberger's home for what, essentially, boiled down to relentless tattling.

"Somewhere, in the back of my mind, something began to feel off. I'd been racking my brain all day trying to think of something Miriam or Leroy had said in their account of Sadie's death that would have propelled either of them to kill Elizabeth. Sure, they'd been scared— scared enough to keep quiet, as we well know. But to kill? It didn't fit. Then, as Ben continued talking about Josiah, I started to wonder if *Josiah* could have been the one who wanted to keep Elizabeth from talking."

"How did you know he had me in the woods?"

"When Josiah started emerging as a strong possibility, I called your cell. Annie answered and told me you'd gone off into the woods to look for the driver of a broken-down buggy. I put her on speaker so Ben could ask her questions about the horse. Eventually, he figured out it was Josiah's and that he'd probably walked back to his home through the woods. When Annie heard that, she begged me to come and find you. She said Josiah was crazy with his guns. That sometimes she saw him pointing one at her as she walked back and forth from her farm to Eva's. That he liked to scare her with them when she'd done something wrong. And then, just before she started to cry, she said she hoped you hadn't made him mad."

Jakob raked a hand through his already-tousled hair, his eyes trained on hers. "I don't know if it was hearing Annie say that, or knowing you the way I do, or a combination of both, but I couldn't shake the feeling that maybe I wasn't the only one with Josiah on my radar for Elizabeth's death."

"And so you came . . ." she whispered, watching him.

He leaned forward, brushed a gentle kiss across her forehead, and then flashed the smile she'd grown to love as much as the man himself. "You bet I did. And faster than I've ever driven in my life, that's for sure."

"I'm so glad you did."

This time when he kissed her, he went straight for her lips. "So am I, Claire. So am I."

When he pulled away, she allowed her focus to drift toward the fire, the flickering flames adding an extra layer of warmth and contentment to her heart. But as she sat there, reveling in his presence, she couldn't help but revisit the turning point in an otherwise harrowing evening.

"I'll always wonder what that tapping sound was that made Josiah turn at the last minute. It was so unexpected yet deliberate-sounding."

"That's because it was deliberate."

She looked back at Jakob. "What do you mean?"

"That was Ben tapping a rock against a tree. It was his way of pulling Josiah's attention off you long enough to give me the upper hand."

"Ben?"

"Ben." Jakob snaked his arm around her shoulders and pulled her up and into his arms. "After we got you back to the inn, safe and sound, I told him he made a great partner."

She nibbled back her answering smile as another reality of the evening elbowed its way to the front. "How is he? How is he taking the news that Elizabeth was murdered? Is he okay?"

"He will be. In time. He's got a lot to get through, a lot to make sense of. But, in the end, he knows that Elizabeth was trying to do the right thing. That, at least, gives him some comfort."

She pressed her cheek against his chest and breathed in his scent. "I hope so. Because Ben is a special man."

Jakob's head bobbed against the top of hers as he planted yet another kiss on her head. "The hardest part about all of this is that it didn't have to happen. If Elizabeth . . . or Michael . . . or Leroy . . . or Miriam had just run for help nineteen years ago, none of this would have happened. Sadie's parents could have mourned their daughter as they had every right to do, four teenagers wouldn't have had to torture themselves for something that wasn't their fault in the beginning, and Elizabeth wouldn't have been gunned down over a secret."

"Or, rather, a misconstrued set of meetings that never would have been necessary if not for that secret," she corrected as she pulled away.

"It's wild to think Josiah didn't even know about Sadie—that his whole basis for killing Elizabeth was over a feared relationship that didn't exist."

She closed her eyes against the memory of Josiah's gun trained on her chest, the fear it had unleashed in her heart still there for the taking. "But it was that way with me, too. I tried to tell him that Leroy was just helping me pet the new horse, but Josiah refused to believe me. He actually accused me of hiring Annie to get close to Leroy . . ."

"He's a sick man, Claire. But you're safe now. I promise."

Safe . . .

Shaking off the image of Josiah once and for all, she forced herself to move on. "Most of what happened after you showed up is still a little fuzzy for me. I know you asked me some questions, I know you took notes, and I know you brought me back to the inn, but what happened to Annie? Is she okay?"

"She'll be fine. She's with her father and from what Ben told me this morning, Atlee is taking good care of his little girl."

"I'm glad. Annie wants nothing more than to spend time with that man." Reaching up, she tapped the handsome detective on the nose and motioned toward the entertainment cabinet in the corner of the room. "And *I* want nothing more than to snuggle up with *you* on this couch and have that movie date I sort of ruined the other night."

"Are you serious?"

It felt good to laugh but it felt even better to feel his touch on the side of her face. "You bet I am."

"I'll make the popcorn."

The delicious mysteries of Berkley Prime Crime for gourmet detectives

Julie Hyzy
WHITE HOUSE CHEF MYSTERIES

B. B. Haywood
CANDY HOLLIDAY MURDER MYSTERIES

Jenn McKinlay
CUPCAKE BAKERY MYSTERIES

Laura Childs
TEA SHOP MYSTERIES

Claudia Bishop
HEMLOCK FALLS MYSTERIES

Nancy Fairbanks
CULINARY MYSTERIES

Cleo C
COFFEEHOUS

Solving crime

pengui

Photo by Carrie Schechter

While spending a rainy afternoon at a friend's house more than thirty years ago, **LAURA BRADFORD** fell in love with writing over a stack of blank paper, a box of crayons, and a freshly sharpened number two pencil. From that moment forward, she never wanted to do or be anything else. Today, Laura is a bestselling mystery and award-winning romance author. She lives in Yorktown Heights, New York, with her husband and their blended brood. Visit her website at laurabradford.com.

ISBN 978-0-425-27302-9

Living among the Amish of Heavenly, Pennsylvania, shop owner Claire Weatherly has come to appreciate a simpler, more peaceful way of life. But secrets within the close-knit community can certainly complicate things—especially when they lead to murder...

After the Stoltzfus barn catches fire, Claire is awed by the response of the community. Hundreds of Amish men gather together to raise a new barn for the family in a matter of days. But in the midst of the work, a human skeleton is unearthed. Found with the remains is half of a friendship bracelet last seen on Sadie Lehman, an Amish teen long believed to have left her strict upbringing for the allure of English ways.

Now Detective Jakob Fisher—once a member of the Amish community himself—is determined to solve the young woman's murder. With Claire's help, he must dig into the past and bring to light long-buried secrets—secrets that someone is willing to kill to protect...

Praise for the national bestselling Amish Mysteries

"Delightful...Well-portrayed characters and authentic Amish lore make this a memorable read."
—*PUBLISHERS WEEKLY*

"The best cozy mystery debut I've read this year."
—HARLAN COBEN on *Hearse and Buggy*

ISBN 978-0-425-27302-9

5 0 7 9 9

9 780425 273029

EAN

$7.99 U.S.
$9.99 CAN